BETTER WED THAN DEAD

The Working Stiffs Mystery Series

Trudy, Madly, Deeply
Sex, Lies, and Snickerdoodles
There's Something About Marty
You Can't Go Gnome Again
Dogs, Lies, and Alibis
No Wedding For Old Men
Crazy, Stupid, Dead
A Kiwi Before Dying
Farewell, Mr. Lovely
Better Wed Than Dead

BETTER WED THAN DEAD

A WORKING STIFFS MYSTERY
BOOK 10

Wendy Delaney

Sugarbaker Press

Copyright © 2024 by Wendy Delaney

All rights reserved. No part of this publication may be reproduced, distributed or transmitted in any form or by any means, including photocopying, recording, or other electronic or mechanical methods, without the prior written permission of the publisher, except in the case of brief quotations embodied in critical reviews and certain other non-commercial uses permitted by copyright law. For permission requests, write to the publisher at the address below.

Sugarbaker Press
PO Box 1164
Boerne, TX 78006-1164

This is a work of fiction. Names, characters, places, and incidents are a product of the author's imagination. Locales and public names are sometimes used for atmospheric purposes. Any resemblance to actual people, living or dead, or to businesses, companies, events, institutions, or locales is completely coincidental.

Cover by Llewellen Designs

Printed in the United States of America

Better Wed Than Dead/Wendy Delaney – 1st edition, October 2024

ISBN: 978-0-9986597-9-4

Acknowledgments

Writing is typically regarded as a solitary process, but it's really not. At least not for me. Other opinions and some timely professional expertise is always needed on a story's journey, and *Better Wed Than Dead*'s journey toward publication proved to be no exception.

Many thanks to fellow author, Kathy Coatney, for helping me get "unstuck" along the way. Also for being the first set of eyes on my work. I couldn't be more grateful for your feedback and encouragement.

Elizabeth Flynn, editor extraordinaire who rocks the best socks, I will never be the grammarian you are, but I'm better having worked with you. Thank you!

Jeff, my love and "guy stuff" advisor, I couldn't have written this series without you. Nor would I have wanted to.

"K," my "all things law enforcement" consultant, thank you for your timely assistance so that Steve doesn't take a misstep because of my ignorance.

As always, my heartfelt gratitude goes out to my dream team of beta-readers: Heather Chargualaf, Lori Dubiel, Jan Dobbins, Christie Marks, Susan Cambra, Melissa Hogan, Cindy Nelson, Denise Fluhr, Vicki Huskey, Amber Lassig, Beth Rosin, Brenda Randolph, Donna Peterson, Deidre Herzog, Toni Mortensen, Mattie Piela, Rebecca Reitze, Melanie McCready, Beth Carpenter, Mary-Jane Grandinetti Rader, Jenna Scully, Kimber Mohr, and Connie Lightner.

Lastly, thank you, dear reader. This book is for you.

Chapter One

"What do you think the holdup is?" my grandmother asked, twisting in her seat to look down the length of the white aisle runner as I had just done. And just like me, I knew she had only seen a pacing wedding planner—the same smiling woman who had stepped in front of us to nervously announce that there was going to be a slight delay.

That had been at least twenty not-so-slight minutes ago. And she no longer appeared to be smiling.

"I have no idea, Gram." I pulled at the sleeve of my fiancé's suit jacket to reveal his trusty Timex.

Steve patted my thigh. "It's five minutes later than the last time you checked."

I squeezed his hand. "Something has to be very wrong."

"You don't know that," he said. "But if we don't see the bride pretty darned soon, there's gonna be two hundred people thinking the same thing."

Hopefully, whatever had caused the delay wasn't anything more serious than Renee Ireland needing more hairspray to guard against the cool breeze that was whipping the escapees from my French twist into my face.

But since Judge Navarro had stepped away from the gazebo covered with garlands of hydrangeas and peach and white roses to take a stroll around the Rainshadow Ridge koi pond, I knew someone must have informed the officiant that he wouldn't be needed anytime soon.

"If you ask me, someone has cold feet," my mother gloated with enough volume for the friends of the groom sitting across the aisle from us to hear.

If my actress mother ever wanted to play the part of a pissy wedding guest, it seemed that Marietta was using every resentment she held against Renee to perfect her performance. Specifically, Renee Ireland was a gorgeous former model, was six years younger, and was the ex-girlfriend of my mother's current husband.

But today, first and foremost on Marietta's acrimony list was that everything about Renee's wedding trumped the ceremony that had taken place in this exact garden spot almost two years ago to the day—the blustery June evening that my mother and Barry Ferris exchanged their vows.

With half of the Port Merritt's merchants in attendance for their favorite newspaperwoman's wedding, there were twice as many guests. There were also showier flowers with more ornate sprays of roses, hydrangeas, and calla lilies tied to the back of each chair lining the white aisle runner. But most of all, instead of the gray murk that had threatened rain two years ago, it was a perfectly lovely, blue-sky day.

At least it looked perfect.

Since the wedding party was nowhere in sight for a ceremony that should have started at five, I wondered if my mother could be right. Either Renee or Adam, the obstetrician she had met on a ski slope last winter, could be having second thoughts about tying the knot.

Gram and Barry quickly shushed the prickly actress sitting between them. But seconds after she huffed another breath of displeasure, the distinguished-looking man in a tailored suit sitting across from Steve rose to face us.

"There was a medical emergency that Adam had to deal with," he said in a low baritone as he fixed his gaze on Marietta.

Yep, he'd heard her loud and clear.

"But I'm sure he'll be back soon," the man added with such calm assurance that I suspected that he worked with the groom in some professional capacity.

After he moved on to deliver his assurances to some of the guests behind us, Gram elbowed me. "Remember when you drove me to that medical building in Port Townsend last year to check out that funny mole I had on my back?"

I nodded. "Uh-huh."

She glanced back in his direction. "That's the dermatologist I saw. I think he works in the same building as Renee's beau."

"Okay." That meant that my impression of the guy had been right. It also made me wonder about the "medical emergency" he might have been privy to.

But I didn't think about that for long because I could

see Judge Navarro heading back toward the gazebo with a taller version of George Clooney in a tuxedo by his side.

The crowd that had been fidgeting in their seats began to buzz with anticipation that the two men would soon take their places in front of the gazebo.

"About dang time," my great-uncle Duke groused from his aisle seat behind Steve.

"Hush!" Alice, his wife of fifty-five years, muttered. "I swear, you haven't stopped bellyaching about coming here since we left the house."

Duke's irritation rumbled deep in his throat like the growl of Fozzie, my chow mix. "You wanted to come to this wingding, not me."

I could only hope Duke would be more enthusiastic about attending my wedding, especially since he was the one I'd asked to walk me down the aisle in three weeks.

"Renee's a friend," Alice snapped.

Steve turned to me with a knowing look.

No doubt because we had heard the same thing from my mother when she insisted that we all RSVP.

Only he and I knew better than to believe her.

Renee Ireland and Marietta had developed a good working relationship over the last couple of years. Since Renee was a reporter for the *Port Merritt Gazette*, that was something that had helped to publicize my mother's local appearances.

Marietta also probably saw this wedding as another opportunity to get her name in the paper.

Whatever.

I knew why I had come today.

Because next month we would be standing in front of that white gazebo with the same lacey wraparound garlands, and if Steve thought that would look too much like something out of a Disney princess movie, I needed him to tell me. Before it was too late.

"She's been a good customer, too," Alice added as if Duke needed to be reminded of their working relationship with Renee. "Asking me to make her wedding cake, which I worked on late into the night, and now I want to enjoy myself. So, behave!"

"Yeah!" Lucille, Alice's pal and Duke's longest-tenured waitress, chimed in behind me. "And shush, it's starting. Ooh, nice dress." She tapped my grandmother on the shoulder. "You could wear something like that to Char's wedding. That shade of blue would look great on you."

"It certainly looks lovely on her," Gram said of the plump lady being escorted down the aisle by a tall, lanky senior to the front row on the groom's side, where two twenty-somethings were sitting. "And I like that jacket, but it looks expensive."

I smiled at her. "I bet it's not *that* expensive, and she's right. Something like that would look really nice on you."

Gram dismissively flicked her wrist. "I already have a dress—the one I wore to your mother's wedding."

"Yes, but you've already had pictures taken in that one," Marietta said, leaning in our direction. "I've been telling you this for weeks. We need to go shopping to get you a different dress for Charmaine's wedding pictures."

Mrs. Dewsbury, who owned the antique store on the same block as Duke's Cafe, looked back over her shoulder to give my grandmother a look as if to ask, *"Can't you control your children?"*

Marietta heaved an indignant sigh. "Oh, please. We're not being that loud."

Gram clamped her hand around her daughter's wrist, giving her the silent message that I used to receive in church every time I was fidgeting. "And this is nothing we need to discuss now," she said, turning to look back at the next approaching member of the wedding party.

"Fine," my mother whispered through gritted teeth.

She wasn't the only one whispering as a slender, silver-streaked blonde with a million-dollar smile started walking down the aisle on the arm of a younger and more wiry version of the groom. A brother, I assumed.

I immediately recognized the blonde as the longtime Seattle television news anchor I had watched as I was growing up. "Holy smokes," I muttered, adding to the growing buzz of the crowd. "That's Joan Germain."

Alice shot me a quizzical look. "You didn't know? She's Renee's mother. She's been to lunch at the cafe a couple of times with Renee."

Not when I had waitressed there for a couple of months after my divorce finalized. Nor had I heard anyone mention Renee's connection to her famous mother.

"I had no idea," I said, studying the graceful woman in the cinnamon beaded sheath gliding toward us.

I glanced past Gram to catch my mother staring wide-eyed at the other local celebrity in attendance. Clearly, Renee hadn't done any name-dropping during the hours-long interview Marietta had given her for the *Gazette* over a year ago.

And why would she? Renee had wanted her interview with the wife of her ex to go smoothly. She had been professional and deferential, doing and saying all the right things to shine the spotlight solely on my mother and her attempt to make a comeback in a new movie.

Today, that D-list celebrity wasn't in the spotlight and had to accept the fact that Renee's wedding was going to be quite the shiny affair.

Aside from starting a half hour late.

Joan Germain gave Steve a nod of recognition as she passed our row.

I leaned into him. "You know her?"

"I've met her," he said. "Back when I was with Seattle PD. I worked security on a couple of benefits she hosted. Nice lady."

What the police detective to my right wasn't telling me was that his ex-girlfriend, a rising TV star now working in the Los Angeles market, had probably introduced them.

Just as well. I wanted to enjoy this day with the man I loved, not chat about our exes.

"I'm sure she is," I whispered, watching Joan take her seat in the front row.

Next, three bridesmaids in off-the-shoulder coral chiffon and lace made their way to the front. They all looked to be in their mid- to late forties. The one leading the procession was tall and had Renee's coloring. With the way Joan was beaming at her, I assumed this was a younger daughter.

Once the three women took their places opposite

Adam and his brother, the familiar chords of the wedding march began piping through the speakers located throughout the garden. Everyone then turned to watch the bride, perfectly gorgeous in blush organza and lace, make her entrance on the arm of an athletic-looking man in his seventies, who towered over six-foot-tall Renee.

"Wow," I whispered in Steve's ear. "He must be at least six-seven."

"Six-eight," Steve said over his shoulder, keeping his voice low. "Played basketball for the Huskies back in the day. Could have gone pro if it wasn't for a bum knee. Became an investment banker instead. You've heard of Mercer and Morton?"

Only because I had once ferried over to Seattle to deliver a subpoena to a witness working in their steel and glass high-rise.

Without waiting for a reply, Steve nodded at Renee's father as they passed. "That's Richard Mercer."

"Mercer? As in Mercer Street?" Named after one of Seattle's founding fathers.

He shrugged. "Not sure about that. All I know is that he grew up in Seattle and then went to the UW."

"Wow," I repeated. "A Mercer."

That earned me another glare from Mrs. Dewsbury.

I didn't care. I was too fascinated with what I was learning about Renee Mercer Ireland, a possible descendant of Seattle royalty.

Glancing over at Marietta, I could see that I wasn't the only one who was viewing Renee in a new light.

Around twenty minutes later, while the wedding party

posed by the gazebo for pictures, my mother grabbed me by the wrist and pulled me away from the banquet table where Steve and I had just sat down with my best friend Roxanne and her husband Eddie.

"You'll have to excuse Charmaine for a few minutes," Marietta abruptly announced.

"Hey," I protested, almost tripping in my strappy slingbacks as I tried to keep up with her racewalker pace. "Slow down, or one of us is going to do a face-plant in this grass." And I had a feeling it was going to be me because I didn't live in heels like she did.

Holding me tight to her side, she led me away from the reception area that had been set up in the rose garden behind the koi pond. "Just keep moving."

"What is going on?"

"Funny you should ask that," Marietta said as if it were anything but.

She glanced back over her shoulder, toward the sound of the laughter coming from the rose garden. "Am I the only one who didn't know?"

"Know what?" I didn't need to ask. I could tell by her tone that my mother's hackles were up.

I was also losing feeling in my right hand.

"It's bad enough that my own husband didn't tell me. As if I can't handle the truth. I don't need you to hold out on me, too." Releasing me, Marietta pointed to a wrought iron bench on the grass between the pond and a boxwood hedge. "Sit."

I took a seat on the rock-hard bench and rubbed my wrist while she loomed over me like an interrogator in five-inch stilettos.

"Before you jump to any conclusions," I said, checking our surroundings to make sure we wouldn't be overheard, "I didn't know any more about Renee's background than you did."

"Joan Germain?" Marietta balled her hands into fists as if she wanted to punch someone. "Seriously, Charmaine. Joan flippin' Germain's her mother?! And her father is probably worth millions!"

"Probably, but—"

"And now Renee's married to a doctor. Did you take a good look at him? He's a total hunk!"

"Yes, but—"

My mother groaned. "Why didn't Barry tell me any of this? I would've been—"

"Nicer to her?" I interjected with a sweet as sugar smile that I hoped would lighten the mood.

She narrowed her kohl-lined green eyes at me. "I was dealing with a local reporter who could've painted me in a most unflattering light considering the circumstances. But I always did my best to be…well…civil. Even accommodating!"

"Uh-huh. But not especially nice."

"I didn't know," she whined, throwing her hands in the air. "No one ever clued me in about her connections."

As if that should make a difference. "And now you do."

Marietta sighed. "Do you think this wedding was Renee's way of getting back at me for maybe being a teensy bit ungracious at times?"

A teensy bit? "No. If you'll recall," I said, lowering my

voice as the bridesmaid who had been second in the procession rushed by with a cell phone pressed to her ear, "Renee wasn't invited to your wedding, so any similarities between the two are probably because you used the same venue."

"Maybe. It just seems so—"

"What?" a woman cried out. "Oh, honey, no!"

Marietta stood on her tiptoes to peek over the hedge. "It's that bridesmaid," she whispered to me. "Whoever she's talking to just gave her some bad news."

My mother and I stared at one another as the woman started sobbing. Clearly, it was seriously bad news.

I pushed off the bench to see if she needed some help.

"Do her parents know?" she asked, standing statue still on the walkway that led to the changing rooms we had used two years earlier for Marietta's wedding. "Okay, your father and I will be there soon." Her breath hitched as tears streamed down her cheeks. "I'm so...so...sorry."

With her phone held to her heart, the woman seemed oblivious to my presence as I came to her side.

"Forgive me, I couldn't help but overhear," I said. "Are you okay?"

She shook her head, her voice so thick with emotion that it was almost unintelligible. "No, my daughter-in-law... I need..."

"To find her?" I asked, trying to fill in the blanks. "Is she here?"

"No!" the woman sobbed. "She's dead!"

Chapter Two

Early the next afternoon, Roxanne and I arrived with takeout at the house of our pal and new mom, Donna Dearborn.

Just like when we met for lunch last Sunday, we didn't ring the doorbell for fear of waking baby Emily. Instead, I used my spare key and eased the front door open.

"Knock, knock," I whispered.

Wearing baggy, blue cotton pajamas and a cloth diaper draped over her shoulder, Donna stood in the middle of her living room and cradled the wailing three-week-old in her arms. "Don't bother trying to be quiet, she's been refusing to go down for a nap all day."

"Poor baby," Rox said, carrying a cardboard tray with three large to-go cups of coffee as we all looked down at the red-faced baby screaming her tiny lungs out. "You've got to be so tired."

Donna yawned. "She is."

Rox leveled a smirk at Donna before heading back toward the kitchen. "I was referring to you."

"Hey, I'm just fine," Donna said. "In fact, I'm learning to be quite the cat-napper. It's amazing how refreshed you can feel after a twenty-minute nap."

I didn't need to be an expert at reading body language to know she was lying. "Uh-huh. You look dead on your feet. Are you sure you're up for this visit? We could just leave you the food—"

"No, no. Don't let these bleary eyes fool you. I'm very up for it," she said, shifting whimpering Emily to her shoulder. "And speaking of the dead, is it true what they're saying? Someone died at Renee's wedding?"

As per usual, Port Merritt's rumor mill had wasted no time spreading yesterday's big news. Also, as per usual, someone didn't have all their facts straight.

"Not *at* the wedding," I said on my way to the kitchen. "She got sick before the ceremony was supposed to start and then got rushed to the hospital."

"Oh, but they weren't able to..." Donna said, following me.

"No." I placed the sacks containing our lunch on the knotty pine table sitting in a corner nook that offered a view of the fenced backyard. "Unfortunately."

"How sad, for everyone involved." Patting Emily's back like an automaton, Donna yawned again.

Her husband Ian may have taken his ten-year-old daughter and their golden retriever out for a couple of hours so that we could have some uninterrupted girl time, but Donna obviously needed sleep more than conversation.

Especially this particular conversation, since the events of yesterday had kept me up most of the night.

Donna rested her head against Emily's as her cries

transitioned to hiccups. "What do you think happened?"

"Are you sure you want to get into this now?" I smiled sympathetically. "There's no rush. We brought deli salads and sandwiches that will keep just fine if—"

"In fact, why don't you let me take her so that you can have one of those *refreshing* naps," suggested Rox, the only experienced mom of the three of us.

"Really, I'm okay. Or I will be once this little girl decides that it's okay to sleep for a couple of hours at a time. Besides," Donna added, gently rubbing her baby's back. "I want to hear all about this wedding I didn't get to go to. So start at the beginning and tell me everything."

By the time I finished my turkey on whole wheat, Rox had regaled Donna with a description of what everyone had worn, which of our mutual friends had been in attendance, and the crowd reaction to Joan Germain.

Then Rox looked at me, effectively passing me the baton to finish with the not-so-happy part of the story.

Skipping over the pissy reason why Marietta had dragged me away from the reception, I told Donna that we were at the right place and right time to overhear that phone call.

"We could tell something was wrong, but we didn't learn until later that it was the girl's husband calling his mom with the bad news," I said.

"Which was what, exactly?" Donna softly asked, glancing down at the baby who had finally quieted on her lap. "That despite all their efforts at the hospital, she died?"

I didn't feel right about providing any specifics, so I nodded and fast-forwarded to the moment when I came back to the reception and Rox asked me where I had been.

"That's when I found out what had happened," she said between bites of her club sandwich. "Word seemed to spread pretty quickly once all the family had been informed. For a while there, it was the only thing people wanted to talk about."

"Oh, this is so sad." Donna shook her head, her long, blond ponytail sweeping over her shoulder. "Do they know what it was that made her so sick? Was it food poisoning or something?"

"She had some sort of condition. I really don't know the details," I said, minimizing what little I had heard from various family members yesterday.

"But it sounds like it came on pretty quickly," Rox added. "She went from acting perfectly healthy to having trouble breathing a few minutes after she finished doing Renee's makeup."

I cocked my head to give my chatty best friend the visual clue that we shouldn't volunteer too many specifics to one of the biggest gossips in Port Merritt.

Rox's brown eyes widened with confusion. "What? Isn't that what Renee's cousin told us? Or was she a sister-in-law? Half the time I didn't know who the heck I was talking to at the reception."

After my mother and I escorted Nora Mercer to the bridal party's changing room to give her a quiet place to grieve the loss of her daughter-in-law, and I went back to the reception to retrieve her husband, I felt much the same way. I wasn't always sure who was who.

Except for poor Natalie Mercer.

I had overheard enough to learn that Natalie was the twenty-four-year-old who died. So had Rox and my mother, along with Lucille and Alice. No wonder word had spread.

"That was Renee's cousin who sat down with us. I'm pretty sure she said her name was Amanda." She had been the one who pointed out Nora's husband to me. She was also the one who accompanied us back to the changing room and then, after hearing the sad news, returned to the reception to begin the process of informing the family.

"Amanda," Rox repeated, reaching for her coffee. "That's right. She'd said she'd been with Natalie Mercer for hours, her doing the bridal party's hair while Natalie did their makeup."

Donna, the owner of Donatello's, the most popular cut and curl in Port Merritt, looked up from the sub sandwich she had started to unwrap. "The girl's last name is Mercer? As in Mercer Street?"

"No relation," Rox said. "I asked Amanda because I had thought the same thing."

So much for the Seattle founding father connection. Still, there was a money and a Joan Germain connection. That had been more than enough to impress my mother.

"And you say that Amanda's a hairdresser?" Donna asked. "Where? Maybe I know her."

Rox shrugged. "I don't know. Seattle somewhere."

I nodded. "Yeah, she works at some downtown salon. I didn't catch the name."

"And Natalie, the girl who died, worked with her at

that salon?" Donna asked.

"No, Amanda said she was a schoolteacher. Taught first grade, I think," I said, trying to remember our brief conversation. "She was just skilled with makeup, so when Nora heard that Renee was looking for someone to do the makeup for the wedding party, she hired Natalie to do the job. I got the impression that she thought it would be fun. Keeping it all in the family."

"Some fun," Donna said. "The girl ended up dead."

"Yeah." I didn't know what to say beyond that, so I took a sip of coffee and hoped that Donna would turn her focus to eating instead of talking.

"So now what happens?" Donna asked, spooning pasta salad onto the stoneware plate in front of her. "Will there be an investigation?"

Since I was the only one at the table with a deputy coroner badge, I knew that question had been for me. "Not necessary since she died under medical supervision."

"Really?" Donna glanced down at the sleeping baby on her lap. "Twenty years from now, if this little one went from feeling okay one minute to not being able to breathe the next, I'd want some answers."

"I get that." And I did. "But when somebody dies at the hospital, unless the doctor contacts the coroner to request an investigation, that's the end of it."

At least normally.

Chapter Three

When I made it up to the third floor of the courthouse the next morning and walked into the offices of the Chimacam County Prosecutor/Coroner, I greeted the receptionist, just like I always did.

Then, I rounded the corner to check in with Patsy Faraday, my boss's legal assistant and my unofficial manager. "Good morning," I said with the expectation that Patsy would immediately glance at the domed anniversary clock on her desk, just like she always did.

This was her version of having me punch a timeclock.

I knew she used it to reinforce the pecking order. And she knew I knew. Not that this mattered one iota.

It was our morning ritual.

Except for today.

Instead of glancing at the clock, Patsy's head swiveled toward the sound of raised voices in the office of the woman serving her third term as prosecutor/coroner.

Frankie Rickard's office door was no more than fifteen feet away from where I was standing. When it was closed, as it was this morning, it was a rare occurrence to hear any trace of conversation. Because sixty-three-year-old

Frankie was the epitome of even-tempered professionalism, it was even more rare to hear someone yelling at her.

"Is everything okay in there?" I asked, trying to get a good look at the couple occupying Frankie's visitor chairs. It sure didn't sound okay, but as long as no one made any sudden moves, I didn't think I'd need to fetch the sheriff's deputy, who was sitting out in the hall like the third-floor bouncer.

"I'm sure it's nothing to be overly concerned about," Patsy said.

Maybe. But something at least *somewhat* concerning was definitely up.

She picked up the short stack of files that had been sitting on the cabinet behind her and handed them to me. "Happy Monday."

In other words, go away and make yourself useful.

Fine. Don't tell me what's going on.

After I stopped in the breakroom to make a fresh pot of coffee, I headed down the hall and proceeded to do the usual Monday morning chitchat with the legal assistants and secretaries who looked up from their computer monitors as I passed.

Not one of them gave me any indication that today was especially different from any other Monday, so when I made my way to my desk at the end of the hall, I assumed that Frankie's visitors were connected to some case we would all eventually hear about.

Then, my desk phone started ringing. Since Frankie's name was displayed as the caller, I wondered if I might hear about that case sooner than I had thought.

"Charmaine," she said when I answered. "Would you please come to my office."

Frankie sounded like her usual self, so I concluded that the couple I had seen in there with her had left.

Two minutes later, after Frankie asked me to take a seat in one of the Georgian high-backed chairs that was still warm from the previous occupant, I learned that I couldn't have been more wrong.

Her visitors had been moved to a conference room.

"There are some unanswered questions as to why their twenty-four-year-old daughter died so suddenly over the weekend," Frankie went on to say before reaching across her desk to hand me a blue file folder.

Blue was the color used in the office to distinguish coroner's cases from criminal cases. Since I was the death investigator's assistant who typically did the initial legwork, I immediately understood why I had been called in. And since we were talking about a death that occurred on Renee's wedding day, I wasn't a bit surprised to see Natalie Mercer's name on the folder tab.

"I spoke with Dr. Cardinale, who treated her in the ER," Frankie said when I opened the folder to the yellow sheet of paper with her neat handwriting. "He said that she presented with the classic symptoms of a heart attack."

I knew Kyle Cardinale—a gorgeous hunk of manflesh I had briefly crushed on three years ago. But I also knew him to be a very experienced ER doctor. Someone who probably saw dozens of heart attack victims each year, so if he said Natalie Mercer died as a result of some sort of coronary issue, I would have no reason to doubt his judgment.

"But Mr. and Mrs. Riley insist that their daughter had been the picture of health ever since she got a pacemaker as a teenager, so it's an unusual case," Frankie continued, tucking back a strand that had escaped from the cinnamon roll at the nape of her neck. "It's even more unusual that she became unresponsive so quickly."

"Wait. She had a heart attack despite having a pacemaker?" I asked.

Frankie nodded. "That's not uncommon. What's concerning, though, is the fact that she had no history of heart attack, confirmed by Dr. Cardinale when he consulted with Natalie's cardiologist. The pacemaker was working just fine at her last six-month checkup. But he agreed with the parents. With the pacemaker to regulate her heartbeat, Natalie had been living a normal, healthy life."

"Until Saturday," I said.

Frankie leaned back in her desk chair. "Until she collapsed a couple of hours before a wedding on Saturday. I'm going to have a talk with the cardiologist—see what other information he can offer about her condition. I'm also sending her fluids to the crime lab to see if anything shows up on tox. Once the results come back, I'll make a determination about an investigation. Right now, though, I'd like you to take Mr. and Mrs. Riley's statement, then talk to the husband, and everyone who was with Natalie Saturday afternoon."

That didn't include me, but it was time to confess to

my boss that I had already talked to some of these people. "Just so you know, I was at that wedding and heard about how Natalie had to be rushed to the hospital."

Frankie's gaze sharpened. "You knew her?"

"No, but I met some of her in-laws. You know, the way you do when you're mingling at a reception."

"Mingling," she said, a flicker of a smile at her peony-painted lips. "Knowing you, that means putting yourself into position to hear all sorts of interesting bits of conversation."

There was no denying it. "That happened a couple of times. I wouldn't say I heard anything terribly useful, but I know at least one person that I'd like to follow up with." Amanda, Renee's cousin, who had told me that she'd been with Natalie most of the day.

"Good. See if they can meet with you today or tomorrow. First, though, talk to the Rileys. They're in the small conference room."

I had my marching orders, so I gathered up the file folder. "Got it. Do you want to see them after I've taken their statement?"

"I do not. I've been yelled at enough for one day." Frankie looked at me over her computer monitor. "And I've already told them how we are going to proceed on this. Same as I told you, so we should all be on the same page."

"Okay." That helped to give me a sense of what to expect once I sat down with the Rileys.

"Just don't be surprised if it gets loud," Frankie added. "They just lost their daughter, and emotionally they're as raw as can be."

"Got it," I repeated with an even greater sense of what was waiting for me in that conference room. And it wasn't something I looked forward to experiencing.

"Is there anything else?" she asked a few seconds later, probably because I had yet to move.

"No." I swallowed the lump in my throat and pasted a smile on my face. "I'm good."

I wasn't, but I knew exactly what to do.

I'd taken dozens of statements. Grieving parents, husbands, wives, siblings. I simply had to compartmentalize my emotions and let them tell me their stories.

"I wish I could tell you it gets easier," Frankie said as I reached her door. "But you'd know I was lying."

I nodded. "Yes, I would." Not because she referred to me as her "human lie detector." Experience had already taught me that hard truth.

Chapter Four

"Mr. and Mrs. Riley," I said as I opened the conference room door. "I'm sorry to keep you waiting."

The couple I saw in Frankie's office turned to face me, their faces ashen as if the events of Saturday had drained every ounce of life from them.

"I'm Charmaine Digby." I didn't wait for them to introduce themselves. Frankie had made a note of their names and contact information in their daughter's file. Instead, I grabbed a legal pad and pen from the side table near the door. "I understand that you've already met with Ms. Rickard. I'm one of her deputies and would like to ask you some follow-up questions, if that would be okay."

They each gave me a solemn nod.

Kayla Riley, sitting closest to the door, looked to be in her late forties. On a normal day, she was probably quite striking. Slender, thick wavy hair the color of molasses, full unpainted lips, perfectly arched brows. If I hadn't already known that she had just lost her daughter, one glance at her puffy eyelids would have informed me that this was not a normal day.

Paul Riley, a large, steely-haired fifty-something in a

charcoal long-sleeved T-shirt, hadn't shaved, the silvery stubble adding to his pallor. He regarded me from behind black rectangular frames, a crease dividing his thick eyebrows, and then looked away, clearly unimpressed.

Yeah, I didn't look the part of a deputy coroner. I had my hair up in a ponytail and I was wearing a jeans jacket from Valu-Mart instead of a wool suit like Frankie. I had also eaten a muffin in my car a half hour earlier and did a quick wipe of my chin just in case.

With that I was as ready as I was going to get, and I shifted my focus to the task at hand.

They each had a bottle of water on the table in front of them so I assumed I could dispense with the hostess duties. What I didn't see on the table was a box of tissues, and I grabbed one from the side table.

Tears often flowed during meetings here with family members—something I had learned to anticipate. And since Saturday had already provided me a preview of the story I was about to hear, I knew it was going to be a sad one.

I took a chair opposite them and placed the tissue box at the center of the eight-person oval table. "First of all, my condolences for your loss."

Mr. Riley folded his arms across his chest and huffed a breath. I took that as a sign that he didn't want to hear any other niceties from me.

I didn't blame him. There was nothing I could say to ease their pain, so I picked up my pen to signal that I was ready to begin the interview. "I know you've already provided some preliminary information to Ms. Rickard, but

I wonder if we could start from the beginning."

Mr. Riley made no eye contact with me, but his wife nodded as if she'd be their chief spokesperson.

"Why don't you tell me about Natalie?" I gently asked to give her an opportunity to find her voice before diving into the events of Saturday.

"She was sweet," Mrs. Riley said, reaching for a tissue as tears spilled over her dark lashes. "Wonderful with children. I wasn't a bit surprised when she decided to go into teaching. It was a perfect fit for her."

I smiled across the table at her. "It sounds it."

"Everybody loved her. The kids in her class, her family and friends. And Lucas..." She slowly shook her head. "He was crazy about her."

"Lucas?" This was the first time I'd heard the name mentioned since Saturday. "He was Natalie's husband?"

Kayla Riley's lips stretched into a sad smile. "She told me she knew from the first time they kissed that he was the one."

Her husband hung his head. "And now she's dead, so can we get on with this, please?"

"Of course," I said. "Is there anything else that you feel we should know about Natalie?"

"Yeah, she shouldn't be dead!" he barked.

I had probably walked into that one, but at least he was no longer stewing in silence.

"I understand," I said. "Let's talk about more recent events. When was the last time you talked with your daughter?"

"A week ago Sunday." Mrs. Riley dabbed her eyes.

"Natalie and Lucas came for dinner."

"And how did she seem?" I asked.

"Fine!" Mr. Riley exclaimed, dialing up his volume.

I met his wife's gaze. "How did she seem to you?"

"She was her usual happy self," Mrs. Riley said. "Almost giddy when she told me that they were trying to have a baby."

I made a note of the last time they saw Natalie. "She didn't mention any health issues or concerns?"

Mrs. Riley shook her head. "No, everything was fine. Completely normal. And it wasn't like she didn't tell us what was going on. She knew we wanted to hear about every visit she had with Dr. Kessler. That's her cardiologist, the one who did her pacemaker surgery. You knew she had a pacemaker, right?"

"Yes, Ms. Rickard told me," I said, scribbling the doctor's name.

"You should also know that her surgery wasn't because she'd had a heart attack," Kayla Riley added. "In high school, Natalie often had dizzy spells and trouble breathing after vigorous exercise. That's when it was discovered that she had an irregular heartbeat. But once she got that pacemaker, those problems went away."

I had never heard of anyone this young getting a pacemaker. "How old was Natalie when she had this surgery?"

"Seventeen," Kayla said.

I did the math. Seven years ago. "And when was the last doctor's visit that she told you about?"

She turned to her husband. "It was last month, right?"

He nodded.

"It was a routine checkup," she said to me. "You know, to check the battery and make sure the unit is working like it should."

I made a note of this May checkup, probably the same one that Kyle Cardinale had told Frankie about. "And what did Natalie say about it?"

"That everything was perfectly fine!" Mrs. Riley was now the one raising her voice, fresh tears spilling down her pale cheeks. "Just like I've been telling you!"

"I understand," I said, wanting to assure Natalie's mother that I didn't doubt her, especially since the results of this checkup had already been confirmed by Kyle.

"I don't think you do." She grabbed another tissue and swiped at the cascading tears. "My daughter was not a fragile flower. She was an energetic twenty-four-year-old. Heck, she even ran in the Seattle half-marathon last November and kept in shape by running five miles almost every day. Does that sound like someone who'd collapse at a wedding?"

I didn't want to be the one to tell her that it wasn't unheard of for athletes to collapse from a hidden medical issue. "No, but—"

"There's something else going on," Kayla Riley said. "I'm sure of it."

Was she seriously suggesting that her daughter had been murdered? "What do you mean by 'something else'?"

"I don't know!" she exclaimed, choking back a sob. "Something!"

Mr. Riley squinted across the table at me. "Something happened that afternoon," he said, picking up where his wife left off. "Lucas said that someone called to tell him that Nat was having trouble breathing. All of a sudden like."

I had heard the same thing from Amanda at the reception Saturday. "And you're not aware of anything like that happening before?"

"Not in the last seven years. Back then it was just physical exertion that made my daughter feel like she couldn't catch her breath. Tell me." His dark eyes narrowed to slits. "What was she doing Saturday that would make her feel that way?"

I had no answer for him.

"Even if the pacemaker's battery were starting to fail, she was standing around, getting ready for a wedding, not running wind sprints!" Paul Riley pounded the table with his fist, making me jump. "This shouldn't have happened."

I looked to his wife to see if she had anything to add, preferably without yelling at me. "What else would you like included in your statement?"

Kayla Riley took a breath and slowly released it. "I don't know what else there is to say. It's just that we know our daughter, and everything that we've been told since Lucas called us from the hospital makes no sense. There's just no way that she had a heart attack."

Which led us back to Kayla's "something else" theory. "We should know more after we get the toxicology results back from the crime lab."

Mr. Riley flattened his palms on the table. "Which we've been told will take a couple of months. What are you people gonna do in the meantime?"

As far as I knew from my meeting with Frankie before I stepped into this conference room, I was the only "people" who had been assigned a role in this preliminary investigation. "We'll be speaking with as many witnesses as—"

"Who's 'we'?" he asked, cutting me off.

My cheeks burned as if they had been set on fire. "I've been asked to conduct the interviews."

Now, Paul Riley looked even more unimpressed.

On that not-so-high note I thought I should bring the first of my interviews to a conclusion. "Is there anything else that you'd like us to know?"

Kayla turned to her husband and lowered her voice. "What about those threatening texts Natalie got after they announced their engagement?"

He shook his head. "Ancient history."

Not so fast. "Did you say 'threatening texts'?"

Chapter Five

Natalie Mercer's parents could provide few details about the disturbing texts their daughter received over a year and a half ago.

All they knew was what Natalie had told them back then. The texts started the week after Lucas and Natalie broke the news of their engagement to both sets of parents. She said they had been sent from an unknown number and never amounted to much more than angry name-calling.

When Natalie received one of the texts while Lucas and she were at the Rileys' house for Thanksgiving, she handed him her phone and jokingly told him that his girlfriend was "at it again."

Since the threats didn't escalate and the anonymous texts ended months before the wedding, Natalie never mentioned them again.

"I think she was so happy with the new job and to be marrying Lucas that she simply put them out of her mind," Mrs. Riley had told me minutes earlier. "I always thought they were a little scary. Clearly harassment."

If I had started to receive weird anonymous texts

within days of getting engaged to Steve, I would have been scared too. Especially if the harassment went on for weeks.

"And then it just stops, which makes it even more weird," I muttered under my breath after I walked the Rileys to the door.

When, I wondered.

Standing in the lobby, I flipped through my several pages of notes only to confirm that I didn't even have an approximate date because I didn't know when Natalie and Lucas got married.

Walking back to my desk, I added that to the mental list of questions I wanted to ask Lucas Mercer. Today, if possible.

Natalie's Port Townsend address had been included in the blue folder, so Lucas should be easy to locate. And from Lucas I should be able to get a last name for his cousin Amanda.

Easy peasy, or so I had thought.

Almost an hour later, I was knocking at the door of a second-floor apartment in rural Port Townsend near the fairgrounds, but the only person to respond was an older woman next door.

"I'm pretty sure they're home," she said as she leaned against her doorjamb with a ceramic mug in her hand. "I always hear 'em leaving for work, but this morning... There hasn't been a peep out of 'em."

Since the neighbor was referring to the couple who

lived here and I knew that only one of the residents was still breathing, I wondered if I had the right apartment number. "Lucas and Natalie live here, right?"

The woman, who looked to be in her late sixties, cast a suspicious glance at the leather portfolio bag my mother had given to me last Christmas. "You a cop?"

I was wearing white jeans and a pink T under my denim jacket—not exactly an ensemble that shouted law enforcement. "No, ma'am."

"Oh, I thought I might see a cop knocking on their door because of all the ruckus last night."

Ruckus?

"Oh, dear. I hope they're okay," I said, trying to sound like a friend of the Mercers as I stepped closer.

She took a quick sip from her mug. "I don't know what's going on. People were coming and going all yesterday, then last night I heard them shouting. The walls here are paper-thin so you hear stuff. Anyway, it sounded like fighting. And then later it turned into the throwing-stuff-and-things-breaking kind of fighting. I was concerned for her safety, so I called the manager. I heard him come to the door a few minutes later, and things quieted down after that."

"*Her* safety," I repeated to make sure I had heard this lady correctly. "You actually heard them arguing?"

The neighbor's eyes widened behind her glasses. "I wouldn't call what I heard an argument. They've had a few of those, but they never sounded like they got physical. That's why I called the manager. Natalie's such a pretty little thing. I didn't want her to get hurt."

It wasn't my business to tell the neighbor that it was too late for that.

I wanted her to elaborate on these arguments, but she sipped on her coffee as if she had divulged enough information to a stranger for one morning.

"Anyway, since they were up so late last night, I guess I'm not surprised that they slept in." She smirked. "Or had to sleep it off."

"In that case, maybe I should knock louder," I said with a smile that I hoped wouldn't betray my growing uneasiness about what I'd see if that door were to swing open.

She nodded. "That's what I'd do, especially if they're expecting you."

Lucas definitely wasn't expecting me, but since this was my best option to speak with him today, I thanked her and went back to pound on his door.

"Hey, Lucas!" I called out as if I were a concerned friend since I could sense the neighbor watching me. "Open up!"

I glanced over at her, and she gave me an encouraging thumbs-up before shutting her door.

Good. Because I could hear someone inside and I was quite sure they didn't need an audience.

I knocked again.

"Jeez, I'm coming," a male voice croaked between expletives.

A couple of seconds later, a pasty-faced tall guy with a serious case of bedhead slumped against the door, his swollen eyelids at half-mast. "What?"

He looked beyond sleepy. More like ready to pass out.

I leaned in and took a whiff. *Oy.* He smelled like a distillery.

Swell. "Lucas Mercer?"

Wearing a sweat-stained T-shirt and boxers, he squinted at me like a mole man. "Whaddya want?"

I held out my laminated deputy coroner badge, but he looked too hungover to focus. "I'm Charmaine Digby with the Chimacam County coroner's office."

Lucas bent at the waist with his nose inches from my badge, a sickly sheen on his sallow face. "Who?"

Criminy. He was definitely too hungover to focus.

After I repeated my name and where I was from, it seemed to register because he nodded.

"I'd like to ask you some questions. May I come in?" I stepped inside without waiting for a response.

The apartment looked like a typical one-bedroom unit that opened to a living room on one side of the door and a kitchen on the other. Not so typical were the chunks of amber glass at the base of an eggshell wall with dark streaks that appeared to have been used for target practice. It reeked of stale beer and from the size of the puddle surrounding the broken glass, only a few of the beer bottles had been empty.

No doubt, this had been part of last night's "ruckus."

Near the broken glass, one of the four oak dining room chairs was lying on its side, but I didn't see any indication of a physical altercation between Lucas and another person.

"Maybe we could talk in here," I said, taking a step

toward an oatmeal sofa that looked like it had been used as a cat scratching post. But the living room smelled a heckuva lot better than the kitchen.

He didn't answer. Instead, Lucas lurched away with his hand over his mouth and ducked into the first room down the hall.

From the sound of the retching, I didn't have to guess what was going on in there.

"I'll make some coffee," I called out. *Because you're gonna need it.*

After twenty minutes, he came into the kitchen dressed in faded blue jeans and an unbuttoned navy Henley. His dark hair was damp and had been finger-combed away from his pale face. He had at least two days' worth of stubble, so he either hadn't taken the time to shave or didn't care to.

I suspected the latter.

Still, Lucas cleaned up pretty well, and he now smelled a thousand percent better, but he moved gingerly like everything hurt.

I was sure the noise I was making sweeping up his broken empties didn't help him feel any better.

"You don't have to do that," he muttered as I dumped the contents of the dustpan into the garbage can under the kitchen sink.

"No big deal. It gave me something to do while I waited." And I didn't want him or anyone else to cut themselves on broken glass.

"Sorry I made you wait. I wasn't... I had to—"

"You needed a few minutes," I said, returning the

broom and dustpan to the closet where I had found them. "I get it."

When I stepped back into the kitchen, I saw him grab an insulated coffee mug from the mottled gray laminate countertop.

I pulled out one of the bottles of lemon-infused water that I saw in his refrigerator when I was looking for milk for the coffee. "Drink this first. You're dehydrated."

Lucas gave the bottle a hard stare. "It's my wife's."

I didn't have the heart to tell this guy that everything in his apartment now belonged to him and him alone. Instead, I took the mug from his hand. "It's okay. Take it into the living room and I'll bring you some coffee. How do you take it? Milk and sugar?"

"Just milk," he said, shuffling away from me.

I poured coffee into his mug, refilled my own, splashed some milk into both and joined him in the living room.

The coffee table in front of the sofa was close enough for Lucas to reach from the velvet armchair he was slumped in, so I set our two mugs down and took a seat to face him.

The light filtering in through the closed curtains wasn't the strongest, but I could see well enough to get a decent read of him as long as he didn't hide behind that coffee mug.

I picked up my notebook and pen from where I had laid them out on the center sofa cushion. "Mr. Mercer, I know this is a difficult time, and I'm very sorry for your loss, but I need to ask you some questions concerning your wife's sudden death."

His bloodshot eyes glistened as he stared down at the half-empty bottle in his hands.

He didn't respond, so I pressed forward. "I'd like to start with how Natalie had been feeling prior to Saturday."

He drained the bottle and exchanged it for his coffee mug. "She seemed fine."

"She didn't mention any problems like shortness of breath or dizziness?" I asked.

"No, nothing like that," he said in a weary monotone.

"I understand Natalie had a pacemaker. Had she been experiencing any issues with it? Any concerns that she mentioned?"

He took a sip of coffee and then shook his head. "No issues, no nothing."

Okay, this matched what Natalie's parents had told me. "You'd known her for how long?"

"A little over three years."

"During those three years did you ever see her pass out from drugs or alcohol?"

Lucas frowned at me. "My wife didn't use drugs and hardly ever drank, so no."

"How about stress? Had she been under a lot of stress lately or upset about anything or with anyone?" *Including you.*

He shook his head. "We were trying to have a baby, but it wasn't anything she was stressing about."

"And everything was cool here at home?" I asked, watching him for a reaction.

"Why wouldn't it be?" Color rose up Lucas's neck while

his volume increased.

"I'm just asking. You know, it's not always smooth sailing in a marriage." Between my mother's three failed marriages and my one, I should know.

"We were doing fine! Everything was great. She was great." He wiped away the tears spilling onto his cheeks with his sleeve. "Perfect."

I believed him. "I ask this because your neighbors mentioned that..." I didn't want to use the word *argue*. Nor did I want to rat out the older lady who was probably trying to listen to every word we said. "That it sounded tense sometimes."

Lucas frowned again. "Tense? With my wife?"

"That things could get a little heated," I added for good measure.

His lips compressed as he stared down at his coffee mug for a couple of seconds. "Whoever told you that doesn't know what they're talking about."

Lie.

No, the lady next door had definitely overheard some arguments.

"Listen," he said, his knuckles turning white around that mug. "My wife just died. I don't know why, but I know for a fact it wasn't because we were having problems. Because we weren't!"

And he was back to telling the truth.

"Okay," I said, scribbling on my notepad. "Is there anything you'd like to add concerning Natalie's health?"

"She saw her cardiologist last month. He said that everything looked good."

I nodded.

"You didn't write that down. Because you'd already heard about that from Kayla and Paul, right?"

I knew better than to divulge any specifics to anyone outside of my office. "I'm not—"

"They called to tell me that they were going to demand an investigation," Lucas rasped. "Like that'll change anything."

"I'm sure they're searching for answers."

His gaze shifted to me, landing like a glancing blow. "If that's what you're here for, it should be obvious by now. I got nothin' for you."

That didn't change the fact that I had more questions for him. "Actually, I think there's something that you might be able to shed some light on. It's come to our attention that Natalie received a number of disturbing texts from an unknown number."

"What?" Lucas winced as if I were giving him mental whiplash.

But he had to have known about them. "I believe it started happening when you announced your engagement."

"Yeah, there were some texts. It wasn't that big of a deal."

"It was suggested that they were threatening."

"Someone was just ranting," he said. "We didn't take them seriously."

Maybe he didn't because he wasn't on the receiving end of the ranting. Or he knew who was sending them. "You never reported them to the police?"

"No. No need."

"I understand that Natalie used to refer to the sender as 'your girlfriend.'"

"She was just kidding around."

Or maybe she was onto something.

"Was the sender someone you'd had a relationship with?" I asked, watching him for a reaction.

He blinked, pressing his lips together for a split second before answering. "No. No way. Like I said, I'd been with my wife for three years."

That last part was true, but I wasn't buying the rest of it.

"So, you never found out who was sending those texts to her?" I asked.

"No."

Nope. He knew, and I suspected that he would be a much better liar if he wasn't hungover.

"And they stopped well before you got married, right?"

"Right."

"Without you taking any action," I said, watching him carefully.

"They just stopped."

I couldn't tell if he was lying. Maybe, maybe not. "And when did you and Natalie get married?"

He teared up again. "Our first anniversary was last Sunday, June nineteenth."

While I made a note of their wedding date, Lucas set his mug on the coffee table with more force than necessary. "What does this have to do with my wife having a heart attack?"

Probably nothing, since the "ranting" happened over a year ago. Still, it was weird.

I politely smiled at him. "Just some details that I've been asked to follow up on."

That wasn't exactly the truth since Frankie knew nothing about the texts, but it helped me move this conversation forward.

"I've also been asked to interview everyone who was in the room with Natalie Saturday afternoon," I added. "Could you provide me with their names?"

Lucas wiped his eyes. "I didn't get there until later, but I know my mother was...Nora Mercer, and my cousin Amanda Sheridan. And my aunt Renee...Renee Ireland. It was her wedding."

So far, he wasn't telling me anything I didn't already know. "When did you arrive at the resort?"

"Around two-thirty."

"You drove there separately then?" Because I knew that all the hair and makeup prep would have to have started closer to noon.

He nodded.

"And where were you when your wife started having trouble breathing?"

He stared at his coffee mug resting on his thigh. "At the bar with my dad and some of the guys. The wedding wasn't supposed to start until five, so we were just hanging out."

"I understand that someone realized that Natalie needed medical attention and called Dr. Wolfe. Do you know who that was?"

"I think it was Renee," Lucas said. "I couldn't say for sure. My mother called me at the same time and then we took off running."

"You and Dr. Wolfe?"

Nodding, Lucas wiped a tear from his cheek. "It was bad. Nat could barely breathe."

"And only your mother, Amanda, and Renee were in the room with you?"

More tears spilled over his lashes. "Huh?"

"Were you aware of other people in the room?"

"I guess, but I wasn't really paying attention." He shuddered. "Nat lying there, trying to breathe, was all I could see."

I believed him and didn't want to pelt this poor guy with any more questions than absolutely necessary. But I still had one lingering thing that we needed to talk about—the "something else happened" theory that his in-laws had insisted upon.

"You said your wife had a heart attack," I said.

Scrubbing his face, he nodded. "That's what I was told. In the ER...that she'd had a fatal heart attack. You know, after she was gone the doctor came out to talk to me."

"But she'd had no warning signs. No issues since getting the pacemaker, right?"

He gave me another nod.

"From what I understand, that's very unusual," I said, trying not to sound like this was something I read on the internet. Which it totally was. "I mean, at the time she started having symptoms, Natalie wasn't stressing her body with exercise, and I doubt that she was overheated in an air-conditioned room."

"What do you want me to say? That it shouldn't have happened?" Lucas stood, his volume increasing as he loomed over me. "That none of this makes any sense?"

He grabbed his mug and disappeared into the kitchen, effectively ending the interview.

Which was fine by me. Since he didn't jump onto the something-else-happened bandwagon, I'd heard enough. At least for now.

After taking a couple of quick slurps of coffee, I grabbed my bag and carried my mug into the kitchen, where I found Lucas staring at the parquet floor.

"I need to get witness statements from your mother and Amanda," I said, dumping the rest of my coffee down the kitchen drain. "May I please have their phone numbers?"

He lifted his head and shot me a weary glare. "Is that really necessary?"

I forced a polite smile. "With these unusual circumstances..." *And because your in-laws insisted.* "Yes."

Huffing a breath, Lucas retreated down the hall and returned with a cell phone in his hand. "I don't have Amanda's number, but I'm sure my mother does. Here's her number," he said, holding up his phone so that I could write it down.

"Thanks." I dropped my notepad into my bag and then pulled out my card from a side pocket and set it on the counter. "If you think of anything that you'd like us to know, don't hesitate to give me a call."

With nothing else to say, I thanked Lucas for his time

and left the apartment. I had made it halfway down the concrete staircase when I heard someone shuffling past the apartment door I had just closed.

I turned and saw Lucas's neighbor.

"Wait up," she said, laboring to follow me down the steps.

I didn't want Lucas to glance out his window and see me talking to this woman, so I went down several more steps before I leaned against the railing to face her.

"So?" The heavyset woman's eyes twinkled with anticipation. "Is everything okay in there?"

Heck, no, it wasn't okay. And I hadn't gone into her neighbor's apartment so that she could gossip to someone else about them, but I knew I needed to tell her something so that she wouldn't pester Lucas.

"There's been some bad news," I told her, leaning in as if I were sharing a secret. "Nothing you need to concern yourself with, though."

She sucked in a wheezing breath. "She's left him! I knew it was just a matter of time."

First, the arguments the neighbor said she overheard and now this. "Why a matter of time?"

She looked at me the way my dog does when I can't keep up on our morning jog. "Well, I sure wouldn't put up with my man two-timin' me."

Chapter Six

Since Lucas Mercer's neighbor had never seen him with another woman and couldn't say with certainty that Natalie suspected that he was cheating on her, I didn't think Frankie would be particularly interested in the woman's speculations.

I, however, was very interested. Especially after Lucas lied to me about the supposed former girlfriend who had been lashing out at his bride-to-be.

Since Kayla Riley had only sung Lucas's praises, if Natalie had thought her husband had another woman in his life, she never breathed a word of it to her mother.

After I slid behind the wheel of my Subaru, I made a note to follow up with Kayla to ask for the name of Natalie's best friend.

Besties typically knew all the dirt.

First things first, though, I needed to talk to Lucas's mother to schedule an interview and to see if she could put me in touch with Amanda.

I had just pulled my phone from my bag when it started ringing.

My stomach clenched when I saw that the caller was

my mother. A call before noon from my mother was never a good thing.

Actually, the same was true about *any* call from my mother. But since Marietta typically slept until noon on the days she wasn't needed on a set—and she hadn't worked in weeks—she had either had a bad night or she was having some sort of emergency and couldn't reach Barry.

"Hi, Mom. Is everything okay?"

"No, everything is not okay," she snapped.

I didn't much care for the tone, but I had long ago given up any hope of experiencing a normal phone conversation with my mother. "What's the matter?"

"For one, your florist just hung up on me."

My grip tightened on my cell phone. "Why are you calling my florist?"

"Because you need more flowers at your wedding."

What the heck? "Since when do you get to make that decision for me?"

Marietta exhaled into the speaker, venting what sounded like a hiss of steam. "I'm your mother and want your special day to look and feel as special as possible."

"You made that point abundantly clear at the florist shop when we picked everything out. It'll be fine and for what it's costing, it's plenty special."

"Don't worry about the cost. Barry and I are happy to pay for this wedding, but really, my darling, you need more flowers. Think of how pretty those chrysanthemum and rose bowls were at Renee's reception."

That's what this was about. Flower envy.

"I don't need flowers at every table. The resort is providing votive candles," I reminded her.

"Oh, please. You *need* flowers at those tables." She emphasized the word *need*, as if my wedding decor were a matter of life and death. "Preferably in Waterford crystal."

Good grief.

"Mother, I'm happy with the candles, but if I change my mind, I'm sure Roxanne and Donna wouldn't mind moving the flowers from the ceremony to the reception."

"Really, Charmaine. We don't want to look cheap about this."

To whom? None of my friends would bat an eye at repurposing the bouquets left stranded by the gazebo. In fact, most everyone I knew had done the exact same thing at their wedding.

No, this was about how Marietta didn't want to be upstaged by Renee Ireland Wolfe, who had already RSVP'd that she and her new husband would be coming to my wedding.

"Trust me. Nothing about this wedding will look cheap." Not even the cake, despite the fact that it wasn't costing her a dime thanks to the generosity of my great-aunt Alice. "So leave it alone and don't call any of the vendors with last-minute changes. *We* aren't going to do that."

"But—"

"And..." Because I knew from my first wedding that my mother would obsess over every little thing. "I've told them to accept changes only from me, so if you try this again, don't be surprised when someone else hangs up on you."

"Really, Charmaine!"

I didn't have time to listen to Marietta huff with all the indignation of a wet cat. "You said that the florist doing exactly what I told them to do was number one. What's the second reason you called?"

"Why are you being so surly when I'm just trying to be helpful?"

Helpful, right. As if wedding planning had become her favorite competitive sport. "I'm not being surly, I'm just busy working."

"Okay, fine. I realize I'm catching you at work, but my darling, you have to convince your grandmother to go shopping with me."

I didn't blame Gram for not wanting to go on a shopping expedition with her daughter. Setting out on a quest with Marietta for the perfect dress and, of course, the obligatory matching shoes typically turned into an all-day marathon.

"If she doesn't want to go shopping, I don't think I'll have any more power of persuasion than you do," I said, starting my car so that I wouldn't have to lie to my mother about needing to end this call.

"She at least listens to you." Marietta paused. "Where are you? You don't sound like you're at the office."

"I'm in my car. You caught me between interviews, but I'm going to have to—"

"Interviews? Like witness interviews?"

"Yes."

My mother sucked in a sharp breath. "Having to do with that girl dying at Renee's wedding?"

"She didn't die *at* the wedding, but yes."

"And you have to meet with all the people who were there with her on Saturday?"

"Yep."

"Excellent!"

Huh?

"If you talk to Adam Wolfe's mother, ask her where she bought her dress," Marietta said. "You know, that pretty blue one with the jacket your grandmother liked."

Oh, yes. After the lady tearfully tells me how horrible it was to see Natalie gasping for air, I'll casually segue to where she shops. You betcha.

"I don't think his mother lives close by," I said, hoping that Marietta would give me the out I was looking for.

"Well, if you call and talk to her, then."

So much for getting that out.

After I disconnected with Marietta I called Lucas's mother, who agreed to see me and provided directions to her Seattle address.

Almost two hours and a ferry ride later, I parked in front of a stately red brick Tudor with a lawn like a putting green near the University District.

Seconds after I pressed the video doorbell, the arched door surrounded by decorative stone swung open, and Nora Mercer graced me with half a smile as she glanced down at my denim jacket.

Yes, once again, my jacket wasn't helping me make the best of first impressions. She on the other hand appeared to have dressed for my visit in a cranberry silk blouse, charcoal slacks, and a coordinating beaded necklace. Either that or she had some other business to attend to later.

Nora was pale without the makeup I had seen her in on Saturday and her chestnut brown hair hung to her shoulders in a long bob. I assumed this was her typical style when she wasn't glammed up for wedding pictures.

"Come in, Charmaine. I hope you didn't have any trouble finding the place."

"No, not at all," I said, stepping onto a pretty cornflower blue and cream area rug covering the lustrous hardwood of the entryway. A marble-topped console table with a bouquet of fragrant star lilies and white carnations stood in bright contrast to the floor-to-ceiling paneling. Opposite it, two lady palms in ceramic pots bookended open double doors to a paneled study with a wall of books.

Bill and Nora Mercer's house looked like something out of a Gothic novel in a dark, every-wood-surface-must-be-polished-by-the-help kind of way. Lucas had definitely come from money, but you wouldn't know it by where he currently lived.

"Your directions were great," I added as she shut the heavy door behind me with a thunk.

Actually, I had taken the wrong exit off the interstate and used the navigation app on my phone to get here, but Lucas's mother didn't need to know that.

"I thought we could talk in the kitchen," Nora said,

leading me past an elegant formal dining room with dark wainscoting and into a large, updated kitchen, where it smelled of vanilla and brown sugar, like she had been baking cookies.

I took another glance at her blouse. It appeared to be flour-free, just like the granite countertop of her sunny kitchen. I could see a plate of what looked like oatmeal cookies at the center of a teak dinette table by a bay window. What I didn't see were any mixing bowls or baking sheets, so Nora or some member of her household staff had tidied up.

She gestured to the dinette set with a hand sporting an enormous diamond-encrusted ring. "Make yourself comfortable."

There were two place settings with dainty china plates, cloth napkins, and silver spoons as if I had come for a tea party instead of a witness interview. I took the closest chair and retrieved my notepad and pen from my bag. "Thank you."

"Would you care for some coffee? I was just about to have some."

I never turned down a chance to get caffeinated, especially when I knew it was going to be a long day. "Sure, thanks."

While she dropped a pod into her single-serve coffee maker, I listened for the presence of someone else in the house. "You have a lovely home."

Nora gave me a polite nod. "We like it."

"It's very quiet," I said as the coffee maker whirred to life as if to make a liar out of me. "I assume your husband isn't at home?"

"No, he's on his way to Port Townsend to check on our son, so it's just us."

For her husband's sake, I hoped Lucas's neighbor wouldn't pelt him with intrusive questions.

"Help yourself to a cookie," Nora said as she plucked a second coffee pod from a storage rack. "I made them this morning." She shot me another half smile, more brittle than the first. "I bake when I'm stressed."

I could relate because baking had long been my coping mechanism of choice. "Me, too."

She held my gaze for a second and then looked away as if to signal that she wasn't interested in bonding with the person who wanted to question her about her son's dead wife.

"I sent the chocolate chip cookies over with my husband," Nora said over the coffee maker's final sputters. "They're Lucas's favorites. Although I doubt he's interested in food right now."

She glanced at me as she placed cream and sugar containers on a lacquered tray along with the two steaming cups of coffee. "How did he seem to you when you were there? I've called and left messages, but I haven't talked to him since Saturday night."

I didn't want to be the one to tell the guy's mother that he seemed beyond hungover. Beyond depressed. Beyond devastated. "He's probably doing as well as can be expected."

As she approached the table, Nora's eyes pooled with tears. "I should have gone over there with Bill, but I have an appearance I have to make at the library tonight. It's something that was scheduled months ago, so I hesitated to cancel, but..." She grabbed a tissue after she set down the tray and wiped her eyes. "Sorry, I'm babbling. I also do that when I'm stressed."

"No, you're fine," I said, reaching for one of the cups. "What are you doing at the library?"

"I'm on a panel with another children's author. We're supposed to talk about the books we write to help kids handle problems they might encounter in life. I probably won't have much to say since I don't seem to be able to help one of my own children right now, but... I made the commitment." Nora took another swipe at her leaky eyes. "I just hope I don't cry through the whole thing."

"I'm sure you'll do fine." After an awkward silence I figured it was time for me to get on with the interview. "I appreciate you seeing me on such short notice."

"Of course," she said, spooning sugar into her coffee. "You said you had some questions about Saturday."

"Yes, the coroner wanted me to follow up with everyone who was in the room with Natalie before she collapsed. Lucas mentioned that you had been there."

Nora nodded. "All of us bridesmaids were there. I didn't realize anything was seriously wrong at first. Natalie just seemed tired, which was understandable considering she'd been on her feet since noon, doing everyone's makeup."

"Who's 'everyone'?" I asked. "For example, who got her makeup done first?"

"Becca went first."

I smiled politely. "I'll need full names and their contact information."

"Oh, I don't know that I have that for everyone. I know I have Becca's, though." Nora stepped to the kitchen counter and returned with the cell phone that had been charging there. "Becca's full name is Rebecca Crenshaw. She's Renee's sister."

After Nora provided me with Rebecca's number and Spokane address, she told me that Natalie did her makeup next.

"Okay," I said after scribbling the number 2 next to Nora's name. "How did she seem to you at that time?"

"Fine. She and I chatted—she was always easy to talk to—and I got caught up on how her summer vacation was going. Everything seemed completely normal."

"And this would have been around what time?"

"I think it was close to twelve-forty when I sat down at the station she'd set up."

"Did you notice if she was drinking?" I'd been a bridesmaid enough times to know that the wedding day typically kicked off with mimosas.

Nora reached for her coffee cup. "No. Becca offered her a mimosa when she first arrived, but Natalie said that she needed to keep a clear head. When I was sitting with her, the only thing I saw her drink was whatever was in the plastic bottle she had next to her."

"Like a water bottle?"

"Water might have been in it. I couldn't tell. It was tall with a straw, like the bottles you see girls using at the gym."

I hadn't been to a gym in years as my flabby thighs would attest, but I knew what she meant.

"Okay," I said, making a note that Natalie hadn't been drinking, so it was unlikely that her death was caused by a drug and alcohol interaction.

While Nora recapped the events of Saturday afternoon—the who was where and when details—I occasionally interrupted to ask what she had observed.

Did Natalie seem tired earlier in the day?

Did anything about her behavior change?

I got the same answer each time: no.

It wasn't until Natalie had started on Renee's makeup that Nora remembered hearing her say something about feeling light-headed.

"What time was that?" I asked.

"Maybe a quarter to three. I thought it might be a blood sugar thing since she hadn't stopped to eat anything, and I tried to get her to eat one of the muffins the resort provided."

"Had Natalie had problems with her blood sugar before?" Because this was the first time I had heard about this.

"No, I do if I go too long without eating, so I just assumed that was the reason."

That wasn't unreasonable. "Did she stop to eat the muffin or anything else?"

Nora gave her head a little shake. "I think she might have had a soda. I remember there was a can of Coke on the table next to her and I thought that might give her a sugar boost."

"Where did the Coke come from? Did she leave the room to get it?" Because Nora hadn't given me that impression until now.

"No, no. Joan, my mother-in-law, ordered room service. Oh, and small world, Natalie even knew the waiter who was taking care of us. Had some classes together at the UW, so they chatted for a few minutes when he delivered our first coffee order. Anyway, when Joan noticed that Renee was getting a little tipsy, she placed another order for coffee, Coke, iced tea—whatever the girls wanted to drink that wasn't alcoholic."

I couldn't help but smile as I remembered how tipsy my ex's sister had been on the morning of her wedding. "Got it. So, your mother-in-law was there with you some of the time?"

Nora nodded. "Joan and Diane, Adam's mother, didn't want their makeup done, but they stuck around after the beverage service arrived. So probably from two on."

Which would put two more potential witnesses in the room around the time Natalie started having symptoms. "Do you have their phone numbers?"

"I don't have Diane's, but I can give you Joan's," Nora said, scrolling through her phone's contact list.

"Great. It would also be helpful if you'd give me Renee's cell number. I doubt she'll be checking in at work while—"

"You can't call her about Natalie's death!" Nora proclaimed as if this would be a breach of post-wedding etiquette. "Have some compassion. She's on her honeymoon."

"I realize that, but—"

"Joan told me that Renee couldn't stop crying that night after the reception. Let her enjoy her honeymoon in peace. You can talk to her after she gets back on the fifteenth."

And I was leaving for my honeymoon on the sixteenth. Swell.

"O-kay." I didn't bother masking my irritation at being told what to do. But I also had to admit that Nora had a point. Waiting until we were both back in town would make no difference in the big scheme of things, given how long the tox screen would take.

I just wouldn't admit it aloud.

"I can give you Joan's number," Nora said as if that were a consolation prize.

Seconds later, I was writing down a number with a local area code. "Does she still live in the Seattle area?"

Please say yes because I'd love to see Joan Germain's house.

"On Queen Anne Hill, so not too far from here."

Excellent! With any luck I could swing by and get her statement today. And try not to totally fangirl out in the process.

I looked back over my notes. "Okay, you were saying that Natalie was working on Renee's makeup."

"Right." Nora fidgeted with her empty coffee cup. "She must've said something about a headache when she was finishing up with Renee, because Renee asked if anyone had any aspirin. I said that I did and came over with the bottle I keep in my purse. I noticed then that Natalie didn't look good and as soon as Renee left with the photographer and Erin to take some pre-wedding pictures, I insisted that Natalie sit down and eat something."

Erin? Was this someone who worked with the photographer or wedding planner?

Tears welled in Nora's eyes. "But she said she was too nauseated to even think about food. For a second, I thought she and Lucas had been keeping a secret. That they had been waiting until after the wedding to make the announcement that she was pregnant." Nora wiped her eyes with her napkin. "Of course, you already know why she was nauseated. I just didn't realize it while it was happening. She was having a heart attack."

Crap. Now I was tearing up. "You couldn't have known."

Nora heaved a sigh. "She knew, though. Natalie was scared when she told me that something was wrong. That's when Adam's mother called him to come quick, and I called Lucas."

I made the correction in my notes about who called Dr. Wolfe. Not that it mattered that much, and Nora didn't need to relive another minute of that day for my benefit. I already knew about the phone call she got from her son hours later.

But I needed her to back up and tell me more about Erin.

While Nora blew her nose, I flipped through my notebook to see if I had any other questions for her. "I think we've covered everything I need for now, but you mentioned someone named Erin as if you knew her."

Nora looked across the table at me, her lips once again curved with that half smile. "I should. Erin Lofgren was Lucas's girlfriend all through high school."

Chapter Seven

Joan Germain didn't answer, so I left her a voice mail to call me. I didn't have Erin Lofgren's number and would have to hunt her down when I got back to the office. Everyone else Nora had mentioned lived out of the area except for Amanda, who had said she could see me between appointments around three.

Perfect! I should be able to get back home in time to make dinner for Steve and myself.

Using my navigation app to guide me to the salon where Amanda Sheridan worked, I headed south toward Pioneer Square. After circling the Seattle stadium district like a vulture, I finally found a place to park.

Just as I reached for my car door handle, my phone started to ring. With the hope that it was Joan returning my call, I pulled it from my bag without checking the caller ID. "Hello."

"May I please speak with Charmaine Digby?" asked a female voice I didn't recognize.

"This is Charmaine."

"This is Avery Olcott, the director of catering at the Rainshadow Ridge Resort."

She said this as if I wouldn't remember sitting down with her and Steve two months ago to finalize the details for our reception. "Hi, Avery."

"I'm calling about the beverage service change you wanted to make."

What beverage service change? "Are you sure you have the right wedding party? Because I haven't asked for a change."

I could hear Avery clicking away at her keyboard. "Yes, Digby and Sixkiller. July sixteenth. The addition of a beverage station was requested by your assistant."

"My *assistant*?" What the heck?!

The only person who would have been brazen enough to pose as my assistant had to have been the pain in my patootie who decided that I needed more flowers.

"I take it you don't have an assistant," Avery said, the only one of the two of us not raising her voice.

"No, I don't." I had a meddling mother who was going to get an earful as soon as I hung up with Avery.

"And you don't want the second beverage station?"

"It's not necessary, and I apologize that my mother called and wasted your time."

Avery chuckled. "It's not the first time that I've had to deal with an overly *helpful* mother of the bride, but it is why I called to confirm before I processed your change order."

After reminding Avery that she had my permission to hang up on my mother the next time she called, I disconnected and promptly called Marietta to let her know that there had better not be a next time.

Of course, she didn't answer. Instead, I got to listen to her sweet as syrup greeting about how sorry she was to have missed my call. "You should be sorry," I wanted to yell, but I didn't. Calling out my mother would only make her defensive and after she'd had some time to brood, she'd become pissy.

The last thing I needed today was a pissy Marietta Moreau in my ear.

"Call me," I said, leaving her a short and not the least bit sweet message. She'd know I wasn't happy with her, and that was enough for now. I had an interview with Amanda Sheridan that I didn't want to be late for.

Five minutes later, after hoofing it three blocks to where Amanda worked in a salon nestled between an art gallery and a Pilates studio, I pushed open a glass door and stepped in front of a water feature constructed with tiers of bronze lotus petals.

Very nice. The trickle of water was calming too, softly telling each new arrival to leave their worries at the door.

If only I could.

Still, the salon's interior set a gracious mood with its sage walls, tall pillar candles flickering on stands, and sleek furnishings. More Beverly Hills meditation studio than south Seattle beauty salon.

And it sure didn't smell like any beauty salon I had ever visited. There was no hair dye and senior-set perm chemicals assailing my nostrils like at Donatello's. Instead, I breathed in a citrusy blend of mandarin orange, lemon verbena, and something else.

Something sensual and earthy.

Something rich, like dollar signs rich, subtly suggesting that this was a salon I couldn't afford on my salary.

Which I already knew, because everything about this place was artfully designed as if it were an extension of the gallery next door. From the workstations that looked like they had been carved out of black marble to the surreal artwork with green and blue swirls hung between ornate oval mirrors. All the stylists were fashionably dressed in black and were busy with clients.

I didn't see Amanda anywhere, so I headed for the reception desk that was separated from the salon's inner sanctum by a wall of glass cubes. The wall looked frosty, like it had been chiseled from ice. The same could be said about the twenty-something receptionist with the heavily lined cat's eyes.

Wearing black like the five stylists working behind her, she lowered her spiky lashes to glance at my Valu-Mart ensemble, and then flared her nostrils as if she didn't care for the odor of the unwashed that had wafted in with me. "May I help you?"

"I'm here to see Amanda."

The receptionist turned to a computer monitor and tapped her keyboard with a blood red acrylic nail. "Your name?"

"Charmaine. I don't have an appointment but she's expecting me."

Ms. Cat's Eye picked up her phone and relayed the message, then shifted her gaze to me. "She'll be with you in a moment."

She immediately went back to her phone as if I had

been dismissed.

Fine. I didn't want to talk to you either.

A couple of minutes after my butt sank into a fringed chair the color of an eggplant, Amanda Sheridan stepped past the reception desk and extended her hand to me.

"Charmaine, it's good to see you again." Amanda cringed as I got to my feet. "Sorry, did that come off as weird? I mean, considering the reason you wanted to talk to me."

"No, not weird at all." I was just happy that she could squeeze me in between appointments.

I noticed that Amanda had an expensive leather bag slung over her shoulder. Black, of course, in keeping with what I assumed was her work uniform. On her feet she wore comfy-looking black and olive camouflage sneakers instead of the heels I saw on the other stylists. This made her shorter than I remembered—just under my five feet six inches—but she exuded the same helpful attitude as when I first met her at Renee's reception.

"My three-thirty called and canceled, so that gives us a little more time. Want to get a coffee?" she said, heading for the door without waiting for an answer.

I didn't need more caffeine in my system, but if that would provide us a quiet place to talk, I was all for it.

"They usually aren't busy this time of day," Amanda said, striding toward the Seattle Beanery across the street. "So we shouldn't have any trouble getting a table."

I could see at least three unoccupied tables near the front window. "Perfect." Even more perfect, the notes of the jazzy piano solo I heard when we entered were muted, maybe in deference to the two guys focusing on their laptops along the far wall.

I pointed to the table at the opposite corner, where we wouldn't be overheard, asked Amanda what she wanted, and then went to the counter to place our order.

A couple minutes later, after stuffing the receipt into my jacket pocket so that I could expense our cappuccinos, I carried our two cups to a retro pedestal table that looked like it had been rescued from a 1950s soda shop.

Amanda didn't react when I set down the white porcelain cups. Instead, she grimaced at the cell phone in her hand.

"Everything okay?" I asked, taking the red vinyl seat across from her.

Blowing out a sigh, Amanda reached for her cup, setting the violet-streaked curls of her updo into motion. "It's nothing, and thanks for the coffee. It was just my daughter informing me that the pork chops I bought for our dinner have gone into a casserole that she's taking to Lucas."

I knew about the cookies his mother had baked him. Add to that a casserole from his cousin. Second cousin? However they were related to one another. I remembered seeing another casserole dish below that case of water in his refrigerator. A cake carrier on the counter, too. I doubted the grieving widower would be interested in food anytime soon, but there would be plenty available when his appetite returned.

Assuming that all this well-intended sustenance didn't get tossed at the nearest wall.

Amanda looked at me over the rim of her cup, her amber eyes wide as if she thought she'd made another blunder. "Don't get me wrong. I think she's wonderful to do this for him, but I hadn't planned on stopping at the store on the way home. Although now it's probably stopping for takeout."

I could relate to not wanting to cook after a long day and made a mental note to ask Steve if he wanted to go out for dinner.

For now, I needed to take our focus off of food.

"Speaking of Lucas," I said, pulling my notebook and pen from the bag by my feet. "Do you see one another often?"

Amanda's delicate brow crinkled slightly as she returned her cup to the saucer. "You mean socially?"

I meant anything that would get her talking about the nature of their relationship and nodded.

"I probably see him two or three times a year. You know, family get-togethers—holidays, weddings—that sort of thing."

"How about Natalie? Were you close to her?"

"Not especially close," Amanda said again with the crinkled brow. "I mean, we were friendly. She was sweet. Really easy to be around."

"Did Natalie ever say anything to make you think that she and Lucas might be having problems?"

Amanda lowered her voice as if we were two gossipy girlfriends. "No. Were they?"

"I'm just asking to get a sense of Natalie's home life." And to see if I could verify what Lucas's neighbor had told me. "No rumors or family gossip about them?"

"Not that I ever heard."

This was getting me nowhere. "Okay, let me ask you about Saturday specifically. Did you see Natalie when she first arrived at the room you were using to do hair and makeup?"

"Yes, she got there shortly after my daughter and I did."

"Your daughter was there with you?" Nora hadn't mentioned that she had been in the room.

"We drove there together," Amanda said between sips. "Sydney helped me carry stuff in and then spent most of the afternoon by the pool with Kerry, Lucas's sister. They're close to the same age and always hang out with one another at family occasions."

I made a note of the girls' names. "Who all was in the room over the course of the next several hours? Think of everyone who came in and out. Food service people, everyone."

Amanda used her fingers to list the members of the wedding party, providing me with the same names that Nora had along with a description of the waiter. She hadn't been able to remember the names of the photographer and her assistant, but I already had that from Nora.

"Oh, and Syd and Kerry came in a couple of times to get something to eat," she added as if it were an afterthought.

I added them to my list. "Did you see anyone give Natalie anything to eat or drink?"

She shook her head. "I was doing hair, so I had my

back to her most of the time. I know she had a water bottle next to her. Other than that, I don't think I saw her drink anything. Same with food. We had some stuff in the room, but I never saw her touch it."

Which was very close to what Nora told me. "Were you in the room when Natalie started feeling sick?"

Amanda nodded. "I was busy chatting with my aunt Joan, so I'm afraid I wasn't paying much attention. At least not until Renee said something about needing aspirin."

She went on to tell me how Adam was called and rushed in with Lucas, basically confirming what I had heard from Nora.

"It's so sad," Amanda said after finishing the last of her cappuccino. "I knew Natalie had some sort of heart problem, but I thought that her pacemaker had taken care of it. Obviously not."

There was nothing I could say to that, so I snapped my notebook shut to let Amanda know that I had everything I needed from her. "This was very helpful. Thank you."

She gazed across the table at me. "Can I ask you a question?"

I didn't know if I'd be able to answer it, but she could certainly ask. "Sure."

"Why did you ask me if anyone gave Natalie something to drink? She died because of her heart condition, right?"

I forced a smile. "I'm just trying to reconstruct what happened that day." And be careful with my answer.

Amanda continued to stare at me. "And you asked a lot of questions about Lucas. You don't suspect—"

"Really, I'm just trying to be thorough."

"I don't understand, though. You said when you called that the coroner wanted to know more about what happened before Natalie was rushed to the hospital."

"She's also trying to be thorough." I added an extra dollop of sincerity to my smile and hoped that this vague reason would satisfy Amanda's curiosity.

"But Natalie died from a heart attack, right?" she asked, clearly unsatisfied.

"That's what it looks like."

She leaned forward on her elbows. "What it looks like?! What's that supposed to mean?"

Crap.

That was a very direct question that I couldn't answer.

Even if I knew the answer, I couldn't divulge any specifics.

"It means that Natalie died of an apparent heart attack, but there could be some contributing factor," I said, mentally kicking myself as soon as I saw her eyes widen.

"A contributing factor. You mean like a drug interaction?"

"I really don't know." *Honest!* "I'm just asking—"

"Oh, my gosh! The aspirin!" Amanda sucked in a breath. "What if the aspirin Nora gave her wasn't an aspirin?"

Chapter Eight

"Where are you?" Steve asked when I called him from a burger stand near the Seattle waterfront. "You sound like you're on a ferry."

"Close." I looked beyond the people eating at the two picnic tables behind the building to see the five-twenty ferry shrink to a speck on the glistening horizon. The ferry I had hoped to be on.

"I'm waiting for my order at that burger place we ate at the last time we went to a Seahawks game," I said over the squawk of seagulls fighting over scraps near an overflowing trash can.

"Why?" he asked while I moved closer to the pick-up window so I could hear when my name was called.

"Because I'm hungry."

"Besides that. Why are you in Seattle this late in the day?"

"I'm working. Or at least I was. Now I'm killing a little time before I meet somebody at the library."

"You have a hot date with a librarian?" Steve asked, adding a smoldering timbre to his voice. "Should I be jealous?"

"Hardly. Someone I need to follow up with is speaking there tonight."

"Does this someone have a name?"

I looked behind me to make sure I wouldn't be overheard and saw nothing but hungry gulls on the prowl. "Nora Mercer."

"Mercer," he repeated after a moment of hesitation. "I assume this has to do with the girl who died Saturday."

"Her family wants an investigation, so Frankie asked me to get statements from as many people who were with her as possible."

"And you have to go to the library tonight to do this?" Steve asked while Fozzie barked in the background.

"It's a long story." Which I knew he wouldn't appreciate, so I decided to change the subject. "Are you at my house?"

"You texted and asked me to feed your dog, so I fed the mutt. I would've fed you too if you'd been here, because I picked up Chinese and got that kung pao chicken you like."

"Oh." I couldn't keep the ache out of my voice because I wished I was home with him instead of waiting for an overpriced veggie burger with no mayonnaise or cheese. Not the juicy hamburger I craved since I wanted to lose four more pounds before my wedding, but my stomach had been growling for the last hour.

"I'll save you some chicken," Steve said as if that would console me. "You have to hurry home to me, though."

I didn't want to admit that I wouldn't get home for at least another three hours. "I'll be there as soon as I can.

And thanks."

"For getting you your kung pao chicken? I always order that for you. I'm nothing if not trainable."

"Yes, you are. But I meant thanks for being the guy I want to hurry home to."

He chuckled. "That's the way it's supposed to be, isn't it? I mean, we *are* getting married."

Steve had been one of my best friends since we were kids, but I had never allowed myself to think of him as anything more. Not until almost three years ago, when we kissed for the first time and he became that guy to me — that *forever* guy I wanted to wake up next to.

"Absolutely," I said, hearing my name being called. "Gotta go. Save me some fried rice, okay?"

"Some of *my* fried rice? That'll cost you."

"I'm sure we can work something out in trade."

"Oh, you can be sure of that," he said with enough smolder to melt my iPhone.

Maybe Nora Mercer would get to the library early for her author panel and I could ask her about that aspirin bottle and then hightail it to the dock in time to catch the seven-ten ferry. That would get me home and into Steve's arms around eight. That seemed doable.

An hour after I left the burger stand, I took a seat in the back row of a Seattle library meeting room, where my prospect of making that ferry was becoming less doable by the second.

Because not only had Nora Mercer not arrived early,

she was three minutes late.

The librarian who had been chatting with a silver-haired woman sitting alone at a long table stepped up to a lectern and smiled at the dozen expectant faces looking back at her. "Let's give Ms. Mercer another minute, then we'll begin."

If I wanted to catch that ferry, I didn't have another minute to give her.

Not when I had a hot cop waiting for me.

I'd have to make another trip to Seattle to get that aspirin bottle. Ideally, the same day I interviewed Joan Germain.

Although who knew when that would be, since she had yet to call me back.

It wasn't the first time a local celebrity had ignored the message I had left her. Case in point, my mother, who had been dodging me the last few hours, letting all my calls go to voice mail.

I was going to have to have a face-to-face talk with her. With both women. Just not tonight. Tonight, I needed to get home to Steve.

Fortunately, I was sitting near the door and could quietly slip out. But just as I grabbed my bag, the woman I had been waiting for appeared in the doorway and my plans changed. Again.

I had absolutely no interest in hearing about the children's books these women had written, but it appeared that one of Nora Mercer's family members did. Because Joan Germain was standing right behind her.

Good luck dodging me now, Joan.

"I am so sorry to have kept you waiting," Nora announced apologetically as she rushed to the front of the room.

"It's entirely my fault." Joan Germain placed her hand over her heart as if she were making a confession. "I asked to tag along and made us late."

Heads turned and some of the women in the audience tittered with excitement at the sight of the famous local broadcaster.

Joan smiled at them with the same ease that she had demonstrated at her daughter's wedding Saturday and then took the aisle seat in the back row with me.

The librarian at the lectern beamed with pride. "We're happy you're here, and I couldn't be more pleased to introduce our speakers," the diminutive woman said, reading from her prepared remarks.

While she read the silver-haired author's bio, I moved closer to Joan so that only one seat separated us. "Hello, again," I whispered while giving her a friendly smile.

She blinked, the curl at her raspberry-painted lips flash-frozen in place. "Hi..."

"Charmaine. I'm the one who called and left you a message a few hours ago."

"A message?" she said, feigning innocence as if she didn't have the foggiest notion what I was talking about.

She did.

No matter. I no longer needed her to call me back. "I work for the Chimacam County coroner and need to ask you a few questions about Saturday." I pointed toward the door. "Maybe we should step into the hallway."

Joan glanced at her daughter-in-law, who was watching us intently from twenty-five feet away. "But we don't want to miss—"

"It will only take a couple of minutes," I said, rising from my chair.

The smile dropped from her lips as she vented a breath of annoyance, but Joan Germain opened the door and I followed her out of the meeting room.

There were several aqua and purple chairs that could double as patio furniture lined up between the room we had just exited and the one across the hall.

Both meeting room doors were shut and the closest person I saw wasn't within earshot, so I stepped toward the colorful seating arrangement. "Shall we sit here?"

Without waiting for a response, I lowered myself to the purple chair on the end and pulled out my notebook.

Joan took the chair next to me and with perfect posture promptly smoothed the front of her green leaf print tunic as if a TV camera lurked nearby.

Force of habit, I guessed.

I flashed her a friendly smile. "I know you want to get back in there to hear Nora, so let's—"

"Nora mentioned that you were at Renee's wedding." Narrowing her blue eyes, Joan did a quick scan of my face. "I didn't recognize you at first. Sorry about that. You were there with Detective Sixkiller, right?"

It figured that she'd remember seeing Steve. He had that effect on women. "Right."

"Nora also mentioned that you were asking about everyone who was with Natalie Saturday afternoon."

Thank you for providing the perfect segue. "Which is why I wanted to talk to you."

Her gaze intensified. "I don't understand. No coroner launches an investigation when death occurs from natural causes."

This woman had too much experience from interviewing coroners and death investigators to accept anything less than the absolute truth from me. "There's no official investigation. We're just doing some information-gathering because of the unusual circumstances surrounding Natalie's death."

"I see," Joan said, crossing her legs. "Well, I doubt that there's anything I can tell you that you don't already know."

I spent the next couple of minutes asking her the same questions I had asked Nora and Amanda.

No, she hadn't seen anyone give Natalie anything to eat or drink. Just the aspirin that Nora gave her.

No, she had never seen or heard anything about her grandson Lucas and Natalie having any problems at home.

"How about what you observed when you were in the room with Natalie," I said. "Did anything strike you as unusual?"

"Unusual?" Joan stared blankly at the meeting room door. "I guess it was unusual to see Erin, Lucas's old girlfriend, there. After all this time, it seemed like a strange coincidence for her to appear out of the blue as the photographer's assistant."

No kidding.

"Any interaction between Erin and Natalie?" I asked after making a note of Erin's job.

"They seemed friendly, but..." Joan shook her head. "I really didn't pay that much attention."

"So, no awkwardness because of some lingering feelings?"

"Feelings on Erin's part?" she asked. "You mean for Lucas?"

I nodded.

"No, they pretty much went their separate ways after high school, which has been what? Six years ago."

"I ask because Natalie received some threatening texts shortly after she and Lucas announced their engagement."

Joan's pupils dilated, signaling an interesting reaction. "Really."

"I got the impression that Natalie thought they were from an old girlfriend."

"Hmm." She turned away as if she knew I could read her body language. "I truly can't imagine."

Truly? It looked to me like she could imagine it just fine. "So, no ideas about the sender?"

"It could have been anyone," she said with a dismissive wave. "But to try to connect some old texts to a girl having a heart attack is quite a leap."

Maybe, but it sure seemed like this family matriarch knew more than she was willing to say. "I—"

"If there's nothing else, I'd really like to get back in there before my daughter-in-law thinks I've abandoned her." Joan Germain pushed to her feet. "Lovely to see you again."

Okay, she had reason to brush me off because she was missing Nora's presentation, but Joan Germain was acting like she couldn't get away from me fast enough.

She definitely knew who had sent those texts. Or at least suspected someone. But who?

Chapter Nine

When I stepped through my back door at ten twenty-two, the black chow mix with the wagging curly tail seemed much happier to see me than the unsmiling cop flipping on the light over the kitchen sink.

"Hello, sweetheart," I said, setting my bag on a corner of the tile counter so that I could bury my fingers in Fozzie's thick mane. "Did you miss me?"

"He's been wondering when you were gonna get home." Steve glanced at the oven's digital clock, his eyes shining dark as onyx. "Kind of late for a school night, isn't it? Did everything go okay?"

"Yep. Things started late at the library, but it went okay." Closing the distance between us, I linked my hands behind his neck. "And then true to my word. I skedaddled home as soon as I could." With my mission accomplished because I had Nora Mercer's aspirin bottle in an evidence bag, but staying to talk to her after her author panel had pushed my departure time from Seattle back another hour.

"I do like a woman true to her word." A hint of a smile curled Steve's lips as he wrapped his arms around me.

"Especially this one."

While I pulled him close to plant a kiss on those lips, Fozzie tried to wedge between our legs to demand his share of our attention.

"Mutt, you're cramping my style," Steve said, pointing toward the plush dog bed that he bought Fozzie for Christmas. "Go lie down."

After a whimper of protest about his banishment, Fozzie made a soft landing on his cushy bed, where he could still see us from the dining room.

"Good boy." Steve turned back to me with a devilish twinkle in his chocolate brown eyes. "Now, where were we before we were so rudely interrupted?"

I ran my hands over his solid shoulders. "I believe you were about to make good on your promise to save me some fried rice."

"About that..."

Slack-jawed, I gave him a shove. "You didn't!"

Steve shrugged. "I saved *some* for you."

I opened the refrigerator to see the evidence to support that statement, grabbed the one and only takeout container, and opened it. A thin layer of fried rice covered a meager portion of kung pao chicken. "This is it?"

"That's it."

"You ate half my chicken," I said, sounding as grumbly as my empty stomach because I hadn't finished my rubbery veggie burger.

"Well, technically, it was *my* chicken since I'm the one who paid for it."

"But you said that you bought it for me."

"Yeah, you got me there. What can I say? I got hungry waiting for you, and you had nothing else to eat here."

"I beg your pardon." I pointed at the vegetable bin. "I have carrots and apples and lettuce—"

"And there's a bag of dog food in your mostly empty pantry, which I also won't be eating."

"Because you'd rather eat my kung pao chicken."

Steve grinned. "In my defense, it smelled way too good to resist."

"That's a weak argument. Would never hold up in court." I sniffed the white box, which really did smell good. It would smell even better hot, so I popped it into the microwave.

"Maybe." Leaning into me, Steve flattened his palms on the counter and then nuzzled my neck. "You smell good, too."

Luxuriating in his body heat, I tilted my head back to give him easier access to the flesh he was exploring. "I suppose you won't be able to resist me either," I said, accompanied by an exaggerated sigh, giving it my all to sound disinterested.

"Nope. Not a chance. Especially when you owe me."

The microwave dinged as if signaling the end of round one and I gave his chest a poke. "I owe you nothing, chicken thief."

"How quickly they forget," Steve said, rubbing above his heart as if I had wounded him.

"What?"

"Our agreement."

I grabbed a fork, took the takeout box from the

microwave, and speared a bite of chicken. "I'm sure I don't know what you're talking about."

With a smug smile I savored the perfectly seasoned chicken melting in my mouth as well as the carnal gleam darkening Steve's eyes.

"Then, allow me to refresh your memory," he said, turning the page of some imaginary notebook on his palm. "Ah, here it is, and I quote, 'We'll work something out in trade.'"

I pointed my fork at him. "That was said in good faith and trust that you'd save me more than three paltry grains of rice."

"I'm pretty sure there's at least ten in there."

I looked into the box I was holding and saw a lot more than that, but this was an argument I had no intention of winning. "Maybe."

His grin was back, only now it was lopsided. "So, what's all that delicious rice worth to you?"

"Well, I don't know. I'm gonna have to think about what I have to offer." I seductively licked my lips, and then to my horror, the tip of my tongue grazed something hanging from the corner of my mouth.

Steve laughed. "Yeah, you have a little piece of something there."

"You could have told me!" I groaned, reaching past him for a paper towel.

"I didn't want to interrupt," he said while I wiped every trace of food and lip gloss from my mouth. "I liked what you were doing with your tongue."

So had I, but that moment was now long gone. As was

my appetite for the rest of the takeout. "Uh-huh. So sexy."

"Are you done eating?" Steve asked, watching me return the white box to the refrigerator.

"I'm quite done."

He took my hand when I tried to toss the paper towel into the garbage can under the sink. "You didn't eat much."

"I had enough."

He disposed of the paper towel for me and then pulled me into his arms. "I don't know about that."

Were we talking about food or something else?

"Because," he continued, "a minute ago, you were about to offer me something."

We were definitely not talking about food. "Was I?"

"I seem to recall you said you were thinking about it."

"That's right!" I said in mock surprise. "I was."

Steve lowered his lips to mine for a series of delicious kisses. "Anything come to mind?"

"Oh, yes."

"Something you'd like to share?"

I glanced down at the bulge straining the zipper of his blue jeans. "Something *you'd* like to share?"

Smiling, he looked at me with so much love in his eyes I could feel my heart thud with delight. Then, after one last sweet kiss, he led me to the bedroom.

That would be a *yes*.

Steve got called out early the next morning and kissed me goodbye around three. Unfortunately, I couldn't get back to sleep, so after a pre-dawn run with Fozzie and a long, hot shower, I dressed for work and headed over to Duke's to help Alice with the baking.

"Oh, dear," my great-aunt said, looking up from her mixing bowl when the kitchen screen door banged shut behind me. "Anytime you're here before five means something's wrong."

I stifled a yawn. "Nothing's wrong."

Not entirely true because my interfering mother seemed to be giving me the silent treatment after the last message I left her, but that was nothing worth losing sleep over.

Alice smirked. "The dark circles under your eyes beg to differ."

I knew I should have applied more of the concealer my mother hyped as her secret weapon in her Glorious Organics infomercials. Heck, given how *Night of the Undead*-ish I had looked a half hour earlier as I flat-ironed my hair, I probably needed more of an arsenal. That and an IV drip of caffeine.

"And good morning to you, too," I said as I stowed my portfolio bag in the locker I'd been using for the last twenty years.

After I pulled an apron from the hook by the door and tied the strings over the waistband of my khakis, I joined Alice at her butcher block worktable.

She let the spoon clatter to the rim of the stainless steel bowl. "What is it? You can tell me."

"Nothing." I reached to a shelf behind me and pulled out an identical bowl since I typically helped with the cookies and muffins. "I just woke up early," I said, omitting any mention of Steve, whom she loved, but Alice and I had always had a "don't ask, don't tell" policy about his sleepovers.

Duke turned from where he had been hovering over his doughnut fryer with wooden tongs. "What'd you say?" he demanded like a man who had forgotten to turn on his hearing aids. "Oh, hey, Char."

Alice waved him off. "We weren't talkin' to you." She lowered her voice. "I swear that man gets more deaf every year."

"I heard that just fine." He shifted his gaze from me to the wall clock and then back to me. "What's up? Something wrong?"

Good grief. "Nothing's wrong. I was just up early and didn't have much at home for breakfast."

I had used this line countless times in the last few years. It gave me the cover I needed to lend a helping hand to my seventy-eight-year-old great-aunt without her asking for it while giving me a couple of hours of baking therapy.

Duke scoffed.

"Really," I added. "You might as well put me to work."

Before turning back to tend to his doughy flock sizzling in their oil bath, he winked. "About time you earned your keep around here."

"Yeah, yeah," I said to my favorite curmudgeon as I headed toward the coffee station.

We both knew that I had more than earned my keep here over the years. I was Duke's emergency waitress when he was shorthanded on the weekends and his on-call pastry chef whenever Alice was under the weather.

After I returned with a mug of Duke's notoriously foul coffee and refilled their cups, Alice shot me a look of resignation. "Since you insist." She pushed her spiral-bound recipe book toward me, just like she had hundreds of times in the past. "Not that you need it. You probably have everything memorized."

True, but I always liked seeing the notes she had neatly written in the margins. They were the good-to-know tips she had shared with me the first summer I worked here.

"Thanks. So, what'll it be, some cookies to start with?" I knew better than to suggest that I help with the pies. Stocking the rotating display case for Duke's pie happy hour was Alice's domain.

"You should have more important things to do than to come here and bake cookies."

"I like baking cookies," I said, turning to her snickerdoodle recipe. "What's your pleasure? Three dozen each of the usual assortment?" That didn't typically include snickerdoodles, but I woke up hungry and craved something cinnamon-sweet, so today it would.

"Fine." Alice pulled a brick of butter from a nearby industrial refrigerator and dropped it onto the table with a thud. "Just tell me. You're troubled by that girl dying Saturday, aren't you?"

Where was this coming from?

"No, not at all." Shoot, that made me sound like I had all the compassion of a block of ice. "I mean, it's sad that she passed away so young, and I sympathize with everyone at the wedding who knew her. But *I* didn't know her, so I'm not losing sleep over the situation, if that's what you're concerned about."

Alice's hazel eyes widened behind her trifocal lenses, and I half-expected her to call me an unfeeling jerk. Or a heartless ice queen.

Instead, she moved her wooden stool closer to the end of the table where I was standing and slipped onto the seat. "But I heard you've launched an investigation, so there must be something...you know...*troubling* about how she died."

Sheesh! Were there no secrets in this town?

"I don't know what you've heard, but it's not true." Technically.

"Really." Alice knit her graying brows. "Then you didn't talk to the girl's parents yesterday?"

Clearly, there were no secrets in this town, and this revelation was *so* not one I wanted to hear.

"I..." I didn't know what to say. To buy myself a little time, I grabbed a knife from the tub of utensils on the storage rack and sliced down the middle of the brick for the cup of butter I needed.

"They came in to buy a couple of muffins for the ferry ride home," Alice said, filling the silence.

"Oh." I looked up at her. "But how do you know—"

"They saw your picture. Said they met you at the courthouse."

"*My* picture?" What the heck?

Then I remembered that the local paper's announcement of my engagement was still tacked to the bulletin board behind the cash register. "Oh, yeah. We should probably take that down." Although it was a little late now.

"Nonsense." She reached for her coffee cup. "It'll stay up until it gets replaced by your wedding announcement. People always like to see good news. Gives us all something positive to talk about."

I stifled a groan. It appeared to have given Natalie's parents something to talk about since they had volunteered some information about meeting with me.

"I'm surprised they recognized me," I said, scooping sugar into my bowl.

Alice swallowed a slurp of coffee. "It's a very nice picture of you and Steve. I guess the girl's mom even said something about that."

She guessed? Then this story had been relayed to her by one of the waitresses working the register.

I hesitated to ask which one, but at the same time I had to know. "Who'd she say that to?"

Please don't let it be Lucille.
Please don't let it be Lucille.
Please, please, please don't let it be Lucille.

"Lucille," Alice said. "She's the one who told me."

Gah!

As I imagined who else the queen bee of Gossip Central had told, I clenched my molars hard enough to turn them into dust.

"Unbelievable," I muttered under my breath, adding a few expletives on my way to the refrigerator for a carton of eggs. Because the news of my very preliminary investigation had to be making the rounds on Port Merritt's gossip circuit faster than a kitchen grease fire.

"It's true then," Alice said, her eyes tracking me as I approached. "Someone slipped something into that girl's drink."

I gaped at her. "What?!"

Chapter Ten

An hour and six dozen cookies later, Lucille sat across the worktable from my great-aunt, exchanging dirty looks like two misbehaving kids who had been sent to the vice principal's office.

"I can't have you laying odds on how Natalie Mercer died," I said, trying to keep the anger out of my voice as I scooped perfect rounds of chocolate chip cookie dough onto a baking sheet.

Lucille waved me off. "It was just some friendly wagering with some of the regulars. And if someone had kept their trap shut, it would've been no big deal," she added with a glare at Alice.

"You're blaming me for this mess?" Alice pushed up from her seat at the ding of her pie timer. "Puh-lease."

"You were the blabbermouth, not me," Lucille groused, swiveling off her stool as if this meeting had been adjourned.

I pointed my cookie scoop at her before she could squeak away on her white orthopedic shoes. "Not so fast. We're not done."

Settling back down, she contorted her apricot-painted

lips into a tight smile. "Come on, Char. She's making it sound worse than it is."

"Seriously?" I exclaimed in disbelief while Alice scoffed from where she was transferring her pies to cooling racks fifteen feet away. "You're betting on how that poor girl was killed like this is a game of *Clue*!"

"Will you girls knock it off back there?" Duke barked, swinging open the door to the kitchen like a gunslinger entering a Wild West saloon. "I can hear you from the counter, where we're gonna have some customers soon, so let's get a move on, Luce."

She pressed her palms to the table. "Coming."

"In a minute." I held my scoop like I was going to pelt her platinum bob with cookie dough if she so much as twitched. "You need to understand something first."

Lucille's pale blue eyes shifted to the chocolate chip glob as if I'd gone off the deep end.

Given that I was wielding a cookie scoop, maybe I had, but enough was enough. "I know that prying information out of people is like sport to you, but you have crossed the line this time."

"Excuse me, missy," she said, leaning on her elbows. "Is it my fault that people like to talk to me?"

I dropped the scoop to my bowl like the idle threat it was. "Criminy, Lucille. You've got a betting pool going for how this girl died!"

"With a grand total of five people." She shook her head. "It's nothing."

She couldn't be serious. "It's not nothing. It's my job on the line if this gets back to Frankie."

"Come on, give us some credit. No one's gonna say anything to Frankie. She hardly ever comes in for lunch, so other than Gladys's cousin living next door to her, I'm sure we're in the clear." She blinked. "Well, pretty sure."

I groaned.

"And you can't count," Alice quipped, rejoining us at the table where she had been slicing apples for her last two pies of the morning. "Dolores makes six."

"Oh, yeah. She's the one who put her money on spider venom." Lucille rolled her eyes. "I swear, that gal's seen *Arachnophobia* too many times."

"Ooh, I loved that movie," Alice chimed in.

I slapped the table to get their attention, raising a plume of flour dust in the process. "Listen! Just because Natalie Mercer's parents came to my office with concerns about how their daughter died doesn't mean that there's going to be an investigation."

"Oh, yeah?" Lucille said. "I heard that you took off shortly after you talked to them. You were even seen getting on the ferry to Seattle. Sounds like someone's doin' some investigating to me."

I stared at her in disbelief. "Are you having me followed?"

Lucille's plump cheeks glowed with pride as she inspected her unvarnished nails. "I have my sources."

Good gravy! "Well, don't believe everything your sources tell you because I'm not involved in any official investigation."

"Right," she said with a knowing nod to Alice. "That means what she's doin' is *unofficial*."

I stifled another groan.

Alice pointed her paring knife at Lucille. "Stop that. You know she can't tell us if she's working on a possible homicide."

Homicide! "Let's not call it that." Not to anyone. "Because I can honestly say I am not officially investigating a suspected homicide. That would be the sheriff's job."

Lucille frowned at me. "But the girl's mother said—"

"I know. It's natural to question what happened when a loved one suddenly dies." I looked from Lucille to my great-aunt. "I was asked to take their statements. Beyond that, I have nothing else I can tell you."

"Since I already knew that, you told us diddly squat," Lucille grumbled.

"Which is what I want you to say if anyone from my office hears about your betting pool."

Lucille heaved a sigh. "Whatever."

"Same goes for Steve," I added. "I don't want him to think that you made your bet based on something I told you."

Alice and Lucille locked gazes.

My great-aunt cocked her head impatiently. "You might as well tell her."

This couldn't be good. "Tell me what?"

"About a show she saw a few weeks back," Alice said, ping-ponging between me and Lucille. "One of those newsmagazines. Tell her what you told me. It was very interesting. I even found the story on the internet and read all about it."

"Are you telling this or am I?" Lucille huffed.

"Someone please tell it." *So that we can adjourn this meeting.*

"Fine." Lucille lowered her voice as if she were narrating a true crime drama. "The episode was titled 'The Perfect Murder.'"

Of course it was.

"Wrap it up back there!" Duke bellowed. "It's six o'clock."

"Well, heck!" Lucille glowered. "To be continued unless you want me to just cut to the chase."

I didn't need to hear a dramatic re-enactment of some show. Nor did I need Duke accusing me of distracting one of his waitresses from doing her job. "We're all pressed for time here, so go ahead and tell me why it was a perfect murder."

Lucille pushed up from the table. "She killed him with eye drops. That's what caused his heart to stop. An overdose of regular ol' eye drops. Who would've thunk it, huh?"

Eye drops?

She started to squeak away and then turned back to face me. "So, let me know if that Mercer gal died from an eye drop overdose. I got five bucks riding on that."

Two hours later, after getting a curt nod of approval from Patsy for arriving to work early, I went straight to my computer to search for the news story that my great-aunt Alice had found.

Sure enough, the victim's original manner of death had

been acute myocardial infarction but was later updated to homicide by the coroner when a lab tech found a high concentration of tetrahydrozoline in the guy's blood.

"Wow," I muttered as I combed through page after page of true crime show-worthy murders motivated by everything from insurance money to revenge by a jilted lover.

Maybe Lucille and I wouldn't have "thunk" that common, over-the-counter eye drops could be used to kill someone, but clearly plenty of other people had. And they had almost gotten away with murder.

The eye drops were tasteless, odorless, and readily available. And tetrahydrozoline wasn't a drug typically tested for by crime labs, meaning that lethal quantities in the blood and urine could go unnoticed unless more specialized tests were conducted.

Holy crap!

I went back to the news story and printed a copy to show Frankie.

She had to know, I thought as I tightened my fist around the one-page printout like a baton in a relay race and charged toward her office.

"There's no coffee," one of the junior assistant prosecuting attorneys griped at me as I blasted past the breakroom.

I knew that was my invitation to rectify his caffeine emergency. And that wasn't gonna happen. Not this morning. Because the red canister behind the coffee maker was at least half-full, and I had more important things to do.

Like solving the mystery of how a seemingly healthy twenty-four-year-old could suddenly die of a heart attack.

"You could make some, Brett," I said without breaking stride. *It only takes a minute.*

"Isn't making the coffee your job?" he called after me.

Yep. This was something we both knew, but would it kill the jerk to start a fresh pot?

I raised the printout in my hand as if I were holding the Magna Carta. "Got a meeting," I lied, but if Frankie were available to see me, it would be the truth. "So I won't be available for a few minutes."

"When you're *available* then," he grumbled, falling into step behind me.

Okay, something else I knew about my job was that it wasn't good practice to tick off any of the attorneys, because I often had to work with them during jury selection and help with witness interviews. And those could be stressful enough without dealing with a jerk seeking petty retribution.

I made a mental note to start a pot of coffee as soon as I left Frankie's office, which I was relieved to see was occupied only by my boss.

I rapped on her door and she waved me in.

"Good morning, Charmaine," Frankie said with a welcoming smile as she leaned back in her desk chair. "Were you able to meet with that witness you mentioned yesterday?"

I nodded. "I spoke with her and also took statements from Natalie Mercer's husband and mother-in-law. The husband's grandmother, too."

Her slate blue eyes gleamed with interest behind the lenses of her bifocals. "And?"

"No one saw anything out of the ordinary on Saturday," I said. "I was able to confiscate the aspirin bottle that was used that day, but—"

"What aspirin bottle?"

Heck, I was sorry I mentioned aspirin. I wanted to talk about eye drops, not aspirin.

"When Natalie complained of a headache, she was given a couple of aspirin by her mother-in-law."

Frankie pursed her peony pink lips, momentarily accentuating the puckers surrounding them. "The aspirin should have been benign, but I can check with her cardiologist."

"Assuming it was aspirin," I added.

Her gaze sharpened. "Did the mother-in-law give you any reason to think it wasn't aspirin?"

"No, I—"

"Should be easy enough to check the contents of the bottle."

I knew I wouldn't be the one checking, so it was time to talk about the document in my hand.

"I have a couple of people I want to follow up with, but I found something online that I thought I should mention."

Frankie smiled the way a parent does when their kid does something cute. "Online?"

"Yeah." And I'd find Brett and kiss his belittling butt before mentioning that I first learned about it at Duke's.

I placed the news article I had printed out on Frankie's

desk. "It's about how a woman killed her husband with eye drops."

"An overdose of tetrahydrozoline," Frankie corrected after scanning the article for a grand total of two seconds. "Yes, I remember reading about this case. I think there was even something on TV about it not long ago."

She passed the article back to me, the smile still hanging from her lips.

That was it?

"I thought that...maybe..." I wasn't sure how to complete that sentence without sounding like I was telling the Chimacam County coroner how to do her job.

"That I should add it to the list of drugs I want the lab to test for?" she asked.

Well... "Maybe."

It wasn't my boldest moment in her office, but since Frankie appeared to be humoring me, I wasn't feeling particularly bold.

"Has anyone said anything to make you think that they would have had a motive to harm this girl?" she asked me.

"No." Other than those weird texts than Natalie received over a year ago and Joan Germain's reaction when I mentioned them, I hadn't picked up on anything the least bit hinky. "Nothing. But the sudden onset of symptoms that her husband and mother-in-law described are identical to what's detailed in this article."

Frankie took it back and scanned the page. "And very similar to what Dr. Cardinale described. Well, that decides it," she said, opening a desk drawer.

"Yes!" I whispered to myself as I watched her pull out

a toxicology lab request form, make a checkmark next to *Pending Tox*, and write "Tetrahydrozoline" in the *Drugs Suspected* column.

She then handed it to me. "Please give this to Patsy so that she can send it out today. This article you found should be added to the file."

"Got it," I said, trying to play it cool while my feet itched to do a happy dance.

Her telephone rang and she reached for it. "Good find, Charmaine. Shoot me a report when you're done with your interviews."

I had just been dismissed, and that was fine by me. I'd gotten what I had wanted. I was even coming away with an attagirl as a bonus.

We'd still have to wait a couple of months for the results to come back from the crime lab, and this proved absolutely nothing in the meantime, but it felt like a win.

The world had tilted on its axis a teensy bit in my favor, and unable to contain my joy, I did a mini fist-pump prior to handing the form to Patsy.

"This needs to go to the crime lab," I said, probably sounding way too happy about stating the obvious.

She placed the form on her keyboard and shot me a smug little smile. "I'm well aware."

Yep, there was no *probably* about it.

I took that as my cue to get while the getting was good. "Okay, then."

"Don't leave," Patsy said before I could make a clean getaway. "I have something for you as well."

I stopped with the expectation that she would hand me

a subpoena that needed to be delivered.

Instead, Patsy swung around in her chair and pointed at a cardboard box. "Brett just dropped that off. Said it's a copying project he needs for a meeting tomorrow."

I stepped around her desk to pick up the box stacked with folders and loose paper. Judging solely by the weight, the bastard had saddled me with at least three hours of tedious, mindless copying.

"Brett, you're a butthead," I muttered, shlepping the heavy box to the breakroom before someone else decided to pay me back for not making them coffee.

Chapter Eleven

After the copier overheated and shut itself down like a fussy toddler in need of a nap, I took advantage of the quiet to call Erin—my second attempt of the morning to reach her.

This time Lucas's former girlfriend picked up and agreed to meet me at three at her mother's photography studio in Bellevue, across Lake Washington from Seattle.

Perfect. That gave me plenty of time to finish with the copying, catch up on the filing, and call Renee's sister Rebecca in Spokane.

As it turned out, I finished all three tasks with time to spare because my phone interview with Rebecca took no more than ten minutes. She hadn't seen anything beyond what Nora had already told me.

Unlike Nora, Rebecca was able to supply me with a phone number for Pam Driscoll, the maid of honor and Renee's best friend from college who lived in Kansas City. But when Pam admitted that she'd had three mimosas on an empty stomach and barely remembered Natalie doing her makeup, I knew she wouldn't be of much help.

That left me with one last member of the wedding

party to interview: the bride, who wouldn't be back from honeymooning in Italy for another two weeks. That wasn't ideal for my report, but I'd have plenty of time to follow up with her after I got back from *my* honeymoon.

Despite what I needed to talk to Renee about, I smiled as I flipped my desk calendar to July to check the date of our return flight, and my eyes landed on the sixteenth circled in red.

My wedding date.

The wedding that my mother kept trying to make bigger, grander, more to her taste when it tasted like perfection to me. Which reminded me, Marietta had never called me back. No texts either.

She was still giving me the silent treatment.

"Her choice," I said with a resigned shrug as I reviewed my list of things to do.

I still needed to get the names of the Rainshadow Ridge waitstaff who worked Saturday and follow up with Kayla to ask her about Natalie's friends—anyone she would have confided in.

I could make both those calls while waiting for the ferry, but not if I didn't leave soon because it was already after twelve and I still needed to grab some lunch. Preferably someplace quick and cheap, where no one would be pumping me for information.

I knew just the place, and thirteen minutes after shutting down my computer, I stepped through the back door of my grandmother's house, where my mother was sipping coffee at the kitchen table.

Crap!

"I didn't see your car," I said, pasting a smile on my face. *Because if I had, I wouldn't have come in.*

Marietta didn't so much as glance my way. "Barry dropped me off. He's going to play golf while your grandmother and I go dress shopping."

"Oh, good. You were able to talk her into going." Wore down Gram's defenses was probably closer to the truth.

"No thanks to you," she stated flatly, still not looking at me.

I had zippo time to get into this with her, but I had to say something before I had a pissed-off no-show to my wedding.

"Mom," I said, softening my tone as I sat down next to her. "I realize that you've been trying to help, and I appreciate everything you've done to make my wedding day so very special..."

While I fumbled with how to sweetly tell her to stop trying to change things behind my back, her green cat's eyes cut to me. "I feel a *but* coming on."

Yep, the *but* and everything that followed it needed to be said. "But Steve and I are happy with our plans the way they are. We'll have all the people we love there to celebrate the day with us. That's what will make it special, not more flowers."

Marietta sighed as if I had let all the air out of her. "But the flower bowls would be so pretty."

"And so unnecessary given how much you're already paying for all the bouquets," I added, trying to appeal to the pocketbook of the actress, who hadn't taken a meeting since her attempt to break into the home improvement show market fizzled months ago.

"But sooo pretty." She smiled wistfully. "You saw how lovely they looked at Renee's wedding."

"Yep. But I don't need—"

"I know, honey." My mother patted my hand. "And I hear you. But if you change your mind, let me know. Because, really, how many weddings do we have in this life?"

Marietta's face flushed as if she had counted up the five, soon-to-be six weddings between us. "Don't answer that. You know what I mean."

This time I patted her hand. "I know what you mean. So, are we good?"

My mother pulled me close, enveloping me in a musky jasmine embrace that went straight up into my sinuses. "We're fine, sugar."

With détente achieved, I pushed away from the table before my eyes started watering. "Where's Gram?"

"Changing out of her sweats into something more appropriate for where we're going," Marietta said, looking far too pleased with herself for making her mother dress up to go shopping.

Poor Gram.

"I should tell her I'm here." And ask if it's okay if I make myself a sandwich.

"Is that Char I hear?" my grandmother called out, easing her way downstairs in one of her best slacks and cotton-knit sweater sets.

I stepped to where she could see me from the staircase. "Hey, Gram. I stopped by to see what you were doing for lunch." A little fib, but it sounded better than *I stopped by for you to feed me.*

She lowered her voice to a whisper as she took the last step. "Your mother is taking me out to lunch, then we'll probably hit every hoity-toity boutique on the peninsula. Wanna come?"

"Can't. Gotta head into Seattle for work." I gave her a wink. "But you make it sound so tempting."

"Can't blame a girl for trying." She gave me a quick hug and then sniffed. "You smell like your mom. Did you two kiss and make up? 'Cause she was not happy when she first stepped through the door."

"We're fine." For now, at least.

"Good. It's bad enough she's dragging me shopping, I don't want her to be in a snit while she's doing it."

"What's all the whispering about?" Marietta demanded, coming up behind us. "You two aren't making other lunch plans, are you? Because Mama, I got us reservations at the Grotto. Charmaine, honey, you should join us. It could be like a girls' afternoon out."

Not on a bet. "I have to get back to work, but you two have a great time."

"Right. That could happen," Gram grumbled as she went in search of her car keys.

"Oh, Charmaine, I almost forgot to tell you," Marietta said, seemingly oblivious to her mother's lack of enthusiasm.

Jeez Louise! I didn't have time for any more chitchat with my mother. I had less than an hour to cram a sandwich down my gullet and then beat it to the ferry terminal. "What?"

Her cupid's bow lips curled as if she had been keeping a juicy secret. "I ran into your friend Heather at the Red Apple Market yesterday."

Heather Beckett and I had been besties when we were kids and shared a lifetime of common history (including a relationship with Steve), but it was a stretch to refer to her as *my* friend. Sure, I had invited her to the wedding. Which was a little weird considering how frosty she had been toward me back in high school, but things had warmed of late and it felt even more weird not to. "And...?"

"She asked me where you and Steve were registered."

Between the two of us, Steve and I had everything we needed to make a home together and hadn't wanted to ask for more stuff we'd rarely use. "And you told her we opted not to register anywhere, right?"

Marietta's smile started to fray at the edges. "Not exactly."

My stomach, which had been growling for most of the morning, clenched into a nervous knot. "How not exactly?"

She took my left hand, gently toying with my engagement ring. "Remember that catalog with the espresso maker that you showed me?"

The knot in my stomach twisted at the mention of the monthly mailer I had been receiving ever since I bought Gram a hand-painted tea kettle that she thought was too pretty to use. "Yeah?"

"And do you remember how it could make cappuccinos and iced lattes at the touch of a button?"

Twist. "Yes, and I also remember that when I hinted that I was thinking about buying it for your birthday, you told me it cost too much."

"Because I knew you and Steve were saving for your honeymoon." Marietta gave my hand a squeeze. "Besides, I think you'd enjoy making iced lattes more than me."

I pulled back my hand. "What have you done?"

"My darling, don't be like that. Lots of people have been asking me where you're registered."

That was a big fat lie. "Lots of people?"

"Okay, two people and one of them was Renee when I was chatting with her during the reception. But the point remains, many of your guests will want to buy you something nice, and when she said how easy it was to register online—"

Twist. "Mom!"

"Just at three stores. And Renee was right. It was super easy!"

Chapter Twelve

I had plenty of time during the ferry crossing to Seattle to make my phone calls. Also, eat the peanut butter sandwich I had made but had temporarily lost my appetite for.

I still cringed at the thought of my mother stopping in the middle of the Red Apple wine aisle to pull out her cell phone and show Heather all the places Steve and I were registered. She even suggested getting me the espresso machine, which for the obscene price tag should have also been programmed to say "good morning" in seven languages and dispense a foot massage along with the coffee.

I had ordered my mother to cease and desist and demanded her passwords so I could at least refine these registry wish lists before any of my coworkers pooled their resources to buy the pizza oven she had picked out for Steve.

Marietta probably wasn't wrong about that becoming Steve's favorite gift ever, but it cost more than the espresso machine!

Anyway, we exchanged some words, most of them at a volume that would have made my dog cover his ears.

The harshest one she lobbed at me was "ungrateful,"

right before she stormed out the door with a declaration that she was done trying to help me.

"Promise?" I called after her.

And with that, détente came to an abrupt end, and I really, *really* regretted coming over for lunch.

Gram said that she'd talk to her, but we both knew she would be wasting her breath. "Mayhem Moreau," as my grandfather used to call Marietta when she'd blow into town and turn our world upside down, had been blowing in full force ever since we went to Renee's wedding.

I wasn't sure why everything having to do with my wedding, and that now appeared to include my attitude, suddenly wasn't good enough for my mother. But here I was and with a ferry to catch, I didn't have the headspace or the time to stew about it.

I saved that for after I found a seat far away from a mom with a crying baby on the ferry's observation deck so that I could stew with decent Wi-Fi.

I spent the next ten minutes logged on to each of the store websites where Steve and I were registered so that I could delete everything that cost more than $200. That eliminated almost everything but the spa-quality towels Marietta had picked out, which I could actually use, a marble wine chiller similar to the one that she had, and a personalized wine rack.

"Now all I need is some wine," I said to myself as I ended my selections with an elegant set of long-stemmed glasses. Which gave me an idea of what to say to Heather, since texting her was my next order of business.

We hadn't spoken for weeks, so I wrote and deleted my

message three times before finding the right words to apologize for my mother's ambush at the market.

"Please don't feel obligated to buy us anything," I continued. "But if you absolutely insist, how about one of those bottles of chardonnay that we shared at your house. That was really good." It had been a nice moment between us, too. "And it's something I could actually use...right now, in fact!" I added, trying to end on a fun note while being a little more honest than I had intended.

Heather responded to my text minutes later with "No worries" and a smiley face emoji.

With that final bit of wedding-related business done, I turned my attention to the business I was being paid to conduct and made my phone calls.

The call to Avery, the Rainshadow Ridge catering manager, was quick and easy. I told her I needed to interview the waiter who had served the Ireland–Wolfe bridal party, and she agreed to set it up. All I had to do now was wait for her to get back to me.

My phone conversation with Kayla Riley wasn't quick, and it was anything but easy, because she wanted answers I couldn't provide.

What had I found out? Who had I talked to?

And the hardest question she asked me: "What do you think?"

After all the time I spent reading about the "perfect murder" I didn't know what to think, so I skirted the question and told Kayla that I still had a lot of people to talk to and that I needed the names of Natalie's closest friends.

Kayla was quick to respond with the names of the two

best friends from high school who had been Natalie's bridesmaids: Jenny Bauer and Mika Kumasaka.

She thought one of the girls had married right after high school but had no additional details to offer, so I thanked her and disconnected with minutes to spare to eat my sandwich before I needed to head back down to my car.

Sixteen minutes later, I drove off the ferry and merged into the typical midday traffic of Seattle under an almost cloudless cerulean sky.

Thirty-two minutes after that, I was northbound on I-405 when my navigation app instructed me to take the next Bellevue exit, then drive straight for four miles and turn right.

After a few blocks, I saw a two-story house with weathered gray shingles and dormer windows that looked like a Cape Cod transplant and my app informed me that I had arrived.

The house looked nothing like the photography studio I had expected to see. But sure enough, a hand-carved wooden sign nestled between two hydrangeas with blooms the size of cantaloupes told me I was at the right place: Liz Lofgren Photography.

There was a guest parking sign affixed to the right half of the garage door, so I pulled into the driveway and parked next to a blue Honda SUV that I assumed belonged to one of the Lofgren ladies.

I was ten minutes early when I climbed out of my car, but if Erin was available I figured the earlier start would help me get ahead of the worst of the commuter traffic.

The first thing I noticed was the quiet. Sure, there was a dog barking somewhere in the distance. I was in one of the many older subdivisions in Bellevue with a name. Robinwoods Garden or something. Neighborhood dogs were practically mandatory.

What I didn't hear was street noise. Instead, a cool breeze jingled the glass windchimes suspended from the porch eaves, while several yellow finches pecked at a bird feeder hanging from a branch of the graceful weeping willow shading half the lawn. Lavender buzzing with busy bees edged the short walkway to the front steps bookended by double-decker boxwoods that looked like they'd had a recent poodle cut.

This place definitely wasn't the photography studio I had envisioned. It was charming and welcoming except for the "By Appointment Only" sign nailed to a shingle over the doorbell.

No problem. I had an appointment with Erin and rang the bell.

I didn't hear any movement inside and then after almost a minute, the fifty-something woman I recognized as the photographer from Renee's wedding appeared at the door.

Fair with freckles dusting her makeup-free cheeks, she was casually dressed in faded blue jeans and a stained chambray shirt with rolled-up sleeves. And by the annoyance tugging at her crow's feet and the messy topknot of nutmeg brown, she hadn't been expecting any visitors.

"Yes?"

"I'm Charmaine Digby," I said, breathing in the aroma

of sauteed onion. "I have a three o'clock appointment with Erin."

"Oh." The woman glanced down at the stain. "Sorry. She told me she was coming over but didn't mention that... Um... I would've—"

"Don't worry about it. It isn't that kind of appointment. I'm with the Chimacam County coroner's office and just have a few questions for her."

Her dark eyes widened. "Because of what happened Saturday."

I gave her a friendly nod to assure this mom that her daughter wasn't in any trouble. Yet, anyway. "Is she here? I realize I'm a little early."

"No, not yet. I'm Liz, her mother." She stepped back from the door. "Please, come in."

As soon as I made my way across the threshold, she darted toward a set of double doors that led to a kitchen.

I noticed that there was another set that was closed at the opposite end of the room. Most likely to keep visitors contained to this living room, which had been converted to a photography studio. To the right of those doors was a black backdrop with a swivel stool surrounded by umbrella lights and reflective screens on pedestals.

"Excuse me a sec," she said. "I have something on the stove."

"It smells good. What are you making?" I asked, meandering past a tidy desk to peruse the framed family portraits and mat boards with smiling brides and grooms on the far wall.

"Meatloaf." She reappeared at the doorway with a

pleasant smile. "Now that the burner's off, it's nothing that needs my immediate attention. Would you like something to drink?"

"No, thanks. I'm good." And preferred to maximize whatever alone time I had with Liz talking instead of drinking. "Since it looks like it might be a few minutes until Erin gets here, could I ask you a couple of questions about Saturday?"

Liz dropped the smile. "Sure." Stepping into the room, she motioned toward the French vanilla leather sofa in front of a picture window with buttercream blinds. "We can talk here," she said, removing two tapestry throw pillows before dropping into the matching loveseat.

Fortunately, the blinds were open, providing plenty of natural light—the next best thing to me shining one of those umbrella lights at her face.

I pulled out my notebook and set my bag on the cushion next to me. "I realize that you were busy taking pictures of the bride and the wedding party Saturday, but were you in the room when they were getting their makeup done?"

"Yes, Renee... She was the bride—"

"I know." I didn't want her to use our time giving me a who's who when I already knew the major players. "I was there. Friend of the family." Sort of.

"Oh." Liz locked her gaze on mine. "I thought you looked familiar. Maybe I got you in a background shot of the ceremony."

This wasn't anything I cared about, but I squeezed out a smile. "Maybe. You were telling me about being in the room with Renee."

"Right. I took several shots of Renee while she was getting ready. A couple of Renee with her bridesmaids. Her mom. Also earlier, toasting the bride with all the bridesmaids raising their mimosas." Liz shrugged. "You name it, I probably captured it with my camera."

This sounded promising. "Any pictures with Natalie, the makeup artist?"

"She wasn't a member of the wedding party, so no," Liz said. "Nothing more than her hand in a few shots."

Dang! "How about shots of the area where Natalie was working? Anything to include water bottles or people standing nearby?"

Liz looked at me quizzically. "I'm paid to create images that the bride and groom will treasure for a lifetime. The only kind of bottle they might want to see in their wedding album is a champagne bottle."

Well, heck. "Got it. Were you in the room when Natalie said something about having a headache?"

Liz nodded. "Nora—at least I think it was Nora—gave her some aspirin. Had her drink something. Renee, Erin, and I left to take some pictures in the rose garden, so I wasn't there when the poor thing got worse."

This matched the chronology of events that everyone else had told me. "What were you and your daughter doing before Renee sat down to get her makeup done?"

"Why?" Liz narrowed her eyes. "What's this about?"

"We're just trying to gain a better understanding of the circumstances that led to Natalie Mercer's death."

"I still don't understand. I thought she got sick because

of food poisoning or something."

I couldn't help her there. I had yet to understand this myself. "Did you see her eat or drink anything earlier in the afternoon?"

"She had a water bottle that she was sipping from. I didn't notice anything else."

Since Liz had her focus on Renee for the majority of the time, I hadn't expected her to pay much attention to Natalie. I made a note about the water bottle just the same. "Okay. Did anything else happen in that room that seemed unusual to you?"

"Unusual? No. It was an older group of ladies and Renee knew exactly what she wanted, so that made it easy for me. We were on schedule and everything was going great until Natalie got sick."

"Did you or your daughter know her personally?" I asked to see what kind of reaction I got.

Liz shook her head. "I'd never met her before. I can't speak for Erin."

True enough. "I understand your daughter knew her husband."

"They dated in high school," she said. "Nothing super-serious."

I wished Erin would get here so that I could find out if that were actually true. "Did they see one another after high school?"

"I don't believe so." Liz furrowed her brow. "Why do you want to know about that?"

"Just asking." *Because it's too weird that your daughter spent any time with her ex-boyfriend's wife who died a few hours later.*

Liz's eyes widened with alarm. "You can't think that—"

"Really," I said, trying to ease her mind. "It's just because it's part of the unusual circumstances of Saturday. That they should run into one another at this wedding. I mean, what are the odds?"

Liz's look of alarm morphed into a death stare. "We are booked for a couple of weddings a week through the end of the year, and I know for a fact that one of those brides is a friend of Erin's from high school. So this might not be as 'unusual' as it seems."

I forced a smile, relieved to hear the sound of a door closing in another part of the house.

Liz pushed to her feet. Clearly, I wasn't the only one ready to bring our conversation to an end.

"That should be Erin," she said. "I'll let the two of you talk in private."

I stood and set down my pen to shake hands if she offered.

She didn't. "Thank you for your time," I said to Liz's back as she stalked toward the kitchen.

Okay. This wasn't the first time that someone I interviewed left in a huff. Usually, it was a good indication that I had scratched the surface to uncover some naked truth.

This time I had just pissed off a protective mom.

"Sorry I'm late." A tall girl with long straight hair the color of maple syrup looked at Liz and then peered through the entryway at me as if checking boxes with her apology. "There was an accident on 148th that backed everything up for miles."

Liz pulled her close to say something I couldn't hear, but with the way both women were huddled in the kitchen, I could guess that she was telling Erin to proceed with caution.

"I'll be in here making dinner," Liz announced, giving her daughter one last worried glance before disappearing from view.

I figured the announcement was for my benefit as much as Erin's. Mama Bear informing us she would be close by if she were needed.

"Charmaine?" Erin said, entering the studio in clunky clogs.

She was a couple of inches taller than me, wearing distressed jeans with enough threadbare holes to be breezy and a gauze peasant shirt that complemented her peachy complexion.

I took her extended hand, which was a little damp, probably because she was nervous. "Yes. Thanks for seeing me, Erin."

Close up, she looked like a young, earth-mother version of Liz. No makeup, lots of freckles, more soap commercial cute than pretty. She also had her mom's dark eyes, but they were dilated, making them look as oily black as Duke's bad coffee.

Yep, she was definitely nervous.

"I hope I didn't keep you waiting long," she said, settling into the loveseat her mother had vacated moments earlier.

"Not at all. I was early and it gave me a chance to chat with your mom."

Erin nodded and then scooted to the edge of the cushion as if she had suddenly remembered her manners. "Would you like something to drink?"

"I'm fine, thanks." I set my notebook and pen on my lap to give this chick the signal that I was ready to begin the interview. But first I needed her to sit back and relax.

I pointed my pen at the equipment in the corner to give her a minute to chill. "What a great-looking setup."

It was probably pretty standard for a photography studio, but I hoped it could serve as an innocuous conversation starter.

She flashed me a brittle smile but said nothing.

Fine. I needed to try again, this time with something requiring a response.

Squaring my shoulders, I met her gaze. "Your mom mentioned that you're booked for a lot of weddings, but you must do a bunch of portrait photography sessions here in the studio."

"It's a big part of her Tuesday through Friday business," Erin said after clearing her throat. "I actually don't have anything to do with that."

"Oh, I just assumed that since we were meeting here that you worked—"

"No, I only work weddings with my mom on the weekend. Other than that, I make jewelry with my roommate." She touched the lapis butterfly hanging from the chain around her neck. "She's the real artist of the two of us, but she's also a slob and our apartment is a disaster area, so I thought it was easier to meet here. There was no one booked for this afternoon. Plus, I knew it was meatloaf night."

Good. Erin seemed more at ease, revealing a little personality. It was now time to see how much she would reveal about last Saturday.

I gave her a friendly nod. "Based on how it smelled when I first got here, I'd want to come over for meatloaf night, too."

"It's the best," she proudly declared while her mother glanced in our direction from the kitchen.

Everything's okay. We're just talking about your meatloaf.

But we all knew that wasn't why I was here.

"Well, we should probably get started so that I don't keep you from your supper," I said, trying to keep my tone light. "As I told you on the phone, the Chimacam County coroner has asked me to talk to everyone who spent time with Natalie Mercer last Saturday."

Erin laced her fingers in her lap, hiding most of the silver rings she was wearing. "Okay."

"Just to get a sense of who you knew in that room where the bride and the wedding party were getting ready, had you met any of the ladies before?" I asked with my pen poised over my notebook.

"I didn't know the bride, but I knew Nora Mercer from when I dated Lucas." She looked at me through enviably long eyelashes. "You know about that, right? That Lucas Mercer was my boyfriend back in high school."

Indeed, I did. "Someone mentioned that. Small world that his aunt Renee hired you guys for her wedding, huh?"

Erin shook her head. "That was crazy. I had no idea

they were related. Not until I saw Nora, who seemed as surprised to see me as I was to see her."

True.

"How about Natalie?" I asked, watching her carefully. "That must have been a surprise to meet Lucas's wife there."

"Not really." She gave me another shake of the head. "We'd met before. And once I realized the entire family was there, it would've been strange not to see her."

I studied her face. Erin was telling me the truth, but this sure wasn't what I had expected to hear. "Where'd you meet the first time?"

"At a wedding two years ago. I was a bridesmaid and Lucas was the best man. He introduced us."

"How'd that go?"

"You know. New girlfriend meeting the old girlfriend is always a little weird. And, of course, she had to be drop-dead gorgeous." Almost shrinking in her seat, Erin muttered an obscenity. "Sorry, that was in poor taste. You know...considering what happened and all."

She was being pretty darned candid, so I was okay with the off-hand remark. "Don't worry about it. So, you two had met before. How'd Natalie seem when you first saw her on Saturday?"

Erin shrugged. "Fine. Friendly, but probably a little shocked to see me there."

"Did you two talk at all?"

"I tried going over to chat for a minute, but one of the bridesmaids was throwing me dirty looks, like I was the help and should only speak if spoken to. So I cut it short and said the kind of 'great to see you again' stuff that you say when you run into someone you barely know."

"How about Lucas? Did you happen to run into him anytime between noon and three?"

She looked down and twisted the ring adorning her index finger. "Not really."

What did that mean? "You knew he'd be there at some point, right?"

"I...well, yes." Erin nodded. "I saw his sister Kerry, and she told me where he was."

"In the bar."

Another nod accompanied by more ring twisting.

"So?" I asked. "What'd you do?"

"Nothing. I thought that if I happened to bump into Lucas I'd act completely cool about it. 'Cause it wasn't like we hadn't both moved on."

Her brittle smile was back and looked so fragile that it was obvious that this girl's heart still had a tender spot for Lucas Mercer. "And did you bump into him? You know, before Natalie got sick?"

"No, I..." Erin pressed her lips together as if considering how much she wanted to admit. "I saw him from a distance when I was setting up for some garden shots. I thought about waving if he looked my way, but I didn't want it to be weird. Like he looks up and there I am, alone in the garden, like a stalker from his past."

Stalker?

Like the kind of stalker who would send her ex-boyfriend's fiancée threatening texts?

Chapter Thirteen

"A stalker," I said to Erin as if I couldn't imagine anything so ridiculous. And, of course, I had no trouble imagining it whatsoever. "Why would he think that of you?"

Staring down at her hands, she shrugged. "I don't know."

Oh, yes she did. "Because you still have feelings for him?"

"It's not that."

It sounded like it was to me.

"It was just a little awkward the last time I saw him," Erin added, playing with her rings again.

Sheesh! I needed this girl to look up so that I could get a good read of her face. "Erin."

She responded by meeting my gaze, and I immediately saw the sadness etched into her features.

"Are you referring to that wedding where you first met Natalie?" I asked.

"It was just hard to see them so happy together, and I had just broken up with a guy." Erin waved her hand as if trying to shoo away the memory. "All emotional stuff that you don't need to hear about."

Emotional stuff that led to Erin sending those texts? Oh, yes. I did so need to hear about it.

The only way to find out was to ask. In some subtle way.

Sure, I could be subtle. But darned if I could think of something to say that wouldn't lead to Erin repeating what her mother had told me minutes earlier: *"Why do you want to know about that?"*

"That had to have been tough," I finally decided upon, injecting so much sympathy into my tone that I sounded like a bereavement counselor. "Were they engaged then?"

Erin cocked her head as if she hadn't heard me right. "What?"

"When you first met Natalie, did she or Lucas tell you that they were getting married?"

"I don't understand," she said with a frown. "What's that got to do with what happened Saturday?"

And there we were—right where I didn't want to go, and I knew this interview would come to an abrupt end if I didn't come up with a good answer.

"I'm just trying to understand what emotions Natalie might have been going through." I racked my brain for a logical connection—something that wouldn't sound accusatory. "If anything happened at that wedding two years ago that could have been upsetting for her on Saturday."

"Happened with me?"

"Yeah. For example, if any follow-up messages were exchanged."

Erin gave me a blank stare. "What do you mean? Like text messages?"

"Yes, exactly like text messages!" a voice in my head screamed.

Sucking in a calming breath, I swallowed the scream before my frustration bubbled to the surface.

"Yes, did you communicate by text?" I asked, channeling the patient energy of that bereavement counselor while I watched for a reaction.

And I saw plenty. Mostly anger. Maybe layered with a hot flush of embarrassment.

Yep, something had happened, and I was quite sure that Liz hadn't known the whole story of her daughter's relationship with Lucas Mercer.

"I humiliated myself enough after Lucas dumped me." Erin's voice was husky with emotion. "I didn't send him any texts!"

Crap. I didn't care about any texts she might have sent to *him.*

"And I don't understand why you're asking me about this!" she added with tears pooling in her eyes.

"That's enough!" Liz announced, stepping into the studio with a paring knife in her hand. "Erin, honey, why don't you come help me in the kitchen."

Erin practically leapt from the loveseat and scurried away like a broken-hearted teen who had been dumped all over again, leaving me alone with a pissed-off mother.

Double crap.

Getting to my feet, I noticed that Liz was pointing her knife at me.

I didn't sense any real threat, but this sure wasn't how I had wanted to wrap up the interview. "I'm sorry if I upset Erin. I—"

"Don't you dare say you were just doing your job," Liz said, her mouth tight with fury.

I wasn't going to. I wanted to tell her that Frankie might have more questions for Erin. If not Frankie, a more skilled interviewer than me because I had already blown my opportunity.

I had made Erin cry while failing to learn if she was my mystery texter.

Way to go, Char.

Liz pointed toward the door with her knife. "Get out."

I immediately grabbed my bag and headed for the door because this interview couldn't have been more over.

Two hours later, after going home to feed Fozzie, I got a text from Steve.

I had hoped he was going to suggest going out to dinner because I was in no mood to cook. I wasn't in much of a mood to eat either.

More than anything I wanted Steve to walk through my front door and take me into his arms. I wanted his heat to warm my bones and make the events of today melt away.

But as I read his text I knew that wouldn't happen until around seven because he needed to finish with a booking.

"No problem," I wrote back. "Dinner out somewhere?"

Within seconds Steve texted me an emoji of a pizza.

"See you there." I hit send, hugged my dog, and wasted no time driving to Eddie's Place, the former brick warehouse that Eddie and Rox had transformed into an eight-lane bowling alley and tavern that served the best pizza in the county.

"Well, look who's here," Rox called out as she wiped the lustrous surface of the massive oak bar. "Did our sign out front for Taco Tuesday lure you in, or are you here to tell your troubles to your favorite bartender?"

I hadn't noticed the sign, and I had no intention of admitting that I just wanted to see her smiling face before she left to pick up twenty-month-old Alex at her mother's.

"What sign?" I said loud enough to be heard over Linda Ronstadt crooning about lost love from the speakers bookending the bar.

"You're the third person to say that." Rox slapped the towel over her shoulder. "I knew we needed a bigger sign."

As I slid onto my usual barstool, I scanned the crowd, which seemed pretty good this early on a Tuesday night. "I don't know. I don't see many empty tables."

What I didn't see was anyone waiting on them. "Who's working tonight? Sofia or Andrea?"

Sofia was the twenty-something who had been waitressing most weekdays for the past year. Andrea was new as of last month—an empty-nesting fireplug with a truck-driving husband who was only home on weekends.

Rox's cocoa brown eyes slanted toward the kitchen door, and I had my answer when Andrea emerged balancing two big platters of tacos and three dinner salads on her sturdy arms.

"Hey, good to see you!" she said, beaming at me with such a happy smile that it lit up her round face.

And my mood immediately lightened as if she had given me an injection of sunshine.

Andrea hadn't waited for a reply, and with her on her merry way to one of the tables behind me, I turned back to Rox. "I've never seen a server so happy to schlep heavy plates of food in my life."

With a grin, Rox tossed a paper coaster in front of me. "With her daughter married and living in Seattle and her son far away in Austin, I think she's just happy to have people to talk to. I sure hope that makes her want to stick around for a while. She's freakin' awesome and everyone loves her."

After my not-so-awesome day, I couldn't help but sigh. "That's nice."

"Well, that was a pithy and underwhelming bit of commentary." Rox searched my expression. "Something wrong?"

"It's just been a frustrating day."

"It sounds like somebody needs a drink. Chardonnay?"

"Sure," I said, setting my cell phone in front of me in case Steve called.

When she placed the long-stemmed glass on my coaster, Rox leaned close to be heard over the din of the bar. "Want to talk about it?"

Yes, but I couldn't tell her anything about work, didn't want to talk about the latest stunt my mother had pulled, and hated to admit how much I wished I could fast-forward three weeks and put all this crapola behind me. "Actually, I—"

"Hold that thought," she said when two of the

mechanics who worked a half block away at Bassett Motor Works waved her down for a pitcher of beer.

I didn't know them well and was relieved when they didn't try to engage me in conversation after we exchanged hellos. They were nice-enough guys, but all I wanted at the moment was to have a quiet drink with my best friend.

"Okay, tell Mama," Rox said a couple of minutes later, after delivering a pizza order to a guy at the pick-up counter.

I shrugged. "It's nothing really. Just wedding stress." Along with a mother who wasn't talking to me, and a sudden death that was feeling less natural with each person I spoke to.

"Is that all? That's normal." She inspected my face and worked her way down to the top button of my mocha linen shirt. "You're not breaking out in hives like my cousin did right before her wedding, and you don't appear to be tearing out your hair—"

"Yet!"

She grinned. "You'll be fine, and if there's anything you need help with, you know where to find me."

Andrea appeared next to me and started rattling off a drink order to Rox.

"I mean it, Char," Rox said, looking back at me as she reached for one of the bottles of tequila in front of the bar's antique mirror.

I gave her a thumbs-up, even though I knew there was nothing she could do beyond providing me with an endless supply of emotional support. Along with the occasional glass of wine.

"Whatcha need help with, hon?" Andrea asked, raising her voice to be heard over the combo of a Lynyrd Skynyrd guitar riff and Rox's whirring blender.

I turned to see her aiming that sunny smile at me.

"I draw the line at helping people move. I'm great at volunteering others, though," Andrea quipped. "It's one of my superpowers."

I couldn't help but smile back at this nice lady. "It's good to have a superpower." Or at least I had thought so when I first discovered I could discern things everyone else seemed to be blind to. My "superpower" hadn't seemed so super lately.

"So, what is it? Wedding jitters?" Andrea asked. "I realize you barely know me, but I'm a good listener."

"It's the wedding and..." A litany of things I couldn't discuss and didn't want swirling around in my brain like a tornado. "There's just a lot of stuff going on that I have to deal with."

Andrea's light blue eyes crinkled with good humor. "Well, dear girl, if there's one thing I've learned in my fifty-eight years, there's always stuff to deal with. It's unavoidable." She winked. "That's why God made pizza—to make 'stuffy' days more bearable."

"And cookies," I added.

"And hugs," she said, wrapping an arm around me to give me a quick squeeze.

Rox was right. This woman *was* awesome. The same age as my mother, but there didn't seem to be an ounce of drama lurking behind Andrea's warm gaze. And she dispensed motherly hugs with no agenda. "Would you adopt me?"

Andrea chuckled. "No can do. Wouldn't wanna make my cat more jealous than she already gets when my husband comes home. What I can do is feed you if you're ready to order, or are you waitin' for that handsome man of yours?"

"I'm waiting. He's stuck at work for a while, so I'm hanging out with Roxanne until he gets here."

"Sounds like a plan," Andrea said, taking the plastic tray Rox had loaded up with two margaritas, three bottles of Corona, and a diet cola. "Shout out if you need anything."

As she walked away, my cell phone rang. I had expected to see Steve's name as the caller ID. Instead, it was a phone number I recognized from earlier in the day.

The second I answered and heard Kayla Riley's voice, I started walking toward the exit. "Give me a second. It's impossible to hear in here."

I stepped into the parking lot, the thundering clatter of the bowling alley muting when the heavy glass door swung shut behind me. "Sorry about that, Kayla. I couldn't make out what you were saying."

"I said that I was calling to give you a phone number for Jenny Bauer, Natalie's friend I told you about earlier."

"Great!" I quickly put Kayla on speaker and opened my notes app.

"I found her parents' number in an old address book. I called and explained the situation to Jenny's mom, and she gave me her cell phone number." Kayla paused. "You ready?"

I entered the number she gave me into the app and then repeated it back to her over the throaty growl of a motorcycle pulling into a nearby parking spot.

"I tried calling her but didn't get an answer," Kayla said as I tried to put some distance between me and the motorcyclist. "Her mom said she typically goes for a run after work, so that might be why. Anyway, I left a message to let her know that you might be calling."

"Okay. This is super helpful. Thank you."

"Whatever I can do. It occurred to me that Jenny might have Mika's phone number, but that could be a long shot." Kayla sighed. "I wish I had Nat's phone. It would save us so much time."

Her cell phone! Why didn't I think of this sooner? "Who has it? Lucas?"

"I would think so, but I haven't been able to get hold of him either. I suspect I'm the last person he wants to talk to right now."

Maybe. But if Natalie's mother was number one on the list of people Lucas Mercer didn't want to talk to, I was quite sure that I didn't rank far behind.

The second I disconnected I checked the time on my phone. Five thirty-seven. Traffic shouldn't be too awful, not like what I experienced earlier on the bridge to Seattle. If I left now, I should be able to drive to Port Townsend and be back before seven. Preferably with Natalie Mercer's cell phone in an evidence bag.

Maybe my day was looking up.

Chapter Fourteen

Forty-three minutes later, an unsmiling bleached blonde in a ruffled tube top and skinny jeans opened Lucas Mercer's door.

Instead of stale beer assailing my nasal passages like the last time I stood here, I breathed in the familiar notes of two of my companions from earlier in the day: chocolate and brown sugar, along with something else. Her pear scent, maybe.

Was I interrupting another visit by a concerned family member who wanted to make sure Lucas's blood sugar didn't plummet for lack of home-baked cookies?

Could this be Kerry, the younger sister Amanda and Erin had mentioned? She looked vaguely familiar and appeared to be the right age, but if this was Kerry, she was flashing an awful lot of cleavage at her brother.

I was trying to think of a nice way to ask, "Who the heck are you?" when the blonde planted a hand on her slender hip and cracked the gum she'd been chewing.

"May I help you?" she asked, shooting me the weary look I used to get from my then-husband when I wanted to know why he was so late getting home.

I know. The nerve I had to suggest that the cheating bastard I had married was, in fact, a cheating bastard. Never mind that I had caught him kissing our sous chef in the walk-in freezer.

I glanced into the unoccupied living room behind her. "Is Lucas here?"

Her amber-eyed gaze raked over me and then disdain dripped from her glossy lips as if I hadn't passed inspection. "Why?"

"I'd like to speak with him."

"What about?"

Who was this guard dog at Lucas Mercer's door? "I'm with the coroner's office and need to speak with him. May I come in?"

Stepping aside to let me pass, the blonde cracked her gum again. Then she headed down the hall and rapped on the door of the bedroom I had seen Lucas disappear into yesterday. "There's someone here to see you."

"Who is it?" I heard him ask.

She lowered her voice to a stage whisper. "Some woman."

This chick made it sound like I was an enemy who had infiltrated their camp.

The door opened a moment later, and Lucas emerged finger-combing his dark brown hair. It wasn't damp this time, but it had been mussed. That combined with the creases in his faded University of Washington T-shirt made me think he had been lying in bed when I arrived.

Alone, while the cookies were being baked? Probably.

Prior to that... I shifted my gaze to the blonde, who was

glaring at me from the kitchen doorway, and had serious doubts about her being his sister.

"You're back," Lucas said to me as he approached. Aside from the hair, he looked much better than yesterday. Somber but clear-eyed, as if he had managed to get some sleep.

"I'm back." I directed a polite smile at his gum-smacking companion with the hope that she'd get the hint and give us some privacy.

She got the hint, all right. She also let me know what she thought of it by folding her arms under her impressive breasts and mirroring my smile back to me.

Fine. If that's the way you want to play this, let's play.

"And your name is?" I asked her, fishing my notebook from my shoulder bag for dramatic effect.

She came up behind Lucas. "I don't think that's any of your concern."

Making it my concern, I locked gazes with the guy gesturing to her to back off. "Her name?"

"Sydney Sheridan," he said, putting a quick end to playtime with a name I recognized from my interviews.

I looked over his shoulder at her. "You're Amanda's daughter." The casserole and now, cookie baker.

Her eyes gleamed like brandy over ice. "And you're the one my mother told me about. Said you thought Natalie died from a drug interaction."

"What?!" Lucas demanded.

"That's not at all what I said." That was the conclusion that Amanda had jumped to. "There's no evidence of any drug interaction." *Yet.* "And it's not what I'm here to talk to you about."

Lucas blew out a breath of exasperation. "Now what?"

"Do you have Natalie's phone?" I asked.

He hesitated before answering. "Why?"

There was no way that I was going to admit that I wanted it so that I could contact Natalie's closest confidants. "I'd like to borrow it."

"I'm not giving you my wife's phone," he said, raising his voice.

"Besides, don't you need a warrant or something?" Sydney chimed in.

Sheesh, had this chick been watching the same cop shows as Lucille?

I had no desire to engage with her and kept my focus on Lucas. "I wouldn't keep it long. Maybe just a day or two. Of course, if you prefer, I could return tomorrow with a subpoena." Which would never happen unless this became a criminal case after Natalie's labs came back, but I was counting on these two not knowing that. "With a subpoena you get more people involved, more layers of complication... Who knows when you'd get the phone back if we go that route."

"I don't believe this," Lucas muttered, followed by a few choice swear words as he stalked back toward his bedroom.

Since I had this time alone with Sydney, I thought I should take the opportunity to ask her about Saturday. Although the folded arm stance along with the daggers she was shooting at me suggested that she'd be a less than cooperative witness.

"Did your mom mention that I've been talking to everyone who was with Natalie on Saturday?" I asked.

Sydney cracked her gum. "Yeah."

"You were there, right?"

"To help carry stuff in from the car, but after that, Kerry and me hung out at the pool," she said, confirming what Amanda had told me.

Lucas returned with a cell phone in a pearly pink case, effectively ending my chat with his cousin, which was fine given how I needed to hit the road. I could always follow up with her later.

"Here it is." Lucas's voice was flat as if he were emotionally spent. "But I don't think it'll do you much good."

I took the phone from his extended hand. "Why?" It didn't look damaged.

"I don't know her passcode," Lucas said. "It's not her birthday, my birthday, or our anniversary. I tried all those at the hospital, when I needed to call her parents."

I looked up at him. "She didn't write it down somewhere?"

"If she did, I don't know where," Lucas said.

And he wasn't lying. Dang it!

"Hey, pretty girl," Steve said, sliding off his barstool to give me a quick kiss. "I was just about to call you."

I wasn't *that* late getting back from Port Townsend. "Sorry, when'd you get here?"

"A little before seven. Andrea told me that you were here for a few minutes, but then had to go somewhere."

"Yeah, I had an errand." A fool's errand, as it turned out.

While I waved hello to Eddie, who had taken over behind the bar, Steve grabbed his beer. Then I followed him to one of the quieter tables in the far corner.

"What kind of errand?" he asked, taking the chair with his back to the wall.

"It was a work thing. I thought that as long as you were working late, I could use the time to get something done. Anyway..." I smiled at him from across the table. "Enough work crapola." Because I didn't want to talk about this anymore. "What sounds good? You still want that pizza or are you up for some tacos? It *is* Taco Tuesday, you know. Eddie put up a sign and everything."

"I noticed. I also noticed how quickly you changed the subject." Steve's lips curled with amusement. "Is there a reason you don't want to tell me what you were doing?"

"Only because it was a big waste of time," I said.

"Why do I get the feeling that you don't want me to know what you've been up to?"

Because I didn't want to invite a lecture about how I should leave the detecting to the sheriff's department if and when this became a criminal case.

"Please trust me that this isn't worth talking about," I said, hoping he'd drop it.

"Uh-huh." He locked gazes with me for a long moment. "Okay, if you're not gonna tell me, *I've* got something to talk about."

Good, because I was fresh out.

He pulled his phone from the back pocket of his black

slacks. "You'll never guess who texted me today."

I didn't even want to venture a guess. "Who?"

"Your mother."

A groan escaped my lips before I could squelch it. "Should I apologize for whatever she had to say now or later?"

"I'm not sure. She said that she talked to my mother and that... Here," Steve said, handing me his phone. "You read it."

"Your mom called me last night to ask where you two were registered," I said aloud, reading Marietta's text while trying to stave off a full-body cringe. *"We discussed and she will pass along the info to the rest of the fam. Tell Charmaine that she loved the idea of the pizza oven."*

"For heaven's sake!" My mother had been soliciting allies for that stupid pizza oven? It made me wonder who else she had been chatting it up with.

"Since when did you do the registry thing?" Steve asked.

I handed him back his phone. "I didn't. That was my mother's doing."

"Without your knowledge?"

I nodded.

The crease between Steve's eyebrows voiced his displeasure a second before he said anything. "What makes her think that's okay?"

"That's something that we've talked about." One of several somethings.

"And?"

"I've made it abundantly clear that she needs to knock

it the heck off, and now she's giving me the silent treatment."

"I guess that explains why she wanted me to give you a message," Steve said, giving his phone a quizzical look. "But what's this about a pizza oven?"

Using my smartphone, I logged onto the registry website with the pizza oven, found the image, and turned the screen to face him. "She thought someone should buy us this."

Grinning, he took my phone. "Cool!"

"You can't be serious," I said as Andrea arrived to take our order. "Look at how much it costs!"

"Whoops, don't mean to interrupt," she said, "but do you kids need a minute to look at the menu?"

"No, it's fine." After helping out while Rox was on maternity leave, I had the menu memorized, and I hadn't seen Steve reach for a menu in years.

"Yeah, I know what I want," he announced in a mischievous singsong.

Andrea chuckled. "I'm not sure if that means you're ready to order or if you like what you're looking at."

"Both," Steve said, turning the phone so that Andrea could have a look.

"What is that?" She adjusted the half-eye glasses at the end of her nose. "A backyard pizza oven?"

"Yeah, my mother's idea of a wedding present," I said.

Andrea beamed. "Well, isn't that just the coolest idea ever!"

Good grief.

Chapter Fifteen

After we got back to my house and took Fozzie on a walk, I fired up my laptop so that Steve could review everything on our wedding gift registry.

After conceding that the pizza oven cost way too much money, Steve added a steak knife set to replace our mismatched hand-me-downs, and with no muss and no fuss, we were done in under ten minutes. Steve would call his mom to remove any misconceptions Marietta may have given her, and I would talk to my mother and...

Actually, I wasn't sure what I could say to Marietta beyond what I had already said.

The only thing I was sure of was that it would take far longer than ten minutes to get through to her.

After Steve went home and I turned out my bedside light, I lay on my back and stared into the inky darkness as if the answer to this mess were written on the ceiling.

Of course, the ceiling revealed absolutely nothing.

And when morning came and the soft light of dawn chased away the shadows, I had no greater clarity of what to do than when I finally managed to drift off for a few hours.

"Well, sleeping on it didn't help," I said to Fozzie, hot on my heels as I padded into the kitchen to make coffee. "What do you think I should do? Go to her house at lunchtime and have it out with her? Or do we need a cooling-off period so that we don't say something we'll regret?"

Just like the ceiling, my dog had no answers for me, so I made the decision for him.

"Cooling-off period it is." At least twenty-four hours. If I didn't want to break out in hives like Rox's cousin, a mental health break from all things wedding-related could be exactly what I needed.

"After all, tomorrow is another day," I said, quoting Scarlett O'Hara but sounding like a poor imitation of Marietta.

Fozzie barked and then disappeared into the bedroom as if it were too early to deal with my mother.

I couldn't have agreed more.

Four hours later, after I caught up with the filing, I went to my desk phone and called the number that Kayla Riley had given me for Jenny Bauer.

After five rings, a breathy feminine voice came on the line. "Hello?"

"Is this Jenny Bauer?"

"Yes, but it's Jenny Goshen now. Who's this?" she asked after a moment.

"My name is Charmaine Digby. I'm a deputy with the Chimacam County coroner's office. I've been told that you were a close friend of Natalie Mercer."

"Yes, I heard what happened," Jenny said, her tone somber.

"Because her passing was so sudden, we're talking to those closest to her to get a clearer picture of the days leading up to her death." Which was as close to the truth as I was willing to get on this phone call. "Would you have some time to meet today or tomorrow?"

"Um... My mom told me that someone might call about Natalie, but I don't know that I can help you. I haven't seen her for months, not since I moved."

That didn't sound promising. "You moved out of the area?"

"To Bend, Oregon."

Shoot! Bend was over six hours away. "Okay—"

"Sorry to interrupt, but I'm at work," she said. "So I don't have a lot of time to talk right now."

An in-person meeting was out. The next best thing would be a video conference, but since she was busy at work, that meant setting up a time for after-hours, and I had my usual Wednesday dinner with Gram and Steve tonight. Darn it.

"I understand," I said. "Let me ask you a couple of things really quick, then maybe we can schedule a video conference if I have more questions."

"Okay, I guess I can take a few minutes."

"Great. Did Natalie ever talk about how things were going at home?"

"Sure," Jenny said. "We'd catch up on what was going on in our lives. You know, all the typical stuff. Work, vacation plans, movies, books we'd read—that sort of thing."

I did know, but that didn't help shed any light on Natalie's home life.

"Did Natalie ever mention any problems she was having with Lucas? Any arguments?" *Like what the neighbor mentioned.*

"Gosh, not that I know of."

"So, she never confided anything to suggest that things were stressful at home."

"No, never," Jenny said.

"Did she ever give you the impression that they were having issues with alcohol or drugs?"

"What? No! Nat hardly ever touched liquor. Same with Lucas. Ever since they got married, they always seemed to be in training for their next half-marathon, so they had very healthy lifestyles."

Until recently anyway. "So, Natalie never complained to you about Lucas."

"Not at all, Lucas is great. Really easy to get along with. Oh," Jenny added after a moment of hesitation. "Well, I guess she *did* complain about him once."

I tightened my grip on my pen. "What'd she say?"

"I don't remember specifically. I know it was when she and I met for lunch to celebrate her engagement, and just before we left the restaurant, she got a weird text. I remember how Nat's face looked," Jenny said, pausing as though she were playing back the scene. "She was ticked. And when I asked her what was wrong, she showed me the text. It was really off the wall. Lines like 'He's mine.

You can't have him.' There was some garbage about how he'd cheat on her. That Lucas had done it before and how she—whoever this old girlfriend was—should know. Anyway, Nat was frustrated with Lucas that he hadn't made his ex stop because this had been going on for close to a week. And I remember, when I asked Nat about it later, that it was still going on. Not as often, but it was still happening—at least one every night. Some of them were really creepy. And I'm pretty sure that this went on for more than a month."

This was good detail, but it only confirmed what I already knew. "Did Natalie tell you the name of the girl?"

"No, I don't think she ever found out who it was."

"What about one of her other friends? Did you ever hear anyone speculate about who this girl was?"

"If they did, I never heard about it. It's not the kind of thing you talk about at a bridal shower, you know?"

Having had three in the last year, I knew that all too well.

And if that was all Jenny could tell me, I probably didn't need to follow up with a video conference. "Is there anything else you think I should know?"

"I don't think so, and I don't want to give you the wrong impression about Lucas because I know he was crazy about Nat. More than anything, I think she was just frustrated with the situation itself. I mean, he tried talking to the girl, asking her to accept that it was over. She told me as much, but how do you get someone to stop doing something that's totally annoying?"

I wished I knew. Because asking nicely sure hadn't

worked with my mother.

Before Jenny reminded me that she needed to get back to work, I wrapped up the call by asking if she had Mika Kumasaka's contact information.

"She was Nat's friend more than mine, so what I have is from when we were her bridesmaids," Jenny said. "Hold on a sec."

Five minutes later, I called the number Jenny had provided me and listened to a recording of Mika Kumasaka politely telling me that she would be out of the office until a week from Monday, and she would not be checking voice mail.

"Swell," I muttered as I waited for a beep. I then left her a brief message with my name and cell number and why I was calling. If she happened to check her voice mail sometime in the next eleven days and gave me the opportunity to interview her, great. If not, I would follow up with her after she got back from her vacation.

Next, I took a few minutes to review the page of my notebook where I had written the names of every person who had either been in the room long enough on Saturday to interact with Natalie Mercer or handle something she consumed, or had been closely associated with her.

I had written check marks next to all of them except for Renee, Mika Kumasaka, and the employee who had provided the food and beverage service to the bride and her entourage on Saturday. He had been someone Natalie knew, so I was especially eager to talk to him, but I was still waiting on Avery to get back to me with his availability.

That left me with nothing to do but review my notes, all twenty-one pages of them. Lots of quotes and scribbles from each and every interview, but I hadn't seen any indicators that anyone wanted to cause Natalie harm. Nor did I detect anything suspicious in anyone's behavior. Sure, Erin Lofgren sent up more emotional red flags than I could count and her stalker comment was a little weird, but when I asked her about the texts, she didn't have the reaction I had expected to see. And I didn't think she had lied about texting Lucas.

Of course, Lucas wasn't the recipient I cared about. But still, if Erin had sent Natalie those texts—all those weeks of warnings to stay away from her man—I would have expected to pick up on it. To see more tension in her micro-expressions, to see her rising anxiety that I was getting too close to the truth.

What I saw beyond a heart that hadn't entirely mended was inconclusive at best.

Depending on what Frankie wanted to do with the information I had gathered, she might want Erin to come in for an interview. Until then, I had nothing else to do but wait for Avery to call me back.

On second thought, there was one thing I could and should do.

I could go back and ask Lucas about his relationship with Erin. Just make it a straightforward question so that I could read his reaction. Because Lucas had been less than forthcoming about who had been harassing his wife with those texts, and based on what Jenny Goshen had told me, it had definitely been someone he'd had a relationship with.

It was either pay Lucas another visit or get started on Brett's newest copying project that he had for me—a decision that was a no-brainer. Assuming, of course, that Lucas hadn't returned to work, which should be easy enough to check.

I opened my notebook to the last page, where I had inserted a printout of the background check I had run a couple of hours earlier on Lucas Mercer. Skimming past all his known addresses, I came to his employment history and the name of the Port Townsend engineering firm he currently worked for.

Bingo.

A company that size had to have a website, and sure enough, in less than a minute I was calling the number listed at the top of their home page.

The receptionist who answered sounded very enthusiastic when she asked, "How may I direct your call?"

"Lucas Mercer, please," I said.

"Oh." The receptionist's tone softened. "I'm sorry. Mr. Mercer isn't in today. Can someone else be of assistance?"

"Is he expected back tomorrow?" I asked to find out how much information she would offer.

"No, not until Monday. May I—"

"Thank you." That was all I needed to know.

Chapter Sixteen

"A little early for lunch, isn't it?" Patsy said without looking up from her computer monitor as I approached.

I felt like I should have a hall pass to hand over to my self-appointed supervisor. "I have an interview at eleven-thirty." Since it was a few minutes before eleven, giving myself over a half hour to get to Lucas Mercer's apartment should sound about right if Patsy asked me any probing questions. "Which I'll be late for if I don't leave now."

She stopped clicking on her keyboard and shot me a skeptical glance. "And where is this taking place?"

Sheesh, why should she care? "Port Townsend."

"Just the one interview?"

"Yes," I said, keeping my tone carefully neutral, because Brett had nothing on Patsy when it came to payback.

Patsy reached behind her and handed me a white business envelope. "That makes you the perfect person to go to Whidbey Island and deliver this subpoena."

Yeah, perfect. It would require catching the Coupeville ferry out of Port Townsend, adding around three hours of travel time to my day, but it sure beat being cooped up with a temperamental copier, plus it was a gorgeous, blue-sky day to be out on the northern waters of Puget Sound.

Another plus, the subpoena was addressed to a CPA at an accounting firm. I rarely experienced any trouble at businesses with other people around. Maybe it was a safety in numbers thing. All I knew for sure was that it was a whole lot better than serving an unwelcome subpoena to a Christmas tree farm in the middle of nowhere. When I did that last December, the owner threw his coffee mug at me. Empty of coffee as well as Christmas spirit. Rude, too.

I never thought I'd have a job where I needed to be able to bob and weave. Fortunately, that didn't happen very often, because projectiles aimed at my head put a serious damper on my desire to venture outside of the office.

"No problem," I told Patsy. "Depending on traffic and the ferry schedule, I might not make it back before four. In case anyone is looking for me."

"In case anyone is, I'll be happy to let them know." With a fake smile at her fleshy mouth, she waved me away as if I had been dismissed.

"Whatever," I said as the heavy oak door of the prosecutor's office shut behind me.

I said the same thing when the sheriff's deputy sitting twenty feet away made a point of looking at his watch as if I was skipping out of work early.

Okay, technically, I sort of was. Because I didn't have an interview scheduled with Lucas Mercer, but I knew that calling him would be a waste of time. Not only would he most likely hang up on me, I needed to see his reactions as we talked.

Plus, I needed to go to Port Townsend to catch the ferry, so I might as well swing by Lucas's apartment while I was in the area.

Yep, I was providing myself a big slice of justification pie, but if I was ever going to solve the mystery of who sent those texts to Natalie, I needed to have some face time with her husband.

When I was climbing the stairs to Lucas Mercer's apartment forty minutes later, his next-door neighbor was coming down with a trash bag in her hand.

"Oh, it's you again," she said over the slap of her mules hitting the concrete steps. "Weren't you here last night?"

And here I thought Lucille was the only one keeping tabs on my whereabouts.

I smiled politely. "Maybe it was just someone who looked like me." I had twisted my unruly hair into a bun and had only bothered to apply a swish of mascara this morning. Not my best look, but after a longer than usual jog to make up for last night's pizza, I had been pressed for time.

Bracing herself with the handrail, she cocked her head to study my hair, which made me wonder if my bun was listing to one side. "Hunh, maybe. There's been so many comings and goings around here, it's hard to keep track of 'em all."

As if that were her job.

But if she'd noticed the comings and goings of a certain bleached blonde I wanted to hear about it.

I leaned against the railing. "Was one of the people you saw a girl in her early twenties? Shoulder-length blond hair, pretty, close to my height?"

"You sure you're not a cop? 'Cause you ask questions like a cop."

I was sure that Steve would find her observation amusing. "I'm not a cop. This girl's not exactly a friend of mine, so I'd like to avoid running into her here, if you know what I mean."

The neighbor rolled her eyes behind heavy-framed glasses. "If it's the same girl I saw here Monday, I can't blame you a bit. She's a rude little number."

That sounded like Sydney Sheridan to me. "So you haven't seen her since then?"

"Can't say that I have."

Then this lady couldn't tell me when Lucas's cousin left last night. "Okay, thanks," I said, continuing up the steps.

"She left him, didn't she?" the woman asked. "His wife, I mean. 'Cause I haven't seen her for days."

In a manner of speaking, she had left him. "I really can't say." If Lucas Mercer wanted his nosy neighbor to know that his wife had died, he would have told her.

Seconds later, I knocked on his apartment door. This time, Lucas's mother, Nora, came to the door.

I saw no pleasant smile of recognition, nor had I expected one, given that this was my third visit in as many days. Instead, Nora's blue eyes iced over. "Haven't you bothered my son enough?"

Lucas had obviously told his mother that I stopped by again last night. "I'm sorry. I'm not trying to disturb him, I'm—"

"But you *are* disturbing him," she ground out. "He's grieving the loss of his wife! We all are, and we don't need you—"

"Mom." Lucas placed a hand on his mother's shoulder. "Why don't you go in the living room with Dad," he said. "I've got this."

Nora cut me with a razor-edged look of disgust before she left, and then Lucas stepped into the doorway. "What do you want?"

"Is there somewhere we could talk privately?" I asked, because his living room clearly wasn't an option.

He huffed out a breath. "Does this have to be now? We're getting ready to meet with the funeral director."

"It will only take a few minutes." Actually, it would take as long as necessary to get the answers I needed.

"Fine," he bit out and then looked back at his parents. "I'll be outside for a few minutes," he told them.

"But our appointment is in thirty-five minutes," Nora protested. "We need to leave—"

"I'm well aware." Lucas glared at me as he shut the door. "So talk."

I pointed toward the stairway. "It's a nice day. Maybe we could sit at the picnic table near the playground." I had seen a young family using it when I was here last night.

Without uttering another word, he led the way downstairs and then walked behind the building, across a swath of recently mowed grass. No other residents seemed to be around other than a mom pushing her toddler on a swing, and they were too far away to be able to hear us.

Good enough for privacy, I thought, sitting on the bench seat opposite Lucas.

He set his phone next to him on the picnic table. "You've got ten minutes."

"Okay." Ten minutes might be enough time. "As I told you on Monday, because of the suddenness of your wife's cardiac arrest, the coroner asked me to interview everyone who was with her Saturday."

Leaning on his forearms, Lucas appeared to be staring at a knothole in the table.

Since he didn't respond, I took that as my cue to stop serving appetizers and dish up the main course. "After speaking with Erin Lofgren, I wanted to follow up with you about your relationship with her."

"My relationship?" Lucas looked up with a frown and not because of the glare bouncing off the fluffy white clouds above us. "With Erin?"

I nodded. "She mentioned that you were her boyfriend in high school."

"Yeah, so?"

"How would you describe your relationship more recently, say in the last three years?" Which would cover the time he had been with Natalie.

His gaze hardened. "I haven't had a relationship with her. I haven't since I broke up with her."

I didn't see anything to indicate that Lucas wasn't telling the truth. "Erin made it sound like she didn't take the breakup very well."

"Yeah, I could've handled it better," he said, looking back down at that knothole. "I was eighteen. Not an excuse, just not something I was equipped to deal with at the time."

"Because she was upset."

He shot me another hard stare. "What's this got to do with anything?"

"Then she saw you and Natalie together at a friend's wedding."

"Almost *three...years...later*," he said, emphasizing each word as if I needed help doing the math.

"And then someone started harassing Natalie by text message. Someone else I spoke with said she saw some of the texts. Said they contained lines like 'He's mine' and 'You can't have him.' Said that both she and Natalie thought they were from a former girlfriend."

"We've already talked about this."

Yes, and I didn't buy his answer. "The person I spoke with said that you knew who the sender was, and you asked her to stop."

Lucas blew out a breath. "And not long after that she stopped. Why do we have to—"

"Was Erin the sender of those texts?"

He blinked, his mouth opening and closing as if he couldn't decide how to answer. "No."

"Did Erin *ever* communicate with Natalie by text?" I asked again, watching him carefully.

"Not that I know of."

I believed him.

Criminy. If it wasn't Erin... "Then who sent them?"

"No one who had anything to do with Nat's death."

"You're sure about that?" Because I had my doubts.

With tears threatening, making his dark blue eyes look like glistening pools, Lucas shrugged. "Listen, I know Nat's mom thinks that this should be someone's fault. She called and told me pretty much everything that you talked about Monday, but... How do you blame someone for a heart attack?" He wiped his eyes with the sleeve of his black Oxford shirt.

A grieving husband would want to find the person to blame if his wife's heart attack had been brought on by some toxin, like in that "perfect murder" news story, but I didn't want to plant that seed in his mind. Not yet, anyway. Let him get through the funeral first.

"I'm not looking for someone to blame," I said instead. "I'm looking for what caused a healthy twenty-four-year-old woman's heart to stop because, quite honestly, Mr. Mercer, her sudden death doesn't make any sense to me."

His jaw went slack. "What are you saying?"

What more could I say? "That's why I've asked you about those text messages—to find out if the person who sent them is somehow connected to what happened."

"Like someone had it out for my wife and stuck a pin in a voodoo doll to make her collapse?" Contempt curled Lucas's lips. "Give me a big break."

"I'm just saying there's a possible connection there, and if you won't let me follow up on it, maybe—"

"If there's nothing else," he said, getting to his feet as if my ten minutes were up.

"Actually, there is." Before he hurried off, I needed to tie up a loose end that had been niggling at me ever since the neighbor mentioned being concerned about Natalie's safety. "Monday I asked if you ever fought with your wife."

"I already told you we didn't fight."

I wasn't so sure about that, but maybe *fight* was too strong a word. "Your neighbors said that Natalie sounded upset, that you argued sometimes."

Pressing his lips together, Lucas hesitated for a second too long. "It was nothing, really. Sometimes, she'd get frustrated—" His phone started ringing and he answered it as if someone were throwing him a lifeline. "I know. I'm coming."

After disconnecting, Lucas looked back to me. "I have to go."

"I understand, but real quick. Who was with you Sunday night?"

"My parents, my sister for a while. Why?"

"A neighbor heard something that sounded like a fight between you and someone she assumed was Natalie. The manager was eventually called."

"It should be pretty obvious that my neighbor was wrong about that," he said bitterly. "Now I gotta go."

"Who was the woman she heard?" I called out as he headed back the way we came.

Stopping to turn back to me, he raised his hands in surrender. "Who knows? It could've been the TV."

I didn't believe that for a minute.

Chapter Seventeen

Two hours later, I served a subpoena on an accountant who didn't throw anything at me, didn't even raise his voice. Instead, he gave me such a frosty death stare that I couldn't get back to my car fast enough. Already a little spooked, I practically jumped out of my skin when I stepped onto the gravel of the parking lot and my cell phone started ringing.

I didn't care who the caller was. In that moment, priority number one was putting some distance between me and Mr. Frosty's death-ray eyes. Preferably the twenty miles to Coupeville to catch the next ferry back to Port Townsend.

"I can't come to the phone right now," I said, flinging my bag onto the passenger seat so that I could plop my hiney behind the wheel and lock the doors. "Because I'm a little freaked out and need to get outta here. So leave a message, and I'll be happy to call you back when my pulse isn't pounding in my ears."

Then, a minute later, as I booked down Route 525 in blessed peace and quiet while my blood pressure normalized, my phone started ringing again.

Since my mother wasn't speaking to me, two calls in rapid succession could only mean that someone from work was making sure I wasn't shopping for bargains at the outlet mall. My money would be on Patsy.

Fumbling with my bag, I found my phone in a side pocket and glanced at the caller ID. Not Patsy, but it was a number I recognized.

"Hello," I said, putting the phone on speaker as a green and yellow tractor chugged by in the southbound lane.

"Charmaine, it's Avery Olcott. Am I catching you at a bad time?"

"No, it's fine. But I'm in my car and probably miles from the nearest cell tower, so I don't know how long this connection will last."

"I'll be quick. I just wanted to let you know that I spoke with Lenny—he's the staff member who brought food and drink to the Ireland–Wolfe bridal party. He's working today and can make himself available for an interview if you have time to stop by. Lenny's also scheduled for Friday and Saturday if today isn't—"

"No, today works. I'm on Whidbey now but should be able to get there around four." Assuming that I made it onto the two forty-five ferry.

"Okay," Avery said. "I'll let Lenny know to expect you."

"Around four" turned out to be an overly optimistic estimate on my part because I didn't step into the rustic bar of the Rainshadow Ridge Resort until four twenty-one.

I was about to ask the bartender where I could find Lenny when a waiter with a big nose and slicked-back mahogany hair set a round serving tray on the end of the bar.

"Looking for someone?" he asked with a tentative smile.

Since he appeared to be in his mid-twenties, I assumed I had found my interviewee. "Lenny?"

The smile disappeared. "That's me."

"Charmaine Digby with the coroner's office," I said, lowering my voice so that the bartender wouldn't overhear. "I'm sorry I'm late. Is this a good time to talk?"

"Sure. It's pretty slow right now." He turned to the forty-ish brunette behind the bar. "I'm gonna be unavailable for a few."

She nodded and then shot me a look that told me she had been instructed to be cooperative. "Would you care for anything to drink? Complimentary, of course."

I waved her off. I just wanted to get this interview over with and head home to feed my dog before dinner with my grandmother. "I'm good, thanks."

Lenny pointed to a table close to the double doors that I assumed led to the kitchen. "We can sit over there."

"Fine," I said, glancing around as I followed his lead.

A couple was nursing drinks by the floor-to-ceiling window that looked out to the rose garden while an elderly man watched a baseball game at the other end of the bar.

Pretty slow? I had never seen this place so empty. Then again, I had only ever been here on a weekend.

"It'll pick up around five," Lenny said as if reading my thoughts. "So, if we could be done by then..."

"That shouldn't be a problem." If I didn't want to be late, I also needed to be done by five.

I waited for him to reach for one of the high-backed leather chairs and then took the seat opposite him.

To demonstrate that we wouldn't be wasting any time, I opened my notebook and picked up my pen. "I'm sure Avery told you why I wanted to speak with you."

Casting down his gaze, he slowly nodded. "Because of what happened to Natalie Saturday."

"Right. I'm talking to everyone who was in the room with her. Very routine stuff," I added with a smile since he had started blinking as if he had a nervous tic.

He swallowed, his Adam's apple bobbing. "Okay."

"Let's start with your full name."

"Leonard Gerald Gallatin Jr. But I go by Lenny."

I had to ask him to spell the last name. Also repeat his phone number since he rattled it off so quickly.

"I understand that you were acquainted with Natalie," I said, watching him carefully. "How'd you know her?"

"From when I was in college." He blinked. "We had a couple of classes together."

"Okay, and on Saturday you were the only staff member to deliver food and beverages to the bridal party?"

"Yeah, I was the one taking care of them."

"Around what time did you first enter the room?"

He tightly clasped his hands in front of him. "I let myself in around eleven-thirty to deliver the chilled bottles of water that come with the bridal package."

I realized that I should have been more specific. "After several members of the bridal party arrived at noon, when did you bring them something to eat or drink?"

"Around twelve-twenty." Blink, blink. "We always

provide the coffee service within thirty minutes of check-in."

"And how long were you in the room?" I asked.

"Not very long. It's usually just in and out, but Natalie called my name so I stayed for maybe two, three minutes."

"To talk to Natalie?"

"We didn't do much more than say hello," he said between blinks. "Ask what you're doing here. That sort of thing."

"How did she seem?"

"I dunno." Blink, blink. "Fine. Probably more surprised to see me than anything else. I was surprised to see her, too. It had been a few years."

"You said you knew one another from college."

Blinking, Lenny nodded. "Right."

"Ever date?"

He sighed. "I wish. I really liked her."

"Did you have her phone number?"

"I never got up the nerve to ask for it," he said after another blink.

So far, I had believed every word Lenny had told me.

"Did you or someone you know ever text Natalie shortly after she became engaged?" I seriously doubted that this guy had anything to do with harassing Natalie, but I had to make sure.

Lenny cocked his head and blinked in rapid succession. "No. How could I? I didn't have her number."

Again, true.

"Okay, let's get back to the events of Saturday. Did you

see Natalie eat or drink anything?"

"No."

"Did you ever see anyone tamper with the food or beverages either inside or outside of that room?"

Lenny's eyes widened between blinks. "No, and that couldn't happen with the water and the pop that came from the bar. We never open the containers."

Good to know.

"After you left the kitchen or bar with the items for the room, was there a period of time when your cart was unattended?" I asked.

"No, never." Blink, blink. "I could get fired for doing something like that."

"Okay, how about what you observed inside of the room. You said that Natalie seemed fine earlier in the afternoon, when you delivered the coffee. Did you also see her later that afternoon?"

"A little before two, I think," Lenny said, rubbing his eyes as if that might alleviate the blinking. "They had an order for more coffee, tea, and Coke. I also brought more water and fresh ice."

This was the first mention of ice, and I added it to my list of things Natalie could have consumed on Saturday.

"Okay, so you delivered the coffee and stuff around two. Did you interact with Natalie at all?"

"Not really," he said, dropping his hands to his lap. "She looked my way and smiled, but I didn't say anything to her. I was covering the bar and needed to get back. Plus, it was getting crowded in there with some girls who came in from the pool. Loud, too. I don't know that

Natalie would've heard me unless I shouted at her."

I could imagine with all those bodies in one room. "How'd she seem then?"

"Fine." Blink. "At least she looked okay to me. She was busy doing someone's makeup."

"Did you happen to notice anyone handing her something to eat or drink?" Like that can of Coke Nora had mentioned.

"No, I just wheeled in the cart and left."

"Okay, and nothing seemed *off* to you in there?"

"Off?" Lenny stared across the table at me, his eyes signaling his wariness as if he were using Morse code. "You mean off, like someone gave Natalie something to make her sick?"

I nodded, because that's exactly what I meant. "Or if you saw something that looked a little suspicious."

He released a shuddering breath. "Whoa, you think that someone..."

I needed to stop him before he mentioned the magic word, murder. "No, I'm just asking because we need to explore all the possibilities."

"Okay, I get that but..." He shook his head. "I didn't notice anything. I wish I had."

He wasn't the only one who wished that.

Chapter Eighteen

When I turned onto G Street and drove the four blocks to my grandmother's house, I smiled at the sight of the Ford F-150 parked in Steve's driveway.

Since I had dashed home to feed Fozzie and ditch my work clothes for a pair of comfy blue jeans and a cotton pullover, I was arriving too late to help Gram with dinner. But I knew that Steve would be happy to give her a hand. He always did whether I was there or not, and she loved him for it. We both did.

Then I drove past her next-door neighbor's house, a 1920s-era two-story on a narrow lot bordered by a tall hedge—the hedge that had been obscuring a silver Mercedes SUV.

"What now?" I groaned as I parked next to my mother's car.

Marietta knew that Wednesday evening was when Steve and I had dinner with Gram. My mother either wanted something enough to break her silence or this was some sort of setup.

"There she is," my grandmother announced as I stepped through the back door and inhaled the mouth-watering aroma of pot roast. "Just in time, too. Dinner is almost ready. I just need to get the biscuits into the oven."

I locked gazes with Steve, who grinned at me with false cheer before he disappeared into the dining room, leaving me with the elephant in the room. Specifically, at the kitchen table, where Barry was sitting next to my mother, who had yet to acknowledge my presence.

Biscuits, Marietta's favorite pot roast dinner, and Barry. This was definitely a setup.

"Hello, Charmaine," he said, raising his wineglass in greeting with a glance to his wife as if she should follow his example.

She folded her arms under her double Ds. "If I have to be here, she should at least show up on time."

It's lovely to see you, too.

"Mary Jo, mind your manners," Gram snapped. "And say hello to your daughter."

Marietta flicked a delicate wrist, her gold bangles echoing her indifference to her mother's instructions.

Stifling a sigh, I turned to Steve, emerging from the dining room with a glass of white wine that had better be for me.

"What's going on?" I asked when he pressed the wineglass into my hand.

"I'll tell you what's going on," Gram said, taking my drink away from me. "You two girls are going to go upstairs for a chat."

Marietta refolded her arms. "We most certainly are not."

"This isn't up for debate." After setting my wineglass

on the table, Gram grabbed Marietta at the elbow and pulled her out of her seat. "You'll march upstairs to your old room, right now." Then she clasped my wrist with her free hand. "Both of you," she said, leading us toward the stairs like an octogenarian bouncer. "And neither one of you will come down until you've settled your differences."

"Mama, really!" Marietta protested. "This is ridiculous."

I had to agree with my mother on this one and pulled out of Gram's grasp. "I appreciate that you want to smooth things over, but Gram—"

"Save your breath, 'cause I've heard more than enough out of the two of you." She gave my shoulder a little push. "Now, go."

Good grief, I was thirty-seven years old and had just been sent to my room.

"You, too," Gram barked at Marietta. "Get your butts up those stairs and don't come down for dinner until you've apologized to one another."

Seriously? "What do I have to apologize for?"

"Do you see what I have to deal with?" Marietta threw up her hands, her bangles clanging like an exclamation mark.

"Enough!" Red-cheeked, Gram pointed up the stairs. "Move! Or do I have to drag you up there myself?"

Taking the first step, I glanced back at my mother. "Come on." We needed to get this over with before Gram made good on her threat. "Then we can eat."

"Fine!" Marietta fumed as she stomped up the stairs behind me.

She shut the door to the room that we had each slept in as children and then sat perched at the foot of my old double bed and glared out the window.

Kicking off my flip-flops, I leaned back against the headboard and stretched out. I wasn't comfortable sitting this close to a woman who looked like she wanted to grab the pillow behind my back and beat me with it, but I had to be more comfortable than she was.

"I can scoot over," I said, making room for her next to me.

With a shrug, she slipped off her wedge sandals and climbed onto the bed, infusing the space with her musky jasmine scent.

A full minute went by before either one of us spoke.

"How was work today?" she softly asked, sounding like a child forced to make polite adult conversation.

It wasn't what we had been banished upstairs to talk about, but it was a relatively safe subject. "It was okay. Kind of a long day. I had to go to Rainshadow Ridge to do an interview."

"Hunh. Because that girl died there?"

I had already explained more than once that she hadn't died there. "No," I said, careful to keep the exasperation out of my voice. "I just needed to follow up with everyone who had been in contact with her, including the staff."

Marietta turned her head toward me. "The staff! You don't think that someone there—"

"No." Not anymore. "This is routine stuff when something about the death is unusual."

"Hmm..."

After several beats of awkward silence, I figured it was my turn. "How was your day?"

My mother blew out a sigh. "It was okay."

It didn't sound so okay. She wrapped her arms around her knees, creating a coil of tension that I could feel from six inches away.

"I got a workout in and then Barry announced that we were going out to dinner, so I showered and changed and here I am."

And here we were.

"So, he was in on this," I said.

She clicked her tongue. "Yep."

"Steve didn't mention that you were here when I texted that I would be a little late, which makes me think he was in on this too."

"No, I was here when he got your text. Your grandmother threatened to send him home without supper if he said anything."

"Sheesh, she's getting feisty in her old age."

Marietta snorted. "Tell me about it."

"Uh..." I said to keep the conversation going. "How'd your shopping trip go yesterday?"

"Your grandmother didn't tell you?"

"I haven't talked to her since..." I wasn't sure how much I wanted to say about yesterday afternoon.

Marietta nodded as if to spare me. "Then you don't know that she found a dress for the wedding."

I thought that the dress she had worn to Marietta's wedding two years earlier would have been perfectly fine, but I knew voicing that opinion would be a huge mistake at this particular moment. "Great."

"It's lavender—a dress and jacket. It flows beautifully and looks gorgeous on her. You should see it." She released her knees as if she wanted to spring from the bed. "I'll get it. It's hanging—"

I grabbed her wrist, wrapping my fingers around more metal than skin. "Why don't we do that after."

Marietta shot me a tentative glance and I withdrew my hand. "Oh, okay." She settled back next to me. "Yes, we haven't...um...finished our...um..."

"Conversation," I said to put her out of her misery. And while I didn't want to bring up the subject of her efforts to supersede Steve's and my decisions any more than she wanted to hear what I had to say, it was now or never.

"Now that Gram has a dress that she likes..." *And you approve of.* "I hope you'll agree with me that we're all ready for this wedding. We just need to wait for sixteen days to roll by, but hey, who's counting?" I added with a chuckle to keep things light.

Marietta heaved a sigh. "Are you absolutely sure on the flowers. Now's the time to order more if—"

"I'm sure. I'm totally happy with what we picked out."

"Because it's very easy to add—"

"Mom, it doesn't matter that it's easy. I'm happy. You were too that day at the florist."

"I know, but—"

"No buts." I bumped her shoulder with mine. "It's going to be beautiful. You were just at the resort last Saturday, so you know how pretty the grounds look right now. There's never a guarantee with the weather, but if it's sunny and warm like it's been this week, what more could I ask for?"

Heaving another sigh, my mother placed her hand on mine. "Charmaine, you're my baby. I just want you to know that you can ask for more. It's okay. Barry and I can easily afford—"

"It's not about how much you can afford." I squeezed her hand. "It's about believing me when I tell you that Steve and I are happy with the choices we've made."

She huffed a breath. "Fine."

"So, it's not that we don't appreciate your suggestions," I said, trying to keep my tone snark-free. "We just need you to—"

"Butt out?"

"I was going to say be supportive of our decisions, but 'butt out' works too."

"I thought it might." She traced the tip of my right ring finger for several silent seconds. "All I want is for your big day to be perfect. Because, my darling, you deserve the most perfect day possible."

"Everyone I love will be there and I'm marrying a great guy. I can't think of one thing to make it more perfect." Aside from no one collapsing and being rushed to the hospital.

"Okay, then, if you're sure," Marietta said, pulling my hand closer to inspect it. "Lordy, when was your last manicure?!"

I yanked back my hand. "I've been a little busy lately, but I'll—"

"You're not working the Friday before the wedding, are

you?"

I had a bad feeling about where this was going. "No, I took the day to tend to some last-minute details like going to Donna's to get my hair cut." She didn't know it yet, but I was sure Donna would be happy to snip off my split ends.

"Great! We'll go get manicures afterward." Marietta squinted as she scanned my face. "Facials, too."

Swell.

Two hours later, after we watched Barry and Marietta climb into their Mercedes, Gram turned to me with a satisfied smile. "Well, that went even better than I had hoped."

"All that crapola with Mom would've blown over eventually," I said. "You didn't have to force us into a room like it was some sort of cage match."

Gram's mouth stretched into a grin worthy of the Cheshire cat. "It worked, didn't it? Peace has been restored."

"Whatever." I knew I sounded like a pissy teenager and didn't care. She wasn't the one that Marietta would be dragging to the day spa.

"Don't be like that." Gram wagged an arthritic finger at me. "You know someone had to do something, and if it wasn't gonna be you, then it had to be me."

"Remind me not to get on your bad side, Eleanor," Steve said as he brought in the last of the dirty dishes from the dining room.

She smirked. "Excuse me, but I don't have a bad side. I do have very little tolerance for reality show drama in my own home, though, which reminds me. It's after eight and I'm missing my show."

I shooed her into the living room. "Go, get into your comfy chair, and leave the cleanup to us because you've done enough for one day." Truly!

"She'll fall asleep in that chair before eight-thirty," Steve said to me when I grabbed a clean dishtowel and joined him at the sink. "What do you wanna bet?"

That made me think of the betting pool Lucille had organized at Duke's and the eye drops overdose she'd put her money on. "Yeah, probably."

Steve held out a plate for me to dry and when I didn't take it right away, he gave me a long look. "You okay?"

"Sure." I flashed him a smile. "I was just thinking."

"About?"

"About how young Natalie Mercer was to have a heart attack," I said, wanting to be honest with the cop I loved, but also wanting to know if Steve found her death to be the least bit suspicious.

He focused on the plate he was dousing in the sudsy water. "Lots of young people have underlying heart conditions. Just the other day I heard about a high school kid who died after basketball practice."

"Natalie Mercer hadn't been running up and down a basketball court when she collapsed."

He handed me the plate to dry. "No, but my point is that there must've been something wrong, like a congenital defect."

"According to her cardiologist, that was corrected with a pacemaker."

"Could've been something else—maybe something that didn't show up on any of the tests he ran."

"Maybe," I said, putting the plate away in the cabinet. "Could be something that will show up on the tox screen, too."

"That's another possibility. Drug interactions happen all the time, especially when alcohol's involved."

"No one saw her drink anything alcoholic." I turned to face him. "I asked. She wasn't much of a drinker."

"Okay." He passed me another plate to dry. "Could still be some sort of drug interaction, and if it is, it should show up on tox."

The operative word there was *should*. "Right."

"So, it sounds like you've done your part and now you just need to wait and let the crime lab do theirs."

"I hate waiting." I was more of a stir, bake, and serve girl, and he knew it.

"Maybe you need something else to think about in the meantime." Steve's voice was as smooth as chocolate mousse and just as tempting.

I set the plate and towel aside so that there would be nothing between us if he was thinking what I was thinking. "Maybe I do."

"I hear you have something big coming up pretty soon."

Inching closer, I leered at the zipper of his chinos. "One can only hope."

"Hey, get your mind and eyes out of the gutter. I was

referring to our wedding."

"Oh, that," I said with a nonchalant flick of my wrist. "That's days away. Sixteen, to be precise." I linked my hands behind his neck and smiled up at him. "What else have you got that would be a little more immediate?"

Steve's lips curled with carnal intent. "Well, as soon as we're done with the dishes, we could head over to my place and make out."

I gave him a quick kiss. "You're on!"

Chapter Nineteen

The next morning, after I caught up with the filing and did battle with a jam-prone copier, I headed back to my desk, where my phone was ringing with a call from Natalie's mother, who wanted an update.

Since Kayla had also called and spoken with Jenny Goshen, she knew as much as I did. All I could do was assure her that I was still working the case even though the only thing I had on today's docket was to write my report for Frankie.

It took me a while to eliminate all my typos, but after three and a half hours, I finally printed the eight-page document that listed the salient details that each witness, family member, or friend had provided me. I then emailed Frankie a copy before tucking the printed pages inside the blue folder she had handed me on Monday and walking it back to her office.

While I knew it was as complete a report as I could make it, it felt thin and horribly repetitive. Probably because I had copied and pasted *"Witness did not observe anything unusual"* six times.

In fact, only Lucille had suggested that Natalie Mercer

could have ingested some sort of toxin on Saturday, and I certainly wasn't going to mention that in my report.

Amanda had speculated that the aspirin Natalie had taken might have been something more lethal, but according to the imprint on all the tablets in Nora's aspirin bottle, that's exactly what they were—common drugstore aspirin.

No one seemed to have a grudge against Natalie.

No one, aside from her nosy neighbor, had even hinted at trouble that Natalie had been having with anyone.

There was the matter of her having been harassed via text almost two years ago, but I believed Lucas when he told me that he had handled that situation the best he could. Despite the fact that he hadn't wanted to name names. Because of embarrassment? Probably. I hadn't made too much out of it. Lots of us do things in our youth that we're not proud of.

Even Paul Riley had dismissed that ugly period in his daughter's life as ancient history, which I mentioned in my report. Beyond that, Frankie could draw her own conclusions.

All I could tell her with confidence was that Lucas had loved his life with Natalie and had no apparent motivation to cause her harm.

According to their mothers, the couple had been happy and their life together appeared to have been the stuff of romance novels.

Until it wasn't.

And I had a whole lot of nothing to show for the time I had spent getting witness statements. Not that I minded the investment of time. It was better than doing mindless grunt work. My report just felt incomplete, unbaked, and as unsatisfying as fat-free butter.

Of course, the Washington State Patrol crime lab would be the ones doing the baking over the next couple of months. Which was a long time to wait for the toxicology results, but if their analysis could help unravel the mystery of Natalie Mercer's sudden death, I would be satisfied. Grateful, too, because this lingering mystery was driving me crazy.

If it didn't, if there were no elevated levels of any toxins and nothing to help explain why Natalie's heart stopped beating, then maybe Steve was right. She'd had some underlying condition that her cardiologist missed.

There might never be a good explanation for what had happened because there had been no autopsy.

I remembered that there had also been no autopsy performed in the case profiled in that "perfect murder" show. The family members, who had suspected that their loved one hadn't died from a heart attack, had to wait for the toxicology results to prove he had been murdered.

A shiver prickled my skin as I thought about the parallels.

Small towns, limited investigatory resources, and the sudden death of a spouse from an apparent heart attack.

But that was where the similarities ended because Lucas couldn't have been motivated to murder Natalie for her money. She was no heiress and her life insurance payout had an unimpressive number of zeroes.

"And this is no TV show," I muttered to myself as I

entered Frankie's empty office and placed the folder in her inbox. I would have no answers in the next hour. Much to my frustration.

All I could do now was wait.

And maybe eat. Because I was starving.

I checked the time on Patsy's desk glass-domed clock and saw that it was almost one. No wonder I was hungry.

"Do you need something to do?" Patsy asked without masking her annoyance at my invasion of her airspace.

"I have plenty to keep me busy, thanks." That included sitting in on a witness interview with one of the junior prosecutors at two, so I took the next seven minutes to get to the fastest lunch spot I knew.

"You eating or are you just going to stand there and let the cold out?" my great-uncle asked as I inspected the contents of the stainless steel refrigerator where he kept the salad greens.

"Eating." I poured some sugar on the smile I aimed at him. "Did Tuesday's baking earn me lunch if I make it myself?"

"Yes!" Alice called out from her worktable. "And you know you don't have to make it yourself."

Duke smirked. "You heard the boss. Whatcha want?"

"How about a grilled chicken breast for the salad I'm gonna throw together," I said.

He jabbed his spatula in my direction. "You got it."

"Who're you talking to?" Lucille tacked an order to the aluminum wheel over the grill and her eyes brightened at the sight of me. "Ooh, stay right there. I need to talk to you."

I had a feeling that my chicken breast wouldn't be the only thing being grilled for the next few minutes.

"Make it fast," Duke barked when Lucille swung the door open. "We've got hungry customers."

"Yeah, yeah." She squeaked up to the prep table, where I was chopping a tomato. "Any news?"

I shot her a glance. "About?"

Lucille planted her fists on her rounded hips. "What do you think? Our version of the perfect murder."

"Please don't call it that," I bit out between clenched teeth. "It assumes *way* too much."

"Whatever. So? What's the latest?"

"I don't have anything that you'd be interested in," I said, returning to my chopping.

All I had was a boring report that offered nothing to counter Kyle Cardinale's medical opinion that Natalie Mercer had died after suffering a major heart attack.

Lucille tsked. "For real, or are you just sayin' that?"

"Really, I have no news." And I wouldn't tell her if I did.

"Did you tell Frankie about the eye drops?" she asked in a too-loud whisper.

"Shhh!" I dropped my knife to the cutting board. "I can't have anyone hearing us talk about that. That could cost me my job if it got back to her."

"Don't be such a worrywart. No one can hear us. So did you tell Frankie or not?"

"I mentioned it, but it's gonna take a couple of months

to get the toxicology results back, so there's nothing to do in the meantime but wait."

Lucille gave me a smug smile. "I wouldn't be so sure about that if I were you."

I hesitated to ask, but I had to know what she had up her sleeve. "What're you talking about?"

"We've got a funeral to go to."

Two days later, I was sitting with Lucille in the back row of a Port Townsend funeral home chapel, where we were watching Natalie Mercer's family members file past in the center aisle.

Lucille leaned into my shoulder as an elderly couple sat in the two padded chairs next to her. "It's a good thing we got here early. Almost every seat is taken and folks are still coming in."

"Yeah, it's quite the turnout," I said. "Not at all what I expected to see." Especially since Erin Lofgren had just arrived and taken the seat next to Lenny Gallatin.

They didn't appear to be speaking to one another. Nor had there been much more than a cursory glance from Lenny when she sat down next to him. Maybe they didn't know one another. There wasn't more than a handful of unoccupied chairs, so maybe Erin picking that particular one was just a weird coincidence.

But I wasn't big on weird coincidences. Not where Natalie Mercer was concerned.

Other than the Mercer family members I had interviewed days earlier and some familiar faces from Renee's wedding, I didn't recognize anyone else in the crowd.

"Who's the dish sitting behind Joan Germain?" Lucille asked over the soaring voice of Andrea Bocelli coming through a corner speaker. "And why does she keep looking back this way?"

I straightened to see over the big-haired lady in front of me. "That's Sydney Sheridan. Joan's her great-aunt." And as if she knew I was talking about her, Sydney leaned forward to say something to Joan and now both women were looking at me.

"Uh, Char?" Lucille uttered when Joan stepped out from the second row and fixed me with an angry glare. "Did you do something to piss off Joan Germain?"

No doubt my presence here was enough to do the job. "Not intentionally."

Lucille held the funeral program in front of her face as if she had a sudden need to study Natalie's picture. "Well, if you get booted outta here, pretend you don't know me."

I heaved a sigh because the odds of that happening looked more likely with every step Joan took in my direction.

When she came to a halt at the end of my row, she smiled at the elderly couple. "Thank you for coming," she graciously said before shifting her gaze to me. "May I speak with you for a moment?"

Uh-oh.

Feeling like I had been busted crashing a not-so-fun party, I got to my feet and followed Joan through the carpeted foyer and into a large reception room, where a stocky woman in her sixties was placing votive candles on a long table.

"I'm sorry to interrupt you, but could we have the room for a few minutes?" Joan asked her.

The woman looked up with the pleasant expression of someone whose job it was to extend every courtesy. "Of course, Ms. Germain."

After the woman clomped across the hardwood floor in her low, clunky heels and the sound of her steps faded behind a set of double doors, Joan turned to me.

"Your presence here is upsetting my family," she said.

I seriously doubted that any member of her clan could be traumatized by me sitting in the back row. "Sorry, I don't mean to upset anyone."

Joan's eyes narrowed. "This service is for those of us who loved Natalie. Since that clearly doesn't include you, I need to ask you to leave."

Crap. I was afraid that's what she was going to say.

I nodded my understanding. "I'm sorry you feel that way. I just wanted—"

"I don't care. You need to leave."

Okay, then. "I need to go back and get my bag."

"After that, if I see you anywhere on the grounds, you'll be forcibly removed."

That should have sounded like an empty threat, but I could see that Joan Germain meant every word she had said.

Crap, crap, and double crap. Coming to this funeral had just become a big waste of a Saturday afternoon.

"What happened?" Lucille asked me when I reached past her to collect my tote bag.

"I just got the boot," I whispered. "Text me when you're ready to leave, and I'll come back to pick you up."

She gave me a thumbs-up. "I'll fill you in if anything interesting happens."

I doubted that anyone would be making any incriminating speeches or that one of Lucas's old girlfriends would be jumping to her feet to declare her love, but I was sorry that I couldn't hang around as an observer. And that included keeping an eye on Erin Lofgren and Lenny Gallatin.

As I stepped out of the row, I noticed Joan leaning over to say something to Sydney.

Something about me?

Then, the second Joan returned to her seat, Sydney looked back to give me a smug little wave that felt like a parting shot.

Yep, it had definitely been about me. Plus, Sydney was informing me that she was the family member who had engineered my abrupt departure.

Maybe this hadn't been a complete waste of time after all.

Chapter Twenty

"Well?" I asked two and a half hours later, when Lucille's butt touched down on my passenger seat. "How'd it go?"

She looked back at the woman standing by the funeral home's front door and waved as we pulled out of the parking lot. "Great. Deidre's a hoot. She's gonna stop by the cafe the next time she's in town."

"That's nice." And wasn't something I was the least bit interested in unless Deidre had offered Lucille some dirt about the Mercer family. "I ran into her before Joan Germain chased me out of there. I take it Deidre works there."

Lucille nodded. "The funeral director's wife. Some of the stories she had to tell. One was about a stiff who had two wives who didn't know about one another until they each called to make the funeral arrangements. Ooh-whee, can you imagine?"

I didn't even want to try.

"Did she happen to mention anything about Natalie Mercer's funeral that was of any interest?" I asked, merging onto Sims Way.

Lucille pulled a pair of oversized sunglasses from her

purse and slipped them on. "Not really. Although she thought that Joan Germain was even nicer in person than she seemed on TV."

Not to me she wasn't.

"So you and Deidre didn't chat about the way Natalie died?" I would expect everyone who worked there to be discreet, especially with someone she just met, but I had to ask.

"Nah, just that it was a shame that such a pretty thing died so young."

"Okay, did anybody else that you talked to have anything interesting to say?"

"Nope," Lucille said. "Not a one of 'em acted like there was something fishy about how the girl died."

"What about the dish? You talk to her?"

"Who?"

How could she not know who I meant? "Sydney, the blonde that you called the dish."

"Oh, her. No. She was hanging out with a pack of girls her own age. I chatted a little with her mom, though. Got the impression that Sydney can be a handful."

"I bet."

When Lucille didn't respond I glanced over and saw her staring at me expectantly.

"What's that supposed to mean?" she asked.

"Nothing. I met her once and came away with that general opinion."

"Met her socially or officially?"

"Not officially," I said, choosing my words carefully. "Our paths happened to cross a few days ago and during the course of the conversation, she just struck me as someone who's used to getting her own way."

"Hunh," Lucille grunted. "In other words, she's a spoiled brat."

"Maybe." Based on my experience when I met her at Lucas's apartment, Sydney certainly had a bratty attitude. But she also appeared to care deeply for Lucas and be very protective of him. In a hostile and off-putting way, but I had to give her props for the way she stood up to me four nights ago.

Didn't mean I had to like it, or her.

"What else happened?" I asked. "Anything I should know?"

"Nope, it was a pretty tame affair."

"Did Lucas Mercer stay for the reception?"

"Yeah. I'm pretty sure he stayed inside that reception room the entire time I was there." Lucille glanced at me. "Why?"

"Did you see him talking to any girls close to his own age?"

"Sure. The dish, his sister, some of the teachers from Natalie's school—I introduced myself to a few of them. Let's see, who else? There must've been at least a dozen girls in their twenties. All of 'em hung out with the guy for at least a few minutes."

"How about a tall girl with brown hair to the middle of her back and freckles. She arrived a few minutes before I got asked to leave. Sat three or four rows in front of us."

"You mean Erin?" Lucille asked.

Indeed I did. "You know her?"

"I met her last Saturday at the wedding. She was one of the photographers."

That hadn't been Erin's job, but it was close enough so I played along. "Oh yeah, I remember her."

"Nice gal. Didn't stay long after we got through the reception line."

"You went through the line together?" This sounded promising.

"I was right behind her."

"And did you happen to hear what she said to Lucas?"

"It was hard not to," Lucille said.

All right! "And?"

"It was just the kind of stuff everyone says. You know, how sorry she was."

"What'd he say?"

"Who knows? He mumbled something and then they hugged for a long time. She told me after that they used to be close. Poor thing was crying so hard that she left a few minutes later."

"Did she leave alone or was she with a guy?" I asked.

"She left alone, but that young fella she was sitting next to took off a minute or two later."

Which told me that Lenny may or may not have been her date today. And if he had been, who were they trying to fool by leaving separately?

I could feel Lucille's eyes on me in the silent seconds that followed.

"Why are you interested in her?" she finally asked.

"Just curious."

Lucille scoffed. "Curious, my sweet butt. You think

somethin's up with those two."

Maybe. "No, Erin and Lucas Mercer were once in a relationship, like she pretty much admitted to you, so I'm just curious about her is all."

"Right. You're probably trying to decide if that nice girl could've emptied a bottle of eye drops into whatever Natalie Mercer was drinkin' that day."

"Don't be silly," I said, picking up speed as we headed out of town. I had already ruled Erin Lofgren out. Same with Lenny Gallatin.

I hadn't thought that either one of them had anything to do with Natalie's death. But now that it appeared that they knew one another, I wasn't so sure about that.

The next day, after driving Gram home from church, I spent a fun couple of hours having lunch with Rox, Donna, and baby Emily.

I didn't want to think about pretty girls dying way too young, and I made Rox and Donna promise to not mention my wedding. I didn't want to think about that either. Instead, after I ate I held Emily and breathed in her delightful baby scent.

"You are the most perfect little girl I have ever seen," I cooed to the sweet bundle in my arms.

Donna yawned. "She's not so perfect when she wakes her mama up at two in the morning and then won't go back to sleep."

"That'll get better." Rox smiled sympathetically at Donna. "By the time Char gets married, Emily shouldn't be quite so fussy."

"Hey." I gently kicked Rox under Donna's kitchen table. "No mention of the 'M' word today."

"Oops," Rox said. "It slipped out. In two weeks then."

Donna grinned at me. "Actually, it's one day less than two weeks. You ready?"

I scowled at her. "How is this not talking about the wedding?"

"Did I mention the 'W' word?" Donna asked, stabbing a bite of the deli salad I had picked up for our lunch.

"Now you're just being technical," I told her.

She pointed her fork at me as she chewed. "And you're being silly. Why can't we talk about this? I've barely seen you since I had the baby. I feel like I'm missing out on everything."

Emily stirred in my arms as if she sensed that I was upsetting her mommy. "If there was any news, I'd tell you."

"You didn't tell me that you signed up for a wedding registry," Donna said, her tone accusing. "And I only know that because Ian's mom told him to ask Steve if you were registered anywhere."

Rox chuckled. "Char's actually not the one who signed up."

Donna's sapphire eyes widened. "No! Don't tell me that your mother—"

"Yep." I released a sigh. "My mother has been making some unilateral decisions on my behalf that I have spent way too many hours undoing this past week."

"Oh, jeez," Donna said. "I hope you still want those

towels you're registered for. Not to give away what you're getting from us, but..."

"You've seen my ratty towels," I told her. "We desperately need new ones, so thank you. Now, can we drop the subject and talk about something else? In fact, let's talk babies and how they smell so good."

"Did you hear that? She wants to talk about babies." Donna cocked her head at Rox, and they both grinned as if they were in on a private joke.

"Am I missing something?" I asked.

"It's just good timing," Donna said, shifting her grin to me. "Because I know someone who has some baby news."

My jaw dropped when I met Rox's gaze. "Are you?"

She nodded, her brown eyes shiny with happy tears. "Due the first week of February."

I passed Emily to her mother so that I could give Rox a proper hug. "Congratulations!" I knew she and Eddie had wanted to have another child, but Rox hadn't even given me a hint that she might be pregnant.

"I thought that you'd guess when you didn't see me drink any champagne at the reception last Saturday," she said, wiping her eyes.

"I was probably so distracted by what happened that I didn't notice." I didn't want to rain on Rox's parade with any more talk of that sad evening and slapped a smile on my face. "But never mind that because I couldn't be happier for you. Is it okay if I share your news with Steve?"

"Of course," she said. "We're not telling anyone other than family and you guys right now. It's early and Eddie says I look more like I've had one too many paninis instead of someone who's growing a baby, so I probably have a few weeks until it'll become obvious. Assuming, that I'm not constantly puking in the meantime."

"You doing okay?" I asked over Emily's cries as she fussed on Donna's lap.

Rox rapped on the surface of the knotty pine table. "So far, so good, knock wood. The morning sickness is much better than last time."

Pushing back in her chair, Donna smiled apologetically. "I need to change her. Don't say anything important until I get back."

"I know this isn't great timing," Rox said, lowering her voice after Donna left the room.

I stared at my best friend. "What isn't great about it?"

"In another two weeks, I might not be able to fit into my bridesmaid dress."

"A tailor can probably let the seams out. If not, just wear something else. The most important thing is for you to be there with me."

"Aww, thanks. But I feel awful about this." A tear trickled down Rox's cheek. "When we started trying, I had no idea I'd get pregnant so quickly. I just assumed it would take a few months. I mean, I'm your maid of honor. I should be putting all the attention on you instead of—"

"Will you please stop," I said while she used her napkin to blow her nose. "There's nothing to feel bad about, not when I'm the one who postponed the wedding for almost a year. Besides, I'm nothing but happy for you. For me, too, because all our dreams are finally coming true."

"What dreams?" Donna asked, holding Emily close to

her chest like her personal treasure, which she clearly was. "What'd I miss?"

"We were just talking about things we've been dreaming of like that little bundle of joy in your arms." Dreams of the heart that had come true for Rox and Donna, and that I hoped would someday come true for me.

Since Lucas Mercer had told me they were trying to have a baby, I imagined that Natalie had the same kind of dream.

While my heart ached at the thought of her unrealized dream, it also started to beat faster as this thought rattled around in my brain.

What if the person who had sent those texts had known that Natalie and Lucas were trying to start a family, and she wanted to make sure that never happened?

Maybe she viewed last Saturday as her best and last chance to take action on her dream of reuniting with the man she loved.

With all the people coming and going and all the beverages and ice-filled glasses being passed around in that room, it could be fairly easy to add a dose of something lethal. Especially if that something wouldn't show up on the standard toxicology screening.

Holy crap.

Lucille was right. This could be a copycat of the perfect murder.

Chapter Twenty-One

When Steve came over while I was chopping veggies for a stir-fry, I welcomed him with a kiss. Our embrace was then cut short when my dog wedged between us like a disapproving chaperone. Any other day, this would have made me laugh, but with murder on my mind, I couldn't even muster up a smile.

Steve leaned against the counter and watched me wash my hands. "Want some help?"

"Actually, what would help is for you to sit," I said, pointing at the kitchen table. "Because I need to talk to you about something."

His eyes darkened while Fozzie danced at his feet. "Something wrong?"

"Nothing's wrong with me, and this has nothing to do with our wedding."

"Okay," Steve said as if he weren't entirely convinced.

"Want a beer?" I asked as I headed to the refrigerator to grab a bottle of iced tea for myself.

"Sure." Stroking the ears of the furball curled next to his chair, Steve watched me with an expectant stare.

Setting our bottles on the table, I sat next to him,

causing Fozzie to pant excitedly because both his favorite humans were close enough to lavish attention on him.

Sorry, pal. Not now.

I met Steve's gaze. "I have something that I want to run by you...to get your professional opinion."

He twisted off his bottle cap. "Any conversation that starts with you needing my professional opinion is never a good thing."

"Just hear me out, okay?"

"Go for it."

"Based on all the interviews I've done, I'm almost certain that Natalie Mercer was murdered by someone that her husband used to be in a relationship with, and—"

"Why are we talking about this again? Didn't we agree a few days ago that you shouldn't jump to any conclusions before the tox results came back?"

"Yes, but—"

"And yet you want to keep speculating about what could've happened," Steve said, raising his voice, causing Fozzie to whimper as if he didn't want to hear Mom and Dad arguing. "Without having all the facts."

"I realize I don't have all the facts, but will you just listen to what I have to say and *then* tell me what you think?"

He blew out a breath that sounded more like a growl. "Fine. Start talking."

I spent the next ten minutes telling Steve everything I knew, from the suspicions of Natalie's parents to the unlikely odds that Lucas Mercer's ex-girlfriend would show up at the funeral right next to the guy who had been the server last Saturday. I wrapped up by grabbing my laptop and playing him key parts of the "perfect murder" episode that had aired a few weeks earlier.

I just left out that I had first heard about it from Lucille.

"What if this inspired a copycat killing?" I asked, pausing the video with twenty-three minutes to go.

Steve shrugged. "I'll grant you there are some strong similarities."

"Similarities! The way Natalie died is practically identical. In fact, I'd be willing to bet a million bucks... Okay, I don't have that much, so a hundred bucks on a lethal amount of tetrahydrozoline showing up on that toxicology report."

Steve took a long pull of beer. "Even if it does, the fact remains that you *have* to wait for it."

I winced. "I know, but—"

"There's no case without evidence." He twined his fingers with mine. "You work with prosecutors, you know this."

"Yes, I know." I also knew that I sounded bitchy and whiny and didn't care.

"What you have is some reason for suspicion," he said, offering me a hint of a lopsided smile.

"I think it's some pretty good reason, given everything I've learned in the past week."

"Okay, maybe it is, and if the tox report lists a high level of the tetra-whatever stuff in her blood, you can take some satisfaction in the fact that you called this one."

I stared at him in disbelief. "That could be two months from now. Shouldn't we do something in the meantime?"

"Chow Mein, I know you don't want to hear this, but there's nothing to do. Your boss hasn't made this a criminal case and until she does, there can be no official investigation."

"I can't tell you how much I hate hearing that."

Steve enveloped my hand with both of his. "I know, and I get it. But, Char, you're just gonna have to be patient and let the facts drive this case. Trying to drive it yourself will only make you crazy."

"You mean crazier?"

His gaze warmed like chocolate over a low flame. "Your words, not mine."

I groaned. "I absolutely positively hate this."

"Could've fooled me."

"It's not funny. That girl was murdered and there's nothing I can do about it."

Steve released my hand and tapped his fingers for several beats of my racing heart. "Did you write a summary of your interviews for Frankie?"

I nodded. "I submitted it to her on Thursday."

"I take it you saved a copy of it somewhere?"

"It's on my work computer as well as the network."

"Okay, then here's something you can do," Steve said after taking a deep breath. "Make a copy of that document and add everything you know. The episode number of the show and the air date. If you felt that anyone lied to you during your interview or was less than forthcoming—basically all the details you think would be helpful to an investigator."

"Okay, I can do that." Oh boy, was I more than happy

to do that.

"Then, *if,* and I do mean *if,* Frankie feels she has cause and asks Jim Pearson to investigate this girl's death, I'll give him a call to let him know that you've already done some legwork."

Bounding up and over Fozzie, I wrapped my arms around Steve. "Thank you!"

Detective Jim Pearson with the Chimacam County sheriff's department was someone I had worked with on several cases. I liked Jim and knew him to be the kind of guy who would be open to meeting with me, especially if the suggestion came from Steve.

Steve pulled me onto his lap. "Can we agree that this subject is now closed?"

I smiled up at him. "For now."

"For now." He shook his head. "Woman, you're killing me here."

I snuggled closer. "I don't want to kill you. I want to marry you and have your babies."

"Now you're talkin'."

"Oh, on the subject of babies, guess who's pregnant?"

"Who?" he asked.

"Rox."

"Yeah?" He brightened. "Good for them."

"It's a secret for now, so don't say anything to anyone, okay?"

Steve chuckled. "Hadn't planned on mentioning it to Lucille, if that's what you're worried about."

"No, it's just that it's early, and Rox wants to wait until after the first trimester. You know how it is."

"Actually, I don't know much about this stuff. This isn't a subject anyone other than you would talk to me about."

"That's because you're a guy." As soon as the words left my lips I knew that wasn't entirely true.

I only knew that Rox and Eddie were trying to get pregnant with their second child because she had told me in confidence a couple of months ago.

And I had no idea that Donna and Ian had been trying until they announced that they were expecting at a dinner party last fall.

This just wasn't something people often discussed outside of their closest circle of friends, which made me wonder…

Who in Natalie's circle knew she was trying to get pregnant?

Chapter Twenty-Two

"What's your problem?" my great-aunt Alice asked me two days later, when I dropped down on the wooden stool next to her and buried my face in my hands.

"I hate my job." And just wanted to hide out in the sanctuary of her kitchen for the rest of my lunch hour.

She scoffed. "Since when?"

Okay, maybe *hate* was overstating it. And I didn't hate *everything* about my job.

But after spending most of my morning on my knees, going from filing cabinet to filing cabinet in search of a critical manila folder that had gone missing, I was seeing red. Because the junior prosecutor who had all but accused me of losing her case file hadn't bothered to mention that she had found it buried under a pile of paper on her desk.

I only found out thirteen minutes ago, when I passed her in the hallway and I got a "by the way" update that we could call off the hunt. But now she had some copying for me to do instead. As in right away because she had an important meeting.

I swallowed the bile rising in my throat and informed

her that I had a lunch date, but I'd get right on this sudden emergency of hers as soon as I got back. I may have even squeezed out a smile to compensate for my lack of sincerity.

Then, she'd had the nerve to ask that I bring her back a turkey club.

Was that my job? No, but I knew this thirty-year-old was one of Frankie's rising stars and hadn't wanted to get on her bad side.

As a chef I'd had years of experience with dealing with demanding bosses. I could swallow my pride and let this baby prosecutor treat me like her personal servant without letting that smile slip from my face. It was a mask that I knew how to wear. A part I could play while burying my feelings.

For now. To keep the peace. But I didn't know how much more humble pie I could eat.

I'd had worse days as a would-be professional, the topper being when I was fired from my first job out of culinary school because the pastry cream of my banana cream pie wasn't as light and creamy as his mother's.

Okay, in hindsight, I shouldn't have told the head chef that he should have hired his mom. That's what got me fired faster than being booted from Saturday's funeral, but I was green and he was an oak tree of a kitchen czar who used his size to intimidate. There was no way I could have stuck it out much longer than I did. At the time, though, I was devastated and just wanted to curl into a ball and cry.

I questioned the wisdom of my decisions.

Was I on the right career path?

Heck, fifteen years later, was I even *on* a career path?

If I was, it sure wasn't one I could see myself staying on for another fifteen years.

No, what I had was a "good enough for now" job that didn't feel good enough today.

"Hon?" Alice softened her voice, but I had dived so deep into my own head that I startled, my pulse surging. "Did something happen at work?"

"I'm just having a bad day," I told her while I rubbed my aching temples.

She patted my back. "Wanna talk about it?"

"Nope. It's just work crapola that isn't worth discussing." And I didn't want anyone else to know about.

"Want some lunch?" Alice's voice softened. "Or some pie? There isn't anything that a good piece of pie can't fix."

My great-aunt had been using that line on me since the day that ten-year-old me came into Duke's with a scraped knee. Was it any surprise that I carried that as a core belief into culinary school?

"Maybe later," I said. "I just want to sit for a minute."

Alice gave my back one last pat. "I get that. Sometimes you just need to sit and catch your breath. Seems to happen more and more these days."

I looked at her, and it was then that I noticed that she had a mixer bowl full of cake batter that she hadn't touched since I first arrived. "Can I give you a hand with anything?"

She slanted a glance at the stainless steel bowl. "It's waited this long. It can wait a little longer."

That didn't sound like Alice. "Are you doing okay?"

"I'm okay," she said with a weary edge to her voice. "Just feeling my age."

Since she recently turned seventy-eight, my great-aunt had earned the right to feel her age. Still, I didn't like what I was hearing. "Are you sure?"

She smiled, her face crinkling in a million fine lines. "Don't you worry about me. You have enough on your plate right now."

"Hey, this place is like therapy for me, so let me help you get the cake into the oven when you're ready."

"Therapy, huh?" Alice squinted at me. "Maybe for you. You always did like to get your hands in the dough."

"And you were always after me to make sure I had washed them first."

"Well, you were probably eight at the time. Always climbing trees and building forts with Steve. Who knows where those little hands had been?"

"You know I loved those summer mornings when you let me help you bake cookies. Looking back, I realize that you were nice to babysit so that my grandparents could have some time to themselves, but—"

"No, no," she cut in. "Honey, you're not remembering it right. When your granny first told me how much fun you had making cookies at her house, I asked her if I could keep you here with me when she had errands to run. She was the one doing me the favor."

What? "She never told me that."

"What was she supposed to say? Tell you that you were the little girl that I always wanted?" Alice's eyes glistened.

"Telling a little kid that I couldn't have children wasn't something we wanted to do. We almost talked about it the day you asked me if I was somebody's grandma. But you seemed satisfied when I told you that I got to be the next best thing with you."

I hugged her, something I immediately wished I had done more often. "You know I've always loved you and Duke like second grandparents."

Pulling back, Alice kissed my cheek. "You're a dear, and you've made your uncle Duke very happy by asking him to walk you down the aisle."

"Good, because he didn't sound very happy at Renee's wedding."

"He's just been a little grumpy lately."

"No kidding." Last Saturday he had taken his role as a curmudgeon to a new level. "What's up with him?"

"Nothing for you to worry about," Alice said, getting to her feet as if that should be the last word on the subject.

"Are you sure?" Because the only thing she had convinced me of was that there was something brewing that I wasn't supposed to know.

"Absolutely. He just has a lot on his mind right now."

I looked over at the guy in the white T-shirt and baggy cotton trousers flipping burgers at the grill just as he had for most of my life. At seventy-seven, some of the muscle he had acquired in the Navy had gone to flab, and his silver crew cut had thinned, but Darrell "Duke" Duquette was still the imposing figure I had always looked up to.

He was also someone who held his cards close to his vest. Not impossible to read, but Alice was easier. Plus, she never could keep a secret.

I got up and followed her over to the mixer stand. "You'd might as well tell me," I said, picking up the heavy bowl of batter for her. "I'm going to find out eventually."

She scowled at me. "Not today, Charmaine. You've already got enough going on in your life."

Now I had to know the secret that she was trying to keep from me.

While I took the five steps to her worktable, I considered the possibilities given what little she had told me.

Leaning on the handles of the bowl, I studied her face for a reaction. "It's a health issue." Hopefully a minor one, but that would explain why she was so tired.

Alice picked up a cake tin as if she might whack me over the head with it. "Stop looking at me with your lie-dar eyes! You know I hate it when you do that."

"Fine. Answer the question and I will."

"There's no health issue. We're doing okay, even though the mirror tells me I don't look so good anymore."

Again, I wasn't convinced. "If you're doing okay, why did you need to stop and rest just now? I've never seen you do that."

"Honey, I'm old!" she retorted. "See how much stamina you have when you're my age."

"Is that all this is?" Because if it was, why wouldn't she just tell me?

Alice clamped her thin lips together and shook her head. "Sweetheart," she said, easing back down to her stool. "Believe me when I tell you that this old body ain't as strong as it used to be. When we first opened this place,

I thought I could do this forever. But I was thirty-eight. Forty years later, I have to face the fact that my get-up-and-go has got up and went."

I dropped down onto the stool opposite her and watched as she rubbed her eyes. I recognized the exasperation practically oozing from her pores because I had felt it in my own skin minutes earlier.

Like me, I knew she was in need of space, some breathing room. And maybe in need of a decision she didn't feel like she was ready to make.

I reached out to touch her arm. "I'm happy to be here whenever you need me. I'm up early anyway, and I can help with the baking like I did last—"

"Dear girl, you and I both know that's not a permanent solution to a problem that, let's face it, isn't gonna get any better. Besides, you're getting married in a couple of weeks and have your own life to live." Aunt Alice's hazel eyes welled with tears. "That's why we've decided to sell."

Chapter Twenty-Three

"I went to Duke's for lunch yesterday," I said to my grandmother the next evening while I sliced a cucumber for the salad she had asked me to make.

She glanced back at me from her pantry door. "And?"

I wasn't sure how much I should say since Alice's secret wasn't mine to reveal. "I had a chat with Aunt Alice."

Returning with a sack of flour, Gram focused on the cookbook on the counter. "Is that so," she muttered absent-mindedly as if she needed to study the dog-eared page of her favorite chicken and dumpling recipe.

I wasn't buying her act for a second because she knew this recipe like the back of her hand. "You know, don't you?" I asked, setting down my knife.

Gram leaned against the counter and nodded. "Alice came over Sunday afternoon and told me the news."

"I can understand that she's tired of getting up in the middle of the night day after day, week after week. I'd be tired of it too if I'd been running that kitchen as long as she has, but..." I choked down the emotion that had been clogging my throat all day. "They're selling?!"

Even though I'd had over twenty-four hours to get

used the idea that the new owner might turn Duke's Cafe into a sandwich or bagel shop, I couldn't imagine living in Port Merritt without the diner I'd loved since I was a toddler.

"Well," Gram said as if there were more to the story than her sister had divulged to me. "That's what Alice thinks they should do. She has a bucket list of things she wants to accomplish before they get too old."

This was news to me. "Such as?"

"Let's see. The top item on her list was to go to Europe. She and I talked about going shortly after your grandfather passed, but she could never figure out a way to leave the bakery in someone else's hands for more than a week. In all honesty, I don't think she wanted to be away from Duke that long."

I was sure Gram was right about that. Alice rarely went anywhere without Duke.

"Anyway," she continued. "We talked about doing a wine tour in France, seeing the Eiffel Tower, riding a gondola in Venice. She especially wants to go to Rome and throw coins in that fountain from the movies, and then eat her way north to Tuscany."

"What a fun bucket list!" Which would probably take three weeks to do it right, and I had never known Duke to leave his diner in the hands of his assistant manager, Hector, for more than a week. And that time it was to take an Alaskan cruise that Alice had booked to celebrate their fiftieth anniversary.

"It should be," Gram said. "I helped her write it the first time she tried to talk Duke into retiring. I think your grandpa's death made her realize that we may not have as much time as we think. And now, all these years later, the list is a heckuva lot longer and she hasn't checked one thing off of it except for that cruise to Alaska."

"And you told me that Duke said that's gonna be his first and last cruise."

She shrugged. "He's not big on crowds."

"He's a cranky old man!" Who was very particular about the company he kept. "He hates crowds. He still gripes about having to fly down for my graduation from culinary school. And that was fifteen years ago. You think he's gonna want to fly to Paris or Rome?"

"Probably not," Gram said on a sigh. "But Alice has her heart set on it. Honestly, honey, I think she's been wanting to retire for a while, but with the offer they got last week, it seems too good to pass up."

Alice hadn't mentioned that they had already received an offer. "Do you think this is a done deal, then?"

"All I know is that a commercial real estate guy in Seattle called to find out if they were interested in selling because he had a buyer."

I picked up my knife and thought about that while I sliced the rest of the cucumber. "So, Duke's hasn't been listed for sale yet."

"As of Sunday when we talked, no," Gram said. "I got the impression that Duke is dragging his feet about talking to a real estate agent."

"Good." This wasn't a decision I wanted them rushing into.

Heck, this wasn't a decision I wanted them making at

all.

I looked up to see Gram staring at me. "Good?" she asked. "Since when is being a stick in the mud a good thing?"

"It's not, but in this instance it could buy us some time."

She narrowed her eyes. "Time for what?"

"I'm not exactly sure." But my gut told me that if I was going to do something to change Alice's mind about selling, I'd better do it fast.

"Earth to Char," Steve said, interrupting my thoughts while I blankly stared out Gram's kitchen window.

I turned to see that he was looking at me expectantly. "Sorry, what?"

"I said that since you've been drying the same plate for at least three minutes, I'm pretty sure it can't get any drier."

"Oh, I guess I was thinking about something else," I had to admit, stacking it in the cupboard.

He handed me the salad bowl he had just washed. "Something I should know about?"

I nodded. "Soon, just not tonight." Because I needed to talk to Duke first and find out if he was seriously entertaining the offer they had received to sell the diner.

"You're not letting the Natalie Mercer death get to you," Steve asked after a beat of silence. "Are you?"

"No." No more than I was a few days ago, when he and I talked about how suddenly she died. "It's not that. It's something in the family that's going on."

Steve groaned. "What's she done now?"

"Who? My mother?"

"Who else?" he said, giving me a sideways glance.

He had a point. Marietta had been a thorn in my side ever since I made the mistake of asking her to help me plan my wedding. But this latest family drama had nothing to do with her.

Which made me wonder...

Maybe it should.

"Char?" Steve shot me a lopsided smile. "You have a funny look on your face. Do I even want to know what your mom has done?"

"It's not her. I promise I'll tell you the whole story soon." I just needed to figure out my part in it first.

He pushed a strand of hair back from my face with his damp fingers, warming me with his touch. "You know you can tell me anything."

"I know, and I will."

After I sealed that promise with a kiss, I was sorely tempted to lead Steve over to the kitchen table and spill my guts about everything, including the idea ping-ponging in my head. Instead, I deepened the kiss for a much-needed distraction.

"Why do I get the sense that you don't want to talk about this?" he asked when we came up for air.

With my hands clasped behind his neck, I flattened my breasts against his chest. "Because I'd much rather do this," I said, angling for another kiss.

He looked at me with an evil gleam in his eyes. "You

know what this will lead to."
　　I was counting on it.

Chapter Twenty-Four

The next afternoon, Ben Santiago, the head of the criminal division, stopped me in the hallway outside of the breakroom. "Do you have a minute?"

I liked Ben and we'd developed a good working relationship over the last three years, but I knew that there was only one correct answer to his question. "Sure."

He motioned for me to go back into the breakroom, where the coffee maker was sputtering to life with the pot I had just started, and then closed the door behind him. "Is there some problem between Brett and you that I should know about?"

Swell. Brett Kearney must have complained to his boss about me.

"I don't believe so," I said, fighting the urge to adopt a defensive posture. "Why?"

"I was talking to him about the case coming to trial next Tuesday, and he declined your help with jury selection."

"Declined?" I hadn't realized that Brett had earned that option.

"I won't insult you with his exact words, but he made

it clear he doesn't want you in there."

His loss, then, because Brett was horrible at reading people.

Ben crossed his arms over his barrel chest as he leaned against the laminate counter. "Care to explain why he doesn't want to work with you?"

Nope. "Shouldn't you be asking him that question?"

His heavy brows furrowed. "I did. He gave me a BS answer about it being a matter of professional courtesy."

"Really." In other words, Brett was accusing me of not being sufficiently subservient. All because I had once suggested that the butthead could get off his high horse and make a pot of coffee.

"Listen." Ben blew out a stale breath. "I know he's not the easiest personality to deal with around here, but I'd appreciate if you'd make more of an effort with him."

"You want *me* to be the one making the effort?" I said, trying to keep my volume down while my blood pressure spiked. "The guy's a jerk!"

"He's also a jerk who wins, especially when you're there for jury selection."

"Well, Ben, it sounds to me like you should inform Brett that he needs to get over his problem with me."

"I already did."

He hesitated and I felt a "but" coming on.

"But it would be helpful if you could make nice with him," Ben said, looking at me over his horn-rimmed glasses to send me the message that his request wasn't optional.

Make nice with the department man-child. Seriously?

Cocking my head, I held his gaze for several beats to send a message of my own. "I'll give it a shot, but I'm telling you right now that I have nothing to apologize to him for."

Ben scoffed as he reached for the door. "No one's asking you to apologize, Charmaine. Just talk to the guy and clear the air. I need you in there on Tuesday."

Fine.

If I was the one who had to make nice, I wanted to get it over and done with. So, I followed Ben out of the breakroom and down the hall, past his office to where Brett shared a cubicle with Finley, the junior prosecutor who had asked me to bring her back a sandwich a couple of days ago.

I knocked on the cubicle half-wall and they both looked up from their computer monitors.

"Oh, hey. What good timing," Finley said, rifling through the papers in front of her. "I need a couple of files pulled." She handed me a sticky note with the case numbers and then pushed away from her desk. "I'm heading into a meeting, but if you could leave the files in my inbox, that would be great."

"Not a problem." Also not why I had stopped by.

I waited for Finley to leave before turning to Brett, who was either looking annoyed at the interruption or at my existence.

"I was just talking with Ben," I said. "He's asked me to assist you in court Tuesday."

"Yeah, he said he was going to have a talk with you." Brett's thin lips curled with satisfaction.

Considering that he was the one that "Dad" spoke with first, I didn't know what Brett was looking so smug about. "That wasn't necessary because I'm happy to help you with jury selection. It's actually part of my job to act as your consultant."

Brett leaned forward in his chair and lowered his voice. "If you want to keep your job, I suggest you remember your place around here."

My place?

Just as I was about to tell this bozo where he could shove his condescending suggestion, I felt a puzzle piece click into place.

Because the course of action that I had been wrestling with for days had just become clear to me.

"Gosh," I said with a smile. "When you put it that way, I can see that you're absolutely right."

He frowned. "What?"

"See you in court, Brett."

In the meantime, I needed to see if Frankie was in her office.

"What do you mean, you gave notice?" my mother asked three hours later as she led me into her living room. "You told me you liked doing the death investigation stuff, although I always worried about you traveling to who knows where. That always seemed a little dangerous to me, especially after the couple of close calls you had."

"It hasn't been *that* dangerous." Except for the few times I needed the cops to come to my rescue. "And I'm proud to have made a difference with some cases that might have otherwise gone unsolved. But Mom, other than sometimes helping with jury selection, I'm a glorified file clerk."

"But I thought your job was more interesting than that. You get to do your 'lie-dar' thing and be paid for it."

"Occasionally, when they want my help with interviews. But more often than not, all I'm needed to do is make the coffee."

Marietta curled onto her white sectional sofa like a cat and took a sip of the chardonnay I had picked up on my way to her house. "How come you never told me this before?"

Because I had never wanted to invite her criticism of my life choices.

"I didn't want to bore you with it, and I still don't," I said, taking the easy chair opposite her. "I'm actually here to talk to you about something much more interesting."

"Oh?" Her cherry red lips pursed with anticipation. "Do tell." Sucking in a breath, she glanced in the direction of the kitchen. "No, wait. Maybe Barry should be on hand to hear your news. He'll be in with the hors d'oeuvres any minute."

I doubted that my former biology teacher would be happy to hear what I had come to propose, but since he had taken over as Marietta's financial advisor, I wanted him in the room before the conversation went any further.

"Did I hear my name mentioned just now?" Barry said, carrying in a tray of deli meats and cheeses from the kitchen before I had a chance to answer.

Sitting a little straighter, Marietta patted the cushion next to her. "Have a seat, dear. Charmaine wants to talk to us about something."

"I heard you telling your mom that you're quitting your job," Barry said as he eased onto the sofa. "What happened?"

I forced myself to ignore the way my mother was stroking his thigh and locked my eyes on his. "I had a moment of clarity. While I don't entirely hate working at the prosecutor's office, there's something else that I'd rather do."

"And what's that, honey?" Marietta asked while Barry handed her a slice of salami.

"I'd like to buy Duke's Cafe."

Chapter Twenty-Five

Steve had the same stunned expression on his face as Barry when I told him what I planned to propose to Duke and Alice.

"You can't be serious!" he said, looking at me as if I had lost my mind.

I reached across our usual corner table at Eddie's and took his hand. "It's something I've been thinking about since Wednesday, when Alice confided to me that they were selling. But the pieces didn't all come together until this afternoon. That's why I couldn't talk to you about it after dinner at Gram's. Once I accepted the fact that it was time for me to find another job, I saw how perfect this solution is, not just for Duke and Alice, but for me too!"

"Without talking to me first?! These are decisions we should be making together."

Of course, he was right, but my heart was fluttering with so much joy at how everything had come together today that I couldn't concede the point. "I'm talking to you now."

"Char, come on. We can't afford to buy a restaurant."

"We can if my mother lends us the money!" I squealed

with glee.

"Your mother! You're getting us into debt with your mother?" Steve groaned, burying his face in his hands. "This has disaster written all over it."

"Hey, kids." Andrea stepped up to take our order and then froze when she looked at Steve. "Uh-oh. Bad timing on my part again. I'll come back."

"No, it's okay," I told her and ordered a beer for Steve along with our usual meaty combo.

When Andrea headed toward the bar, he scrubbed his face as if he wanted to wash away the last five minutes. "Tell me how this is okay."

"I was actually talking to her."

"Talk to me because I don't understand why you suddenly want to own a diner."

I felt like kicking myself for shutting him out of my thoughts when we were doing the dishes Wednesday. "Because that place is part of me. It has been since I was a kid. I need its smells and tastes, and I don't want to lose it to some stranger when Duke and Alice retire. I love it too much to let it go. It's family. The people who work there are family. You get that, right?" I asked, squeezing his hands.

Steve didn't respond at first. Instead, he stared down at the engagement ring he had placed on my finger. "I get why you'd have an emotional attachment to the place. But think about it—"

"I've been thinking about it. Practically non-stop ever since Alice told me they're selling."

"Which is completely understandable, but it doesn't

mean that you need to become the next Duke or Alice. When was the last time they took any time off?"

"They took a cruise."

"Okay, they took one cruise for a week. Other than that, they've been chained to the daily grind of running a restaurant for the last thirty-plus years. Is that what you really want?"

Not when he put it that way. "Well—"

"And what about when you get pregnant and want to stay home with the baby for a couple of months? How's that gonna work?"

I hadn't thought that far ahead. "I'll have to staff accordingly."

"And what about when our kid's sick and needs to be picked up at school, and I'm unavailable?"

"We'll figure it out," I said, pulling back from his touch. "Stop trying to shoot holes in my plan."

"Chow Mein." Steve reclaimed my hands. "I'm not trying to shoot holes in it. I'm trying to help you think this through."

While I stared across the table at him, Andrea arrived with his beer and a glass of ice water for me.

"Eddie's threatening to come over here to break up your fight," she said. "Just sayin'."

Good grief, had we been that loud? "We're not fighting. We're discussing."

Andrea nodded at me. "Hon, I've had plenty of discussions with my man, and I realize that we have to reach a certain volume to get their full attention. Just know that we can hear you over at the bar."

Swell.

Steve reached for his beer. "Tell Eddie to crank up the music. Problem solved."

It would also be solved in fifteen minutes, when the volume of the flat screens mounted throughout the bar was turned up for tonight's Mariners game. In the meantime, I had a bigger problem sitting across the table from me.

Once Andrea stepped away to take the drink order of the couple sitting two tables over, I met Steve's gaze. "I know that taking over Duke's will present some challenges, but I've given this a lot of thought and I want to do this."

Steve blew out a breath. "I get how you have the experience to pull this off, but do you seriously want to get up at three in the morning to make doughnuts?"

"Absolutely not," I said, shaking my head. "That's gonna be someone else's job. I'll bake the pies and the croissants I plan to add to the menu. The custom cake orders, too. I may have to buy a delivery van if the wedding cake volume takes off, but I'm factoring that into the loan amount."

His mouth quirked with amusement. "You *have* given this some thought."

"Are you kidding? How to make this work is all I've been thinking about."

"And here I thought our wedding would have crossed your mind now and again."

"It does." I aimed a happy smile at the man I loved. "You do. But in the last couple of days Duke's has been top of mind because I truly believe that when I'm not with you, it's where I belong."

Steve slowly nodded, his mouth a flat line. "Okay."

That "okay" looked begrudging at best. "Okay, what?"

"Okay, we'd better talk about what you plan to say to Duke and Alice."

I sprung from my seat and threw my arms around him. "I knew you'd understand how important this is to me!"

"There's one thing I will never understand, though."

I pulled away to look down at his face. "What?"

"Why did you ask your mother to float you the loan?"

I grinned at him. "I needed the money fast, and I knew I could make her an offer she couldn't refuse."

He winced. "Do I dare ask?"

"I'll tell you all about it later tonight," I said, scooting closer in my chair. "Right now, you need to help me with my offer to Duke and Alice."

Chapter Twenty-Six

"I'm heading out," I told Patsy at four the next day. "Do you have anything you want me to mail?"

Just because I was no longer afraid that this woman might rat on me to Frankie for leaving early didn't mean that I wanted her to exact some sort of Brett-level retribution on me because of my short-timer's attitude. I also didn't want to burn any bridges. All my coworkers were potential Duke's Cafe patrons, including Patsy, so I sweetened the pot by adding enough sugar to my smile to induce a diabetic coma. "Or maybe there's some office supplies you need?"

Patsy smirked. "Soon you won't be my problem anymore, so you can drop the charm offensive."

I inched closer. "Come on, Patsy. You know you're gonna miss me around here."

"You've proven yourself to be useful from time to time," she conceded, her fleshy mouth stretching into an honest to goodness smile.

Holy cow! She gave me the Patsy-version of a compliment. A sincere one, too. Amazing, considering the source. "Gee, thanks."

"Frankie has told me that she wants to write you a letter of recommendation." Patsy squared her shoulders as she gave me a regal nod. "You may use me as a reference as well."

"I don't know that I'll need that, but thank you."

Her gray eyes widened. "Really? You already have something lined up for when you get back from your honeymoon?"

"I told Frankie that I'd be happy to work the first couple of weeks of August, until she can find a replacement. After that, yes. I hope to start my new job."

"Good luck with that," Patsy said with surprisingly good humor.

Sure, it was edged with a little sarcasm. This was Patsy, after all. Considering I was leaving early to talk to Duke, I was okay with it.

Because I needed all the luck I could get.

"What are you doin' here?" Duke asked, looking up from where he was slurping a cup of coffee at the counter.

Ninety-three-year-old Stanley, a pie happy hour regular seated next to my great-uncle, pointed his fork at me. "Yeah, shouldn't you be at work?" He squinted at the wall clock, his black horn-rimmed glasses shifting on his bulbous nose. "Like for another forty-five minutes?"

"I got an early release for good behavior," I said as I stepped behind the lemon-yellow Formica counter to pour myself a cup of coffee.

Stanley let out a rheumy chuckle. "Sure you did."

"Help yourself to some pie to go with that coffee if you want," Duke said, eyeing me as if he suspected that I wasn't here for his lousy coffee.

"Can't. Got a wedding dress to fit into." It was the same convenient lie I had used at my mother's house yesterday while my stomach twisted itself into a pretzel.

It had yet to untwist and I wished I had worn something cooler than the shirt dress I had thrown on to give myself a boost of confidence. It looked crisp and cool in summery blue and white stripes, but the combination of the heavy cotton and my nerves had me sweating as if I had run here in my navy espadrilles.

At least those strappy sandals were nice and airy, and my feet weren't sweating. Yet.

While I stirred creamer into my coffee, I searched the cafe for Alice but didn't see her at any of the tables. "Is Aunt Alice here?"

"Lucille drove her home after her shift," Duke said.

Just as I had hoped because I wanted to talk to him alone.

His eyes narrowed the way they did when one of the waitstaff lingered for too long at the cash register. "Why?"

"Something tells me that the young lady didn't stop by for pie," Stanley said, elbowing him. "Wanna sit down, Charmaine? I can move."

"Thanks, Stanley." I locked gazes with Duke. "But I wonder if I could see you in the kitchen for a few minutes."

Frowning, Duke guzzled the rest of his coffee and then got to his feet. "See ya tomorrow, Stan."

I picked up my coffee cup and was about to head toward the double doors when I noticed Stanley waving me over.

"Fair warning," he whispered. "He's in a bad mood."

I was pretty sure I knew the reason why. "Thanks for the heads-up."

"Well, you coming?" Duke snapped at me from the doorway. "You're the one who wanted to talk."

Johnny, Duke's latest cook, pointed his spatula at me as I passed by the cutout window. "You've been warned."

I may have been warned, but I wasn't the least bit deterred. I was a woman on a mission, totally prepared for this moment, thanks to Steve staying up late and talking this through with me.

Unfortunately, once I saw Duke glaring at me from Alice's worktable, everything that I had rehearsed last night melted away like butter in a hot skillet.

Dang it!

"I suppose I don't have to guess what you want to talk about," he said, folding his arms tight across his chest as I sat on the wooden stool across from him.

I glanced behind me at Johnny, standing behind the grill with a portable fan going, and saw no one else within earshot, so I knew this was as private a setting as I could hope for here. "Alice told me that you're selling the cafe."

"We're *thinking* about it," Duke corrected.

"My grandmother said that you have an offer."

He swore under his breath. "Everyone has a big mouth around here."

"So, you do have an offer," I said, watching him

carefully.

He shrugged. "It's just some commercial real estate guy fishing."

"To see if you have any interest in selling."

"Yeah. Unfortunately, Alice took the call, so he thinks we're a hot prospect. Called again a couple of hours ago. Wanted me to know how serious his buyer is about expanding into Port Merritt."

My pulse quickened at the thought of getting into a bidding war with someone with deep pockets. "And?"

"I told him we're not gonna accept the first offer we get and hung up on him." Duke shook his head. "What's he think? That I was born yesterday? There's probably dozens of potential buyers out there."

"You're looking at one," I said, flashing him a smile while trying to ignore the bead of sweat trickling down my back.

He scowled across the table at me. "You're not serious."

"I couldn't be more serious. If you're ready to sell, I'm ready to buy."

"I think I would've heard something if you or Steve hit the lottery," Duke said. "And I'm pretty sure no one in the family's died and left you a small fortune. Where's the money coming from?"

"I've secured a loan. Money won't be a problem."

Cocking his head, he tapped a stubby fingernail against the tabletop for several seconds. "You *are* serious."

"I told you I was. I'm ready and able to make you and

Alice a fair offer."

"What about your job? Not sayin' I'm ready to agree to anything today, but I don't see you turning a profit unless you're putting some long hours in here."

"I've already given Frankie my notice."

"Jeez, Char! I don't even know if I want to sell! You shouldn't have—"

"I would've quit sometime soon anyway. Did Alice mention that we talked a couple of days ago?"

Duke nodded. "She said you were having some problems at work."

"Yep, and they weren't going to get any better, so with the wedding coming up, it was a good time to go. I just hadn't thought it all the way through that day I was here. And then Alice started telling me how she was having some problems of her own. You realize that, right? How the work's starting to take a toll."

"Yeah, I got eyes," he said, looking down at the wood grain of the tabletop. "She's wanted to sell for the last couple of years, but I haven't..."

"I get it." I'd known this man all my life. He didn't need to explain. "It's a big decision."

Duke took a deep breath and slowly released it. "Yeah, but it should be a no-brainer. I promised her that when our bodies tell us that it's time to hang it up, we'd sell to the highest bidder and start traveling to some of those places on that list of hers."

"Like that's something you want to do." My great-aunt would be lucky to get him to agree to go to any of her dream destinations. "Gram should go. She'd be the perfect travel partner for Alice."

"Probably. But I promised." He shrugged a meaty shoulder. "It made her happy."

And it probably bought him some time, but he and I both knew that this situation couldn't go on for much longer.

"What's gonna make *you* happy?" I asked.

"Darned if I know. It won't be a ten-hour flight to Paris, I can tell you that much."

"You like to fish. Think of doing that any time you want instead of standing behind that grill for hours on end."

"Yeah, but the season is only so long."

I thought of the boating trips to the San Juan Islands that he'd take with his buddies. He had always enjoyed those weekends away. "You could buy a boat and sail."

Duke glowered at me. "I'm not wasting my hard-earned money on a boat."

"You could garden. You've got that big backyard. Think of all the stuff you could grow."

"Alice is the gardener. Not me, and stop trying to find things for me to do."

Fine. "Then what were you planning to do when you retired?"

"That's just it," he said with increasing volume. "I never really saw myself retiring."

"So, you're just going to work here until you keel over. Is that what you're saying? Because if Lucille finds you lying in a heap, I don't know if you can count on her to give you mouth-to-mouth resuscitation."

"No." Duke raked his fingers through his short silver

hair. "And that's a fate I'd like to avoid. At all costs!"

I smiled at him. "If you're not ready to make this decision, I'll understand. This is a big deal for all of us. But when the time comes, and you're ready to sell the diner, I want you to sell it to me."

"What if that time doesn't come for another year or two?"

"Then I'll wait." I ran my hands over the smooth surface of the table. "Right here, working as your pastry chef."

His face split into a grin. "Oh, yeah?"

I grinned back. "Well, I do need a job."

"And we're gonna need another pastry chef around here pretty darn soon."

"Which is something we should talk about with Alice, to make sure that she's okay with me taking over in a few weeks. I could follow you home if you're ready to head out."

"I'm ready, but I know she's gonna be on me to sell. That's all I've been hearing ever since she took that guy's call."

"We could talk about that, too." That would definitely get my vote. "I'd like her to know that I want to be your buyer. I just wanted to talk to you first because I wasn't sure how receptive she'd be to the part of my offer that really only concerns you."

Duke furrowed his brow. "What do you mean by that?"

"When Steve was helping me put together my proposal to you, we thought you might not be ready to walk away from this place. So, *when*—notice that I'm saying *when* and not *if* you sell me Duke's Cafe—we'll include in the contract that you have the option to work behind the grill until you're good and ready to retire."

I was sure that Alice would insist that a maximum number of years be stipulated, but Duke didn't need to hear that today.

"Well, you certainly know how to sweeten the pot," he said.

"I'm also being selfish. I don't want to lose one of the best cooks I know."

He grinned. "Okay."

"Okay?" I was almost afraid to ask what he meant. "You'll think about selling to me?"

"Okay, we'd better go talk to the boss and fill her in on the big news."

Now, I wasn't sure what he meant. "That I'll take over for her in a few weeks?"

He pushed up from his stool. "That you're buying the place!"

Chapter Twenty-Seven

"I have big news!" I sang out when I arrived at Rox's house with lunch the next day. "Huge news!"

"You look happy about it," she said, following me into the kitchen. "So, I'm pretty sure your wedding is still on. In fact, please tell me the wedding's still on. At the moment I'm capable of squeezing into my dress—it's a tight squeeze, but I really want to wear it next Saturday."

"The wedding's still on. This has nothing to do with that." I placed the bag with our deli sandwiches on her table and pulled out a chair for her. "You'll want to sit down for this."

Rox froze, her eyes wide. "You're not pregnant, are you?"

"No! Sit." I took the seat opposite her, and my cell phone rang. "Heck, let me see who that is," I said, reaching into my tote.

I didn't recognize the number. "They can leave a message." Unable to repress my joy, I grinned across the table at her. "You ready?"

"Yes! Tell me."

"I'm buying Duke's!" I squealed.

"What?!" Rox blurted out with equal volume and then covered her mouth with her hands. "Oops, don't want to wake Alex. I just put him down at noon."

I cringed. "Oh, sorry."

She turned her head and listened for a second. "We're good. So, tell me, when did this happen?"

"Last night," I said, and then told my best friend everything that had happened since the last time we spoke.

By the time I gave her the details of how Steve joined me at Duke and Alice's house to celebrate the deal we had struck, Rox had finished her sandwich.

"You're right, this is huge," she said as I nibbled on one of the pickles that had come with our lunch. "Not just that you're buying Duke's but that he's willing to sell."

"The timing was right for both of us."

"I hope he gave you a family discount."

I shook my head. "We haven't gotten that far. He's gonna get an appraisal and we'll go from there. The important thing is that they've agreed to sell to me."

"I hope you don't mind me asking," Rox said, "but where are you getting the money?"

"My mother. She's been looking for somewhere to invest her money for a while, so I asked her to invest it in me."

"Dang, girl! Considering your history with your mom, the two of you have come a long way. It wasn't that long ago that you wouldn't have trusted her to be there when you need her."

"We definitely have a history, but she's gotten better in the last few years." Because she was easier to be with?

Because I understood her better than I used to now that she lived in town? I wasn't sure which was true.

Maybe both.

"So does that also mean that she's stopped trying to take over as your wedding planner?"

"Uh...she had."

Rox frowned. "You say that like it's past tense."

"Because I had to strike a deal with her to get her to lend me the money."

"Don't tell me..."

I nodded as my phone rang for the second time. "I had to agree to a short list of her demands—something that should make all the vendors happy since Marietta has to pay extra for every last-minute change."

"Sheesh, your mother is good at getting what she wants," Rox said as I looked at the phone number on my phone—the same number as before. "I should take lessons from her."

"And I should probably take this. Excuse me a second," I said, holding the phone to my ear. "Hello?"

"Is this Charmaine Digby?" the female caller asked.

I didn't recognize her voice. "Yes."

"This is Mika Kumasaka. I left you a message a few minutes ago. I actually called to add something that I forgot to mention."

"I'm so glad you did," I said, rooting around in my tote for a notepad. "Can you talk for a few minutes?"

"No problem."

"Great. Give me a moment to find something to write on." Hoping that Rox would have something bigger than the grocery list I found, I looked at her and gestured for a pen.

Seconds later, Rox placed a ruled tablet and a pen on the table in front of me. "I have laundry to do, so take your time," she whispered to me.

With a grateful nod, I pushed my half-eaten sandwich out of my way and grabbed the pen. "Sorry to keep you waiting, Mika."

"Hey, I'm probably the one who should be apologizing. I wish I'd heard your message earlier. If I had known you were calling about Natalie Mercer, I would've called you from Japan."

I hadn't specifically mentioned Natalie in the voice mail I left Mika a week and a half ago, so she had obviously heard the news about her friend from someone else. "As it turns out, it probably wouldn't have mattered if you had. The coroner's office is still waiting on some test results, so in the meantime I've been getting background information from the friends and family members closest to Natalie."

"Okay. Since it's only been a few minutes since I left you the message, I'm going to assume that you haven't listened to it."

"No, not yet."

"Because I talked to Jenny for over an hour right before I called you. She'd left me a message about giving you my number, but of course, I didn't listen to it until after we got back this morning." Mika choked up. "Sorry, I'm jet-lagged and have been dealing with a death in my family for the past two weeks, so getting hit with this news on top of that... It's a lot."

"I understand, and I'm very sorry for your loss. I promise I won't keep you long."

"No, I'm okay." Sniffing, she took a beat before continuing. "Jenny filled me in on what you want to talk about. Trust me, I can stay on the phone as long as you want because I've seen some things you need to know about."

Whoa.

I sucked in a calming breath while my pulse pounded in my ear. "Before we get to that, let me get some information from you."

"All right."

"You've been friends with Natalie since high school, right?"

"Since middle school, actually."

Just like Donna and me. "Have you stayed in touch with her since her wedding?"

"Oh, sure. I live in Tacoma so it hasn't been as easy to get together as it used to be before she moved to Port Townsend, but we'd meet for lunch or drinks at least once a month. Usually in Bremerton or Seattle."

"When did you last see Natalie?"

"Three weeks ago exactly," Mika said. "I remember because Nat was telling me about doing the makeup for Lucas's aunt's wedding."

"How'd she seem when you were with her?"

"Completely fine."

"She didn't mention any health issues or concerns that she might have been having?"

"No, nothing like that. I knew about her heart

problems back in high school. I even saw her faint a couple of times after gym class. But she hadn't had any issues since the surgery. Heck, she and Lucas have been training to run another half-marathon." She sniffed again. "*Were* training, anyway."

"Let's talk about Lucas." I paused to listen for a reaction to his name.

"Yeah, let's talk about Lucas," Mika said, sounding as if she had some tea to spill.

"Did Natalie ever voice some concern about any of his old girlfriends?"

"Oh, I can tell you that she was plenty worried about that bitch who sent her all those texts. We both were."

"Do you know if she ever found out who the sender was?" *Please say yes.*

"If she did, she didn't tell me."

Dang it!

"But I'm pretty sure I know who it was," Mika added.

My heart skipped a beat. "Who?"

"I don't remember her name."

"Could it have been Erin?" I asked.

"No, that doesn't sound familiar."

"Okay." That made me think that my first instinct about Erin was correct. She had nothing to do with Natalie's death. "Why don't you tell me what you do remember about her?"

"I only saw her once, an hour before Nat's wedding. I was a bridesmaid, and we had finished posing for pictures. So, since we had a little time, I went outside for a smoke, and I saw this girl and Lucas walking behind the church. I didn't think anything of it at first, but then I realized she was crying. She was being all clingy, too, and really loud. Like she didn't care if she made a scene. That's when Lucas pulled her toward some trees like he wanted to get her someplace where they couldn't be overheard. Well, this was the guy that one of my best friends was marrying, so that didn't work for me. So, I followed them and hid behind a bush so that I could hear what they were saying."

Good girl! That's exactly what I would've done.

"Which was what?" I asked.

"It was like something out of a bad movie. She was bawling her eyes out, begging him to not go through with the wedding."

"Holy cow!"

"I know! That's what I thought. She was saying how she loved him and how they could be happy together. 'Give us a chance.' Or maybe it was 'give me a chance.' I don't know. I just remember thinking that this had to be the girl who had been rage-texting Nat all those weeks. You know? Because it was such a desperation play."

"Hold on, I'm writing all that down," I said, frantically scribbling. "What did Lucas say to her? Could you hear?"

"He wasn't nearly as loud as she was, so no. But he had his arm around this girl and let her cry on his shoulder for a couple of minutes. More than anything, it looked like he was just being nice. Then, Lucas's grandmother came out to break things up."

"Joan Germain?" I said, remembering how evasive she was with me when I asked what she knew about the girl who had been harassing Natalie.

"Yeah, the anchorwoman. I had no idea that she was his grandma until she marched out there and told Lucas that his father was looking for him."

"Then what happened?"

"That was pretty much it," Mika said. "Lucas headed back toward the church and the grandmother stayed out there with the girl for a while. I don't know how long. I had to take off before someone caught me spying on them, which I totally was."

"Did you tell Natalie about what you saw?" I asked.

"Not right away. I waited for a couple of months to see if the texts started up again. They hadn't, thankfully, but when I asked about it, Nat could tell that I was keeping something from her. I have a horrible poker face. Anyway, I told her that I saw the girl with Lucas. Not everything she said. I didn't see the point in that. I just wanted Nat to know so that when she ran into her at the next family picnic, she'd know who she was dealing with."

I wasn't sure I heard Mika right. "Wait. Are you saying that this girl is a member of the Mercer family?"

"Nat said that she's Lucas's second cousin."

I drew in a sharp breath. *Sydney!* It had to be. "Describe her."

"Young, at least she looked young to me. Maybe around eighteen, nineteen. She had streaky blond highlights in her hair. Pretty, but she looked ridiculous in the super-tight dress she was wearing. I suppose I might wear something like that if I had her body, but not to a wedding. You know?"

"Uh-huh," I muttered, writing as fast as I could with a shaky hand. Because now I was sure that I knew who she had just described. "Could her name have been Sydney?"

"Sydney! Yeah, that's it. Do you know her?"

"I've met her."

"I never talked to her myself, but Natalie didn't seem at all surprised when I told her about this chick. I guess there was some family event where Lucas's sister told her that Sydney had been crushing on Lucas for years."

This sounded like a lot more than a crush to me. "Did Natalie ever say if she talked to Lucas about Sydney?"

Mika released a frustrated breath. "Yes, but she wouldn't get into it with me. Nat sort of brushed it off like he had the situation handled, and she wasn't concerned about this girl making a play for her husband."

Maybe she should have been.

Chapter Twenty-Eight

An hour later, I pulled into Steve's driveway as he was carrying a big cardboard box to his truck.

"Perfect timing," he said when I took an end and helped carry the box to the tailgate. "I'm cleaning out closets. There's one with old linens that I want you to look at before I get rid of 'em."

"Later. I need to talk to you." I scurried into the living room, sat on his brown leather sectional, and waited for him to join me.

Steve gave me an assessing look before he sat down. "What's goin' on?"

"I need to run something by you."

His gaze tightened with wariness. "Okay."

"I got a call from one of Natalie Mercer's friends," I said. "If this case ever goes to court, I think she'll be a key witness."

"Witness to what exactly?"

"She was an eyewitness to Natalie's husband having a heated conversation with the girl who was sending Natalie a lot of hate mail by text. Of course, it would be tough to prove it was her if she used a burner phone, but it totally makes sense. My witness thinks so, too."

Steve's brow furrowed. "Hold up."

I glared at him. "Don't even think about saying that I'm supposed to be waiting for the lab results."

"Since this won't even be your job when the results come back, I wouldn't dream of it. What I was about to say is that this isn't a case. No crime's been charged."

Details. "Trust me. It's going to be, because I'm positive that this girl did something to cause Natalie's heart attack."

"Just like it can't be proven that she sent those texts, you can't prove that she wanted to hurt the girl, much less kill her. Not without—"

"I know!" I cut in, raising my voice. "It's just that I'm so sure that it's her."

"I've been sure plenty of times. Doesn't mean I'm able do anything about it, though."

I heaved a sigh. "This is so frustrating! There has to be something I can do."

Steve took my hand. "Sorry, babe. Just like we talked about before, you have reason for suspicion. When you factor in some past behavior from… What's her name?"

"Sydney."

"From Sydney, that strengthens the case *if and when* it actually becomes a case."

I slumped against his shoulder. "So, once again, you're telling me that all I can do is write up my notes and hope that Frankie reads them when the labs come back?" Because I was getting really tired of hearing that.

"Hey, I'm not telling you that you can't talk to your

boss about your suspicions. If Frankie didn't value your opinion she wouldn't have hired you. I'm just saying that this doesn't change the fact that she'll continue to wait for the labs to come back before opening an investigation. It's the way it has to be."

"I hate this waiting game. It's just infuriating!"

"Trust me, I know," Steve said, holding me close.

"I knew from the get-go that my job was going to test my patience, but my eyes are now wide open to the fact that I'm not cut out for this kind of work. It's like mixing all the ingredients for a cake and not being able to bake it."

"Maybe you should think about doing something else. Like owning a place where you get to do as much baking as you want."

I buried my face in his T-shirt, breathing in his clean scent. "That's a great idea. Why didn't I think of that?"

"I'm pretty sure you did." Steve kissed the top of my head. "You good?"

That was debatable. "Probably as good as I'm gonna get today."

"Then are you ready to take a look at the stuff in that closet?"

"Sure." But after that, I wanted to take another look at that "perfect murder" video. Because somewhere in that story should be a clue for what I could do next—besides waiting!

An hour later, I fibbed and told Steve that I needed

some me-time to get ready for the fancy restaurant where he wanted to take me to celebrate the deal I had struck with Duke and Alice. I then rushed home, hugged my dog, and grabbed my laptop to watch "The Perfect Murder" for the fourth time.

It occurred to me, while I watched family members recount how they contacted the coroner with their suspicions that their brother had been poisoned, that it could be helpful if Lucas did the same thing.

Maybe it would add a sense of urgency.

Not that Frankie would have any more pull with the crime lab than any other Washington state coroner, but if Natalie's toxicology screening could be expedited as evidence of a suspected homicide, why not try?

I hit pause, leaned back on my living room sofa, and stared at the image of two brothers frozen on the screen. Both had been in agreement that their brother had been murdered for the insurance money.

The motivation was different in Natalie Mercer's case, but the end result was the same: a murder that appeared to be from natural causes.

An almost perfect murder.

Paul and Kayla Riley suspected some sort of foul play, but... "How do I make Lucas feel that way?" I asked the dog snoring at my feet.

But Fozzie wasn't the least bit helpful, probably because nothing I had previously said to Lucas had made him question Natalie's cause of death.

Plus, Fozzie wasn't listening to me.

Which was almost the same problem I was having with

Lucas. He didn't want to hear what I had to say, but if I could convince him to watch this video... Maybe then Lucas would be open to the possibility that Sydney was responsible for his wife's death.

Even Steve thought that the similarities surrounding the two deaths justified my suspicions.

"At least I'll know I tried everything I could think of," I told myself as I reached for my cell phone.

This is it, I thought as I entered Lucas's phone number. With only one week before I left for my honeymoon, this would be my last chance to convince him that Sydney had been the only woman in that room with Natalie who would have wanted her to die.

After five rings I thought I might have to leave Lucas a message, but then he finally answered.

At least I assumed it was him. There was so much background noise I could hardly hear his voice. "Lucas?"

"Yeah," he said as something that sounded a lot like a chainsaw whined nearby.

"It's Charmaine Digby. Do you have a moment to talk?"

"What?"

I repeated what I had just said.

"I can't hear you. Hold on."

I heard the bang of a door and the background noise muted.

"Sorry," he said. "Who's this?"

"It's Charmaine Digby."

He dropped a bomb of a swear word. "When are you gonna give this a rest?"

I'd have to walk away from this investigation the day I was no longer employed by the county. Right now, though, it was in my best interest to not answer that question. "I'm calling because I have a witness who has identified Sydney Sheridan as the person who was harassing your wife by text two years ago."

"Sheesh, not this again."

"Please, just hear me out. I know you don't want to believe it, but I'm almost positive that Sydney poisoned Natalie with something that afternoon of the wedding."

"I'm not listening to anymore—"

"Wait! I'm going to email you a link for a true crime video about a so-called perfect murder. Please watch it. You'll see how similar—"

"Don't call me again."

"Lucas, don't hang up!" I looked down at my phone and saw that he had disconnected.

"Crap!" I exclaimed, waking up Fozzie.

"Sorry, sweetheart." I ran my hands over his ears. "I just had a call that didn't go very well. Want to go for a walk after I send this email?"

He wagged his tail.

"Okay, a walk will be in our future in approximately five minutes," I said, opening the email app on my laptop, while Fozzie huffed his annoyance at being told to wait.

"Yeah? Well, I don't like it either, so you're in good company. At least your gratification will come as soon as Mom figures out what to write."

I had Lucas's work email as well as his personal address in the notebook I kept in my leather portfolio. As I entered them on the address line, I could only hope that he would open one of my emails out of curiosity if nothing else.

If I were in his shoes, I would.

I might have to get over my frustration with someone from the coroner's office accusing my hot second cousin of murder, but nothing short of a tranquilizer gun would allow me to sleep before I satisfied my curiosity.

"What to write," I pondered as I stared at my blinking cursor.

It was vitally important that when Lucas opened my email message, he'd see at a glance what I had tried to tell him when I called. That meant that it had to be short and to the point. No niceties, nothing off-topic.

Even more important, I needed to come up with a compelling subject line so that Lucas wouldn't delete my message on sight.

It took me a minute to think of something that would pique his interest. Lucas was a mechanical engineer who had to have taken some chemistry in college. I doubted that any of his professors had ever mentioned tetrahydrozoline, but with that chemical compound as my subject line, I hoped that Lucas was enough of a science geek to open my email.

Once he did, all I wanted him to do was click on the link. The lab techs the show featured explained how lethal levels of tetrahydrozoline were found in the victim's blood. Since Lucas needed to hear that from them, not me, I wrote just one paragraph:

> *It recently came to my attention that the symptoms Natalie was experiencing when Dr. Wolfe and Dr. Cardinale examined her are virtually identical to what the murder victim experienced as detailed in this video. Please click on the link and watch the first seven minutes. Call me anytime if you want to discuss.*

After proofreading my message, I pasted the link to the video and hit send.

"If those seven minutes don't make a believer out of you..." I didn't know what would.

"Now, stop making yourself crazy with this stuff and walk away," I told myself as I closed my email app.

That was going to be a lot easier said than done, but I had a wedding to turn my attention to. I also had a big fuzzball waiting not so patiently for me.

"Are you ready to go?" I asked Fozzie, who answered by scampering to the door the second I shut down my laptop. "Because I've done all I can do, at least for now."

I only hoped that it was enough.

Chapter Twenty-Nine

Six days later, after I finished packing for my honeymoon, I ate a late breakfast and then picked up my mother for the spa session that she had insisted I needed so that I'd be all glowy for my wedding tomorrow.

I hadn't wanted to squander three precious hours with Marietta when I had so much to do today, including meeting Duke and Alice at their attorney's office. After that I had to get to Donna's house for a quick haircut. If I was lucky, that would leave me thirty minutes before Steve and I needed to leave to pick up his parents at the airport, so I had thought there would be no way that I'd be able to relax enough to enjoy a minute with my mother.

Was I ever wrong!

Since I had spent every night this week packing and moving boxes to Steve's house, the mother/daughter massage and facial package had felt heavenly. My skin looked luminous, the knots in my shoulders had been vanquished, and all the tension of the last few weeks melted like ice cream on a hot summer day.

It was the best I had looked and felt in months.

And my formerly chipped nails, painted in burgundy

to match Rox and Donna's bridesmaid dresses, were utter glossy perfection.

While our nails dried, my mother and I sat side by side in the spa's waiting area. Unfortunately, I couldn't see the clock over the receptionist's desk from there.

"I should've looked at the time before we came in here," I told Marietta. "Did you happen to notice?"

"Sugar, don't worry about the time. You'll tense right back up. We have all day to do whatever you need to get done."

Holding my hands in front of me like a doctor who had just scrubbed for surgery, I eased out of my seat to peek at the clock. "Shoot, it's almost two-thirty. I don't have time to take you home until after my three o'clock appointment. Do you want to browse the antique stores on Main Street while I meet with Duke and Alice?"

"I most certainly do not," she said, sounding like an entitled Hollywood elite who was unaccustomed to being kept waiting. "I thought I made it clear earlier in the car. I'm going in with you."

What?

I dropped back down onto the chair. "No, you said that you understood that we're meeting today to go over the terms of the contract. As in Duke, Alice, and I are meeting."

"You said 'we' and while I wasn't informed of this meeting before today, I feel that 'we' should include me." She shot me a smug smile. "After all, I should be there to ensure that my financial interests are protected, wouldn't you agree?"

Since when did my mother take any interest in a contract that didn't have the name of a production company at the top of it?

"Fine," I conceded through clenched teeth. "But this meeting is really important to me, so do me a favor and let me do the talking."

She flicked a bangled wrist. "I'll be as quiet as a mouse. You'll hardly know I'm there."

A half hour later, when Duke and Alice's attorney stood as Marietta extended her hand like a queen offering a ring to be kissed, I knew having her here for this meeting was a recipe for disaster.

"Ken, how lovely to see you again," she said as he gawked in slack-jawed wonder at her.

I recognized that look. I'd witnessed it all my life.

Gag me with a spoon, Ken Durante was a fan.

"What the heck is she doing here?" Duke demanded, glaring at me with the intensity of a thousand suns.

Yep, we were on the verge of imminent disaster.

Alice patted his arm. "Settle down. Mary Jo is Char's mom and—"

"I'm her financial advisor for this transaction," my mother interjected as she took a seat and smiled across the conference table at Duke.

I dropped down next to Marietta and stared at her in disbelief. This was her being as quiet as a mouse?

"What?" she said in a snappish whisper. "I had to say something. Would you prefer if I called myself your financier?"

I shushed her, preferring that she stop talking, period.

"Your *what*?" Duke growled, looking like Mount Vesuvius about to blow.

There was no point in denying it. "She's lending me the money."

"You didn't tell us that, honey," Alice said.

Marietta huffed. "Why should she? It was a business transaction between the two of us. All you should care about is that she has the funds to buy the cafe."

Duke squinted across the conference table at her. "I don't like your involvement in this."

"Well, Uncle Darrell," my mother said, folding her arms under her impressive chest, "I guess that's tough, because I *am* involved."

He groaned.

"As a partner?" Alice asked me. "Because you also didn't tell us about that."

This conversation was going downhill fast. "No, no. She's just the bank. She'll have nothing to do with the day-to-day operations."

"Nothing?" Marietta looked crushed. "I thought I might be able to help with the menu and help redecorate. You know how I love to work with color palettes."

Color palettes!

Jeez Louise, if I didn't come away from this meeting with an eye twitch it was going to be a minor miracle.

"I don't plan on redecorating or making any major changes." That wouldn't be the least bit conducive to a smooth transition. Plus, it would honk off Duke while he was adjusting to his new role at the cafe. I needed him to be at peace with his decision to hand the reins over to me, and that meant no hovering mothers to raise his blood pressure. Or mine!

"I will be upgrading the coffee, though." I aimed a sugar-sweet smile at Duke. "Soon, because we're gonna be known for our great coffee instead of that rotgut you like."

He smirked. "Whatever."

"As far as the menu is concerned," I said to my mother. "Eventually, I'll expand it. Maybe add some grab-and-go items like breakfast croissants, so I'll need you to help me taste-test later in the year."

Marietta sighed. "Whatever."

I searched the faces of each of my family members, which ranged from moderately miffed in the case of Marietta to the satisfied gleam in Alice's eyes.

"Are we good to move on now?" I asked, fixing my gaze on Duke. Because if he was going to continue to take issue with my mother funding me, now was the time for him to lay his cards on the table.

He gave me a curt nod and turned to his attorney. "Let's review that contract you drew up."

Whew! I grinned across the table at Alice, who winked as she reached for the short stack of papers in front of her.

I did the same, and with Marietta looking over my shoulder, I tried to keep from beaming as I read my name at the top of page one.

This sale was going to happen. I was buying Duke's Cafe!

While Ken read the salient points aloud on each page, I nodded in agreement because it was all as Duke, Alice, and I had discussed when we met earlier in the week with Steve. This included the clause that my great-uncle had wanted, stipulating that he could continue to work at Duke's Cafe until he chose to retire.

Heck, I was willing to agree to just about anything to make this deal happen, so I readily agreed to that, too.

Unfortunately, Alice didn't.

Clearly, she didn't trust her husband to do what was in their best interest as a couple, so we reached a compromise. My great-uncle would be allowed to continue to work at Duke's Cafe for no more than three years, but he could not exceed thirty hours a week, and he had to take three months of vacation a year.

Duke glared at Alice after she rattled off her list of demands, which included a month-long trip to Italy. "You've got to be kidding me," he protested.

"We are going to Italy," she informed him in no uncertain terms. "So take it or leave it."

Duke pointed a sausage finger at his attorney. "Fine. Write it up the way she wants." He turned to Alice. "Anything else you want changed? Speak now or forever hold your peace."

Folding her hands on the conference room table, she smiled contentedly. "I'm happy."

"How 'bout you, boss?" Duke said with a twinkle in his eyes as he looked across the table at me.

He was already calling me *boss*? Sheesh, I couldn't love this old dude more if he were my own grandfather. "I'm happy, too."

He didn't bother asking Marietta if she was happy. Shocker.

"Okay, that should do it," Duke said to Ken. "How long do you think this'll take?"

"I should have the contract ready for everyone to sign when Charmaine is back from her honeymoon and is around to authorize the wire transfer." Ken looked at me. "That's what you wanted to do—to coordinate the sale with your last week at your current job, correct?"

I nodded. "Correct."

Ken turned a page of his day planner to jot a note. "Then we'll schedule an appointment to regroup some time in the first week of August."

After we said our goodbyes to Ken, Marietta excused herself to use the restroom and Duke, Alice, and I stepped onto the sidewalk, where I gave them both a big hug. "I can't thank you enough for doing this for me," I said, feeling as warm and sunny as the day itself. "It's the best wedding present I could've received!"

My great-aunt held me at arm's length. "Child, we didn't do this *for* you. This is like a dream come true to know that the place will be in such good hands, and that our cafe family will be able to keep their jobs." Her eyes misted. "And I'll finally get to Italy. France, too. I've always wanted to see Paris."

"Yeah, yeah," Duke grumbled. "Let's get this kid married off first, and then we can talk about all the places you're gonna drag me off to."

"Ooh, that reminds me." Alice grinned at me. "Your

cake's a beauty, if I do say so myself. It's in the cooler. Wanna see it?"

If I hadn't had so much to get done before Steve's mother and stepfather touched down at SeaTac, I would have jumped at the chance. "I'm sure it's gorgeous. But I want to save that for tomorrow. I also want pictures of you with the cake." I smiled at Duke. "So that's your job before you walk me down the aisle. Because we're gonna display a couple of those pictures on the bulletin board behind the cash register."

He leered at his wife. "I'll be sure to get your good side."

Alice swatted his arm. "No butt shots!" she said as Marietta emerged from the building.

"Whatever are you talking about?" My mother looked to me. "What'd I miss?"

"Nothing, and we need to go," I said, needing to make a quick exit with her before she and Duke started squabbling again. "Donna's waiting for me."

"Okay, sweetie." Alice drew me into her arms. "We'll be there plenty early with the cake, so don't worry about a thing. Tomorrow's gonna be great."

I held her tight. "Thanks for everything." Then I shifted to Duke, who patted my back as he hugged me, just like he did after my grandfather's funeral. I knew then that he would take over as the new father figure in my life. "I love you," I whispered in his ear.

When he pulled back, his eyes shone with tears. "You need to go, so get a move on. We'll save the mushy stuff for when I give my other favorite girl away tomorrow."

Now I was crying.

"You heard the man," Marietta said, hooking her arm in mine. "Save the mushy stuff for tomorrow."

With one last wave goodbye, my mother pulled me away before I dissolved into a weepy mess. "Thanks for getting me out of there," I said between sniffs.

While I looked for my car keys, she handed me a tissue. "Blow your nose and wipe your eyes."

After I blew my nose, Marietta stepped in front of me. "What's your least favorite vegetable?"

"What?" She was giving me mental whiplash.

She clucked her tongue. "Come on, Charmaine. It's not a difficult question. What's your least favorite vegetable?"

"I don't know. Turnips, I guess."

"Think of how a turnip tastes and smells. Absolutely disgusting. I should know because Barry loves the nasty things but insists on cooking the heck out of them."

"Why are we talking about turnips?"

My mother's raspberry red lips curled into a satisfied smile. "Because you, my dear, are no longer crying."

Holy cow, she was right.

She cupped my cheek. "Save those tears for *after* all your wedding pictures have been taken. In the meantime, think turnips!"

Chapter Thirty

Twenty-three hours later, I was sitting in a Rainshadow Ridge Resort changing room while Donna gathered my hair into a loose curly bun.

"What's the matter?" Leaning over me as I sat in front of a full-length mirror, Donna fixed on my reflection. "Are you rethinking the soft curls framing your face? Because I love this look on you."

"No, it's great." I just couldn't stop thinking about Natalie Mercer slowly dying in the room next to ours. "I love it."

"That would be a lot more convincing if you smiled when you said that," Rox quipped while she bounced Emily on her hip.

I bared my teeth in a forced smile.

Rox rolled her eyes. "Oh yes, that's the snarling she-wolf look you want in your wedding pictures. Speaking of which, when's the photographer supposed to show up?"

"Around three," I said. "I figured that would give us plenty of time to get our hair and makeup done."

"I love the smoky eyes your mom gave you. And your dewy foundation…" Donna gave my shoulders a squeeze.

"You look absolutely radiant."

I thought I looked more sweaty than radiant after the spritz Marietta had applied to set my makeup, but as long as Steve thought I looked good when he saw me walking down the aisle, that's all I cared about.

"Thanks," I said and then glanced over at Rox. "What time is it now?"

Supporting Emily in the crook of her arm, Rox reached for the cell phone that I had left on the desk three feet away. "Two-twenty-one."

"Have you seen Steve out there?" I asked. Not that I was worried that he wouldn't show up. I just hadn't seen him since I said good night to him and his family after dinner last night, and it felt strange not to hear from him today. Not even a reply after I texted that I had arrived at the resort.

"He's at the bar with Eddie," she said.

"He is?" This was good news, but why hadn't he returned my text? "Can I have my phone?"

"Will you stop moving, please." Donna scowled at my reflection.

"Sorry." I raised my phone to eye level while Donna fastened crystal-encrusted pins in my hair. I had missed a text from Steve. A call, too. Dang!

"Okay, do *not* move," Donna demanded as she pulled a can of hairspray from her travel toolkit on wheels.

After she had shellacked my hair with enough spray to withstand gale force winds, Donna nodded approvingly. "This has to be some of my best work ever! What do you think?"

She passed me a hand mirror so that I could see how the decorative hair pins created the illusion of sparkling flowers at the edge of my messy bun. "I love it!" Handing her back the mirror, I pushed up from the chair to give Donna a hug. "Thank you!"

"Wow," Rox said while she patted the back of the baby fussing in her arms. "You're the image of perfection, plus look how thin you are. Those jeans you have on are getting downright baggy. Since I'll be the one who'll need help squeezing into her dress, consider me jealous."

"Hey, I'm the one with the mommy pooch," Donna chimed in. "So I'm right there with you. Totally jealous."

Leaning against the edge of the desk, I waved my phone at them. "Stop it, I've lost a grand total of three pounds in the last two months, not even half my goal."

At least my wedding dress fit like a glove. So what if I didn't have a bikini body? I refused to starve myself, especially on my honeymoon in Kaua'i, where I wanted to enjoy every moment. I had a good-enough body for the beach. A strong and healthy body that I hoped would soon grow a baby like Emily.

"Char, you stop it," Rox demanded in a low voice as Emily started to cry. "You look gorgeous and your wedding is gonna be absolutely beautiful. And I think someone's hungry. Time to go to Mama, sweet pea," she said, transferring Emily to Donna's outstretched arms.

While Donna headed to the one bed in the room clear of toiletry bags to nurse her six-week-old, Rox claimed the seat I had just vacated. "I meant to tell you earlier, and I know this is a sore subject, but your mom was right about ordering more flowers. They were still decorating the gazebo when Emily and I went to the bar to say hi to the boys, but everything looks stunning! You're gonna love it."

"I'm sure I will." I also would have loved it if we had stuck to the original plan, but at least my mother was happy.

"Where is my mom, anyway?" I had expected that Marietta would spend as much time primping in here as I was.

"She's *supervising*," Rox said, using her fingers to make air quotes.

"Of course she is." She was probably driving everyone crazy, too, but better them than me. I had been making myself crazy enough worrying about not hearing from Steve.

"How did Steve look when you saw him?" I asked her.

"Fine. A bit casually dressed in shorts and a T-shirt." Rox gave me an assured nod. "But I'm sure he'll be ready to go by five."

I glanced at the creamy tulle and lace confection that I'd soon be wearing. Holy smokes! This was happening. After loving Steve since the third grade, we were getting married.

Married!

My skin tingled at the very thought of walking down the aisle, and then my eyes started to well with hot tears.

No!

"Turnip," I muttered to keep from ruining my makeup. "Turnip, turnip, turnip. I hate turnips!"

Rox leaned in. "Did you just say that you hate turnips?"

"Don't mind me. I'm having a moment," I said, fanning myself. "I probably just need to chill for a little while." And clear my head or I'd be chanting *turnip* like a lunatic for the next few hours. "Do we have any more bottles of water?"

"I think I drank the last one. I'll get some more from the bar and see how things are going out there. Want anything a little stronger?"

"No, thanks." I didn't need any alcohol in me to get even more emotional. "I'll stick with water until the reception."

"Okay," Rox said after checking to see if Donna wanted anything. "I'll be back in a few."

"Take your time." There was certainly no rush since the photographer wouldn't arrive for another half hour. "I'm gonna call Steve."

Right after I checked his message so that I'd know if there were some issue that he had been calling me about. Like why his mother had yet to show up when we had talked last night about Donna doing her hair and makeup.

Of course, it was early, I reminded myself as Rox clicked the door shut. There was probably nothing to worry about.

Please don't let there be anything to worry about, I prayed as I looked down at my phone.

But the call wasn't from Steve. The number was Lucas's, and it had come in almost fifteen minutes ago.

What the heck?!

How had I missed his call? Then I thought of the

person who had tossed my phone onto the bed because it kept ringing while she was doing my makeup.

Had my mother managed to silence my phone in the process?

Probably.

Maybe even intentionally to eliminate the interruption. Sheesh! Today of all days, I didn't need this kind of help from her.

I immediately switched it off silent mode and put it to my ear to listen to his message.

"Charmaine, this is Lucas Mercer," he said, his words coming in rapid-fire succession. "Call me as soon as you can. Sydney is on her way to my apartment, and I'm going to make her watch that video you sent me."

My heart threatened to pound its way through my rib cage as I pressed the button to call him back.

He answered after one ring. "You got my message."

"I just listened to it," I said. "How soon will Sydney be there?"

"The ferry will dock around three, so maybe in forty-five minutes."

I doubted that I could get there any faster than that, but I could try. "I want to be there when she watches that video, and in case she makes a confession I'm bringing a cop with me. Is that okay?"

"Yeah, that's okay," Lucas said, the tension in his voice almost palpable. "Just get here!"

Disconnecting, I grabbed my tote bag from the bed. "I have to go," I told Donna.

"What?" She gaped at me with her baby at her breast.

"Has something happened?"

"It's about to," I said, running out the door.

Chapter Thirty-One

"You need to come with me right now," I told Steve when I found him sitting with Eddie at the bar.

"Hey!" Eddie said while Steve swiveled around to face me. "Isn't it supposed to be bad luck for him to see you before the main event?"

Getting to his feet, Steve's jawline set like tempered steel. "What's wrong?"

"I need you to trust me." I took his hand in mine. "We have to go."

"O-kay," he said, drawing out the word. "The wedding's still on, right?"

Jeez! "The wedding's on, but we *have* to go. Now!"

While I tugged on his hand to get his feet moving, Steve looked back at Eddie. "I guess we're gonna be gone for a little while."

"Okey-dokey. Not what I was expecting to hear today." Eddie raised his glass in mock salute. "But you do you."

"What the heck is going on?" Rox demanded as she stepped into the bar. "I just finished telling your mother that everything was going great, and now you're up and leaving?"

I didn't have time for this. "I'll explain everything when we get back," I said, dashing past her with Steve in tow.

"Char!" she yelled after me. "Where are you going?"

Instead of responding, I picked up the pace.

"Slow down. Where exactly *are* we going?" Steve asked as we marched past the immaculate garden where resort staff members were setting up for our reception.

"I'll tell you in the car. Where'd you park?"

"We're leaving the grounds?" He pulled me to a stop. "Char, what's going on?"

"Please, I need you to trust me. This is super-important. You know I wouldn't ask you to leave if it wasn't."

He held my gaze for several beats of my drumming heart. I didn't know if Steve could see the worry in my eyes, but I could sure see it in his.

"Then let's go," he said, giving my hand a reassuring squeeze.

As we approached the parking lot, I heard my mother, her call as shrill as the eagles that nested on the ridge.

"Charmaine!" she cried out. "Where the heck are you going?"

Pasting a smile on my face, I turned to wave at her. "It's okay. We just have to go somewhere for a little while."

"What?!" Marietta shrieked. "You can't leave! The photographer will be here any minute. You need to get dressed!"

"It's fine. I'll explain later." Much later. But in that moment I needed to beat it toward Steve's F-150 and was never more grateful to be wearing running shoes.

"No, no! You can't go!" she called out, shuffling after us in her four-inch slingbacks. "Tell me you're not eloping! Charmaine! Please, whatever's going on, we can talk about it. You don't have to run off!"

"You'd better give her something or she's gonna try to block my truck with her body," Steve said, breaking into a jog to keep up with me. "And I really don't want to see your mother become a hood ornament."

"She can't move that fast in those heels." But I knew he was right. I needed to say something to ease her mind. "Mom, don't worry. I promise we'll be back."

"When?" She stopped in her tracks. "What do I tell everyone?"

Sheesh, I didn't know.

"Tell them everything's okay," I said as my lungs screamed for oxygen. "We just had to run an errand."

"*An errand!*" she screeched so loudly that a flock of pigeons took flight. "Are you freakin' kidding me?"

I know. Pretty lame, but my brain was too preoccupied to come up with a more creative lie.

"You also might want to find Avery," I said, sucking wind. "And ask her to uncork...some champagne a little early."

I had a feeling that Marietta was going to need it.

"Turn here," I said to Steve twenty minutes after I told him about Lucas's call.

"I can't believe that you're doing this on our wedding day," he grumbled, throwing me a look that promised that this escapade would become family legend, a tale told and retold to our children every anniversary.

As long as we had all those years together, I was okay with that, especially if we got a confession out of Sydney.

"Well, believe it." I pointed at the visitor parking area when Steve pulled into the lot. "There's usually an open spot over there. And trust me when I tell you this girl is as guilty as sin." She even looked the part.

"I trust you, Chow Mein." He shook his head as he parked in front of Lucas's apartment building. "It's just incredibly bad timing."

I glanced at the clock on the dash. Three-fourteen. "If we can get her talking, we might be able to get out of here before four and be back with time to spare." I smiled at Steve. "I wouldn't want to be late for our wedding."

He shot me a lopsided grin. "Yeah, we *really* don't want that. So, you ready to do this?"

"As ready as I'm gonna be," I said, climbing down from his truck.

A minute later, I rapped on Lucas's door, and he silently motioned for us to come inside.

"Is she here?" I whispered as I looked around.

"Not yet," Lucas whispered back.

Then I didn't know why we were whispering. It felt too cloak and dagger, like something out of a *Scooby-Doo* episode, and was making me more nervous than I already was.

"This is Steve," I said, taking a step back so that the men could shake hands. "He's a Port Merritt police detective. I've filled him in with everything I know about your wife's death."

"Lucas Mercer," he whispered in introduction as if the walls were listening.

Considering how nosy his neighbor was, maybe they were.

"You've watched that show—the one about the eye drops?" Lucas asked Steve.

"Yeah. Of course, the toxicology results aren't back yet." Steve shot me a knowing glance. "So we don't know if we're dealing with exactly the same kind of situation."

Whatever. If we heard a confession today, the test results would be frosting on the cake.

"But," Steve continued. "If—"

"I want to question Sydney," I interjected to cut to the chase. "Lucas, I haven't told you this before, but I'm a body language expert. That's why the county coroner asks me to talk to witnesses and assist in investigations." Sometimes, and not for much longer. "And I think that with your help, we can get to the truth of what happened to Natalie."

Lucas's eyes misted. "That's all I want. To know if Sydney had something to do with it."

"Okay." I took a deep breath and tried to ignore the butterflies flapping in my belly. "Here's what I want you to do when Sydney gets here."

Two minutes after we had worked out the basics of our plan, Steve and I were hiding in Lucas's bedroom while we waited for Sydney's arrival.

"Messy room," Steve whispered. "It stinks like old sneakers, too."

"You should've smelled the place the first time I came here. This is a vast improvement."

"Hmm." Steve sniffed my hair. "You smell good, though."

"It's Donna's hairspray."

He lifted my chin and his gaze swept over me. "You look great. Meant to mention that earlier, but someone got me a little distracted."

I gave him a careful peck on the lips so that I didn't ruin the makeup my mother had spent over an hour applying. "Thanks, but try to pretend that it's the first time you're seeing me when I walk down the aisle. And at least you haven't seen me in my dress."

Steve chuckled. "I'll do my best." Then he put his ear to the door and his face turned to stone. "She's here," he mouthed.

I nodded and sent up a silent prayer that we could coax a confession out of Sydney in the next thirty minutes.

It was hard to hear what they were saying from this far away, but by the flirty tone of Lucas's voice, it sounded like he was playing his part exactly how I had suggested.

"I didn't want to be alone," Lucas said, loud and clear.

That was the line I had told him to use to signal that Sydney had taken a seat in the living room. Because when she saw me she was going to know that Lucas had lured her here to be questioned and I wanted her sitting in case she tried to bolt.

"That's our cue," Steve said, opening the bedroom

door.

He entered the hallway first and headed straight toward the entryway to block the door while I stepped into the living room.

Sitting on the sofa next to Lucas, Sydney looked up at me and went rigid. "What is this?" She glared at Lucas. "I thought you... Never mind, I'm leaving."

Lucas grabbed her arm when she stood. "No, you're not," he said, pulling her down with so much force that she almost bounced off the seat cushion.

"Lucas!" Sydney pleaded with him. "That hurt!"

"You'll live." Lucas released her arm. "Unlike my wife."

Retreating to the far end of the sofa, she blanched. "What's that supposed to mean?" Her gaze flicked from me to Steve as he joined us in the living room. "And what are they doing here?"

She was going to find out very soon. "Lucas, do you have something that you'd like Sydney to watch?"

After he positioned his laptop on the coffee table in front of Sydney, Lucas looked at me expectantly, as if he were awaiting instructions. Probably because I had told him that Steve and I didn't have time to go through the entire forty-two-minute episode.

Sitting cross-legged on the floor so that I had a good view of Sydney's face, I gave Lucas a nod that I was ready. "Why don't you start it at the two-minute-fifty-second mark."

Steve, standing a few feet to my right, shot me an amused look.

Yes, I had watched the video three more times to

include the most critical parts and their timestamps in the report I had written for Jim Pearson with the sheriff's department.

I wanted to tell Steve to wipe that smile from his face, but no sooner than it appeared, it disappeared. He was now in cop mode, ready and focused on our subject.

I was ready, too, and took immense satisfaction at the sight of Sydney's pupils dilating when the family member being interviewed said the words *eye drops*.

I knew that in another minute and seventeen seconds the show's medical expert would explain how tetrahydrozoline, a compound in common eye drops, was lethal when a large amount was administered orally.

"His death appeared to be from a heart attack, but his brothers suspected that his money may have been a motivating factor," the host of the show said less than a minute later.

"Please pause it, Lucas." I scooted closer to the sofa, my gaze fixed on Sydney, who was staring at the frozen screen as if she were facing her executioner.

"Natalie's death also appeared to be from a heart attack," I said. "But her parents came to the coroner's office, where I work. They knew that couldn't be right. Lucas knew it too. He just had to get past the shock of losing his wife. He also had to see you for who you are now, not the girl you were before he met Natalie."

Sydney blinked back tears, her breathing ragged.

"That took me some time to understand." I leaned in, wanting her to look at me. "Of course, I'm an outsider. I don't know you two, but I talked to people who did. One of them told me how you begged Lucas not to marry Natalie."

Sydney hung her head, the tears now flowing.

"You loved him," I softly said while motioning to Steve to find her some tissues. "You probably loved him for years, didn't you?" I certainly knew how that felt.

She nodded and took the paper napkins Steve handed to her.

Okay. Finally, a response. It was far from an admission of anything, but it was a start.

"But Natalie came along and everything changed. The texts you sent her after they got engaged had little to no effect. They still got married."

I waited for Sydney to respond, but she only blew her nose.

"But Natalie knew about you, didn't she?" When Sydney said nothing, I looked at Lucas, who nodded.

"And I bet you knew plenty about her. Family members talk, especially the women. It's that way in my family, too. Everybody's in one another's business."

That was a lie. Lucille was the only woman I knew who routinely got into everyone's business, but Sydney didn't need to know that. "So, of course, you knew that Natalie was trying to get pregnant."

Sydney gaped at me. "I... I didn't." She shook her head. "No one told me that."

Nope. She knew. "Your mother probably told you. She and Lucas's mother are such good friends. They probably tell one another everything." I looked at Lucas. "You told your mom you were trying to start a family, right?"

Because Nora had mentioned to me that she first thought Natalie's symptoms were because she was pregnant.

Lucas nodded. "Probably the second week of June. I remember because school was over for Nat."

"So that would've been close to two weeks before your aunt Renee's wedding," I said. "Interesting timing."

Sydney's mouth opened and closed like a fish out of water, her lower lip trembling. "I don't... I'm not sure what you want me to say."

You're just stalling now. "You viewed being together at that wedding as your last chance to get back what should've been yours. Once Lucas and Natalie had a baby, that would slam the door shut on your hopes and dreams. His bond with Natalie would be that much stronger, leaving no room for a future with you."

"No!" Sydney turned to Lucas. "It wasn't like that. You have to believe me."

But I could see that Lucas didn't believe her any more than I did.

"Then, a couple of days after your mom tells you this bit of gossip, this show airs in primetime," I said, thumbing toward the laptop. "You watch it and realize how easy it would be to eliminate the woman who has been standing in your way for the last two years."

"No!" Sydney cried out. "I've never seen this show before. I don't even watch these kinds of shows."

Lie.

"Yes, you do," Lucas countered. "You've told me about some episodes where you knew it had to be the husband who did it. That wasn't true this time, though, was it?"

She reached for him. "Lucas—"

"Don't!" He shifted away from her on the sofa. "I tried to be understanding, to be *sensitive* to your feelings even though Natalie was uncomfortable when you were around. I should've listened to her when she said there was something wrong with you."

"Wrong with me!" Sydney shrieked. "The only thing wrong with me was that I loved you! You once loved me, too. You said you did."

He stared at her in stunned silence. "I didn't mean it that way. I just wanted to get you into—"

"Yes, you did! You loved me, and I loved you. I still love you."

"If you love me so much, how could you do this?" Lucas rasped as tears spilled over his lashes.

I held my breath as we all waited for her answer.

"Because you and I...were supposed to be together!" she blurted out between sobs.

That sounded like a confession to me, and I looked up at Steve. "Is that enough?"

With a nod he pulled out his phone from the back pocket of his cargo shorts. "That's enough for Jim to take her into custody. I'll call him in a sec. Right now, I'm calling Port Townsend PD to ask for a uniform to stay until Jim can get here."

While Steve headed into the kitchen to make his calls, I motioned for Lucas to step into the hallway with me.

"I know hearing all that was hard," I told him, standing where I could keep an eye on Sydney, who was still weeping on the sofa. "Are you okay?"

"I needed to hear it," Lucas said. "After I watched that show, I thought she had to have done something similar. Now I know for sure."

Now we both knew for sure.

He blew out a shaky breath. "I still don't understand how she did it. I talked to my mother and grandmother before I called you and they both said that Sydney hardly spent any time in that room."

"That's what everyone I interviewed said. But somehow she managed to get the eye drops into Natalie's drink."

"Yeah," he muttered as he wiped his eyes. "I guess."

"Sorry." Although saying that I was sorry felt so inadequate for everything this guy had gone through.

"I'm okay, or at least I will be eventually." He glanced back at Sydney. "I don't know how I could've been so blind. I just never thought—"

"Natalie did, though, didn't she? Even though you said that you never fought, maybe she voiced her frustrations about how Sydney flirted with you." Loudly enough for the neighbor to hear.

"I thought it was harmless. That she was overreacting." Lucas's voice cracked as tears trickled down his cheeks. "I should've known... The way Syd kept coming around after...insisting on staying with me."

"It was her that Sunday night. She was the one your neighbor heard." And thought had been in danger. Boy, had that lady been wrong.

"I didn't want her here," Lucas said, choking out the words. "I didn't want anyone but my wife."

Oh, heck, now my tear ducts wanted to join the party.
Turnip, turnip, turnip!

"What happens next?" he asked after pressing the heels of his palms against his eyes.

"Steve's calling the detective who will be handling the case," I said, relieved to have something to focus on besides stupid root vegetables. "He's also requested that a police officer come stay with you until Sydney can be taken into custody. When the cop shows up we'll take off. We're getting married in..." I checked the time on my phone and I yelped as if I'd had a stick jammed up my colon.

It was six minutes after four!

I rushed into the kitchen, where Steve was still on the phone. "We need to go," I said in his other ear.

Steve nodded and held a finger up to give him a moment while he kept talking.

I held up my phone so that he could see the time on the screen. "We need to go *now*!"

"Thanks," Steve said. "I'll be in touch." Pocketing his phone, he turned to Lucas, who was watching us from ten feet away. "Port Townsend PD has been dispatched and should be here any minute. When they get here, we'll take off—"

A series of loud knocks interrupted him, and while Steve opened the door and explained the situation to the uniformed officer, I took Lucas aside.

"Like I started to tell you, we've got a wedding to get to, but this officer will stay with you until someone from the sheriff's department can get here," I said. "I hate to leave you like this, but I'll be back in town in two weeks and will call you then to see how you're doing. If there's anything you need from my office in the meantime, call Francine Rickard."

"Okay," Lucas said, looking a little shellshocked.

With nothing left to say to the poor guy, I threw my arms around him to give him a quick hug. "Thanks for opening that email. Your call totally made my day."

Steve took me by the hand and led me to the door. "I would also like to make your day by getting married, preferably on time."

"Gotta go!" I called back to Lucas.

"Is Jim on his way?" I asked as Steve and I sprinted toward the stairway.

"He'll be here within the hour. Sends his congratulations, by the way."

My heart warmed that Jim remembered this was our wedding day. "Aww, nice guy."

"I meant about getting the confession."

"Oh." That was nice, too.

"You did good in there," Steve said over the rumble of our footfalls on the stairs.

"I didn't do that much. Lucas is the one who got her talking. I think we just helped convince her that there was no way out of this mess."

"Yes, but that wouldn't have happened if you hadn't stumbled upon that video."

"Actually, Lucille gets the credit for that," I said, slightly breathless as we pushed off the last concrete step. "That's one of her favorite shows."

"Why am I not surprised."

"She told me about it because she'd assumed I'd get involved in Natalie's death investigation. And, of course, she was convinced this was a copycat killing. Even backed that up with a five-dollar bet."

"Of course she did. But the fact remains that you did good work in there. You sure you want to hang it all up and take over Duke's?"

I looked at him as we jogged toward his truck. "Absolutely! Almost as much as I want to become your wife."

He grinned. "Good answer."

Chapter Thirty-Two

The second that Steve turned off his ignition and my feet touched the asphalt of the Rainshadow Ridge Resort parking lot, my mother shuffled toward us with Steve's mom, Debbie, by her side.

"Oh, thank goodness!" Marietta exclaimed with outstretched arms. "I was beginning to think you'd never get back!"

"I said we'd be back." I didn't want to be slimed with her cloying perfume, but she crushed me to her bosom before I could make an evasive maneuver. "It just took a little longer than I thought."

Marietta pushed me back with surprising force, her green eyes sparking with fire. "A little! We've been worried sick about you two. When you didn't answer your phones, we didn't know what to think."

"I know, and I'm really sorry." I smiled at the nice lady with the salt and pepper curls who had her arm wrapped around Steve's. "Hi, Debbie. Hi, Gram," I said as my grandmother approached with a champagne glass in her hand.

Lucille lumbered up behind her, with Duke and Alice

bringing up the rear.

Good golly! I appreciated the welcoming committee, but with my wedding scheduled to start in seven minutes, I didn't have time to field questions, especially the ones that I knew would be at Lucille's lips.

"Sorry we couldn't answer your calls. We were dealing with a bit of an emergency." To say the least.

"I'll explain everything later, Mom," Steve said to Debbie.

She cocked her head to give him the *look* of motherly disapproval. "Yes, you will. Right now, though, perhaps you two would like to change into something a bit more formal." Debbie sweetened her expression when she focused on me. "There are quite a few people here who would love to see you two say 'I do,' me included."

"Me, too!" my mother echoed.

"And me!" My grandmother gave me a squeezy hug. "I've been waiting a long time for this day."

"What's goin' on?" Lucille demanded as she descended upon me like a hungry locust. "What'd I miss?"

I shook my head. *Not the time or place, Lucille.* "Nothing."

Lucille gasped. "You got a break in the case, didn't you? That's where you've been!"

Criminy! For years, Lucille's far-out theories had been so ridiculous they'd been laughable, but she had to be right every step of the way this time.

Not only was it incredible, it was incredibly inconvenient at this particular moment.

"What case?" Debbie asked Steve, who grimaced.

"What's she talking about?"

"Char knows exactly what I'm talkin' about." Lucille eased toward me with a wolfish gleam in her eye. "So? Do I win?"

"Win what?" Marietta and Debbie asked in unison while Alice and I groaned.

"Just ignore her, folks," Duke declared. "I've been doing that for forty years and I see no reason why today should be any different."

Lucille stuck out her tongue at him and then turned back to me. "Be a pal and give me a little hint."

"I can't. Sorry." Even if I was no longer afraid of getting fired for having loose lips, I didn't want to say anything that could hurt Jim Pearson's investigation. "You'll have to wait to find out."

She slammed her fists to her hips. "Wait! I hate waiting!"

I hear you, sister. "Me too, and I think we've kept all of you waiting long enough this afternoon."

As if that had been her cue to make an exit, Marietta hooked me with her arm. "So let's get you into that dress!"

"I'll help. Everyone else who isn't gonna get escorted down that aisle, take your seats," Gram declared like the matriarch she was.

"I'll make sure that happens," Duke said, fixing his gaze on Lucille.

"We both will." Alice gave me a wink. "You go get ready, honey. We'll handle things out here."

"And I'll find my husband so that we're ready to go when you are," Debbie said to me.

I nodded and then beamed at Steve. "Sounds perfect."

As they scattered, Gram shooed Marietta and me toward the changing room. "Go, I'll find Roxie and Donna. Last I saw them, they were walking the grounds with their hubbies."

"I'll go with you, Eleanor, but first..." Steve looked back to me. "How long do you need? Ten minutes?"

Before I could answer, Marietta took my chin and inspected my makeup. "Better make it fifteen."

"I'll ask Eddie to make an announcement that we'll be starting a little late." Then he gave me a quick kiss. "See you soon, beautiful."

"You two know that it's bad luck to see the bride before the wedding, right?" Renee joked as she and her husband, Adam, walked toward us.

"Not today it's not." This Saturday had already proven itself to be quite the good luck day.

And it wasn't until Renee was standing in front of me that I realized just how lucky it was. Because she was the one potential witness I had yet to speak with.

"Do you have a second to talk?" I asked her.

While my mother jabbed me in the ribs with her elbow, Renee grinned. "Sure, but don't you have something else you should be doing right now?"

"Yes, she does," Marietta said, answering for me again.

"I'll be really quick, I promise." And to keep that promise, everyone else had to leave. "Gram, I need Steve here, so would you ask Eddie to make that announcement?"

She nodded. "I'll do that right now," she said, setting off toward the rose garden.

I turned to my mother, who had failed to take the hint. "Why don't you wait for me in the changing room."

Marietta lifted her eyes to the cotton candy clouds as if seeking divine intervention. "I swear, you seem determined to give me a heart attack today."

Renee flinched as if my mother's poor choice of words had landed like a physical blow. Her husband had noticed her reaction, too.

"Are you okay?" Adam asked her, his voice barely audible over the click of my mother's heels as she retreated.

"I'm fine." Renee offered him a brittle smile before meeting my gaze. "It's just the first time we've been back since—"

"That's actually what I want to talk to you about," I said. "You might've heard that I've been involved in the preliminary investigation into Natalie's death."

Renee nodded. "My mother called me last night after our flight got in and said that you talked to her."

I was sure that Joan Germain hadn't painted me in a glowing light, but I didn't care. My only concern was what Renee had witnessed when she was sitting within a foot of Natalie for an hour or more. "This is a horrible time to ask you some of the same questions, but when you were getting ready for your wedding, did you see Natalie drink anything?"

Renee's eyes narrowed. "Are you suggesting—"

"No." I didn't want to suggest anything. I wanted her to tell me what she had seen. "I'm just asking what she was drinking."

"Nothing alcoholic when I was with her, just a can of

Coke. Same as me."

A bubble of hope rose inside me. Maybe I had finally found the eyewitness I had been searching for. "Did you happen to notice if someone handed her the can?"

Renee's brow crinkled with awareness, and I no longer hoped, I *knew* that my search was over.

"Sydney, my cousin's daughter, handed us each a can with a straw in it," she said.

"An *open* can." I turned to Steve, who was nodding with a satisfied curl to his lips. "That's it."

That was how Sydney poisoned Natalie—with a doctored can of cola.

"What?" Renee's look of confusion ping-ponged between me and Steve. "Was something in the can she gave to Natalie?"

A whole lot of something, given how quickly Natalie started experiencing symptoms. "We'll have to wait for the lab results to know for sure—"

"And that's as much as we can say about an ongoing investigation," Steve interjected, sounding like a police spokesperson wrapping up a press conference. "Now, if you'll excuse us, my bride and I need to get ready for our wedding."

"But thank you," I said over my shoulder as he pulled me toward my room. "Someone will soon be in touch to get a full statement from you."

"Stop talking, Chow Mein," Steve muttered in warning.

"What? Shouldn't she expect a call from Jim Pearson? You'll tell him that we have an eyewitness, right?"

"I'll make a call when I get to the room."

I took his hand and squeezed it. "Could this day end in a more perfect way?"

"Yes." He brought my hand to his lips and kissed it. "Marry me."

"Oh, I have every intention to," I said to my grinning future husband before he jogged off to his changing room.

Seconds later, I rounded the corner and almost bumped into my mother, who was pacing outside the door of my room chanting, "Turnip, turnip, turnip."

Not you, too!

"What're you doing out here?" I asked.

Marietta flapped her hands like a bird that couldn't achieve liftoff, her eyes glittering with tears. "I don't have a key to the room!"

"Luckily I do, so everything's okay. There's nothing to get upset about."

Her breath hitched. "Easy for you to say. I've been worried sick all day."

After I closed the door behind us, I pulled her in for a hug, stinky perfume and all. "You can stop worrying now. Everything looks beautiful out there and we're all here now, so relax and try to enjoy your role as mother of the bride."

"Did you see the flower bowls?" she asked, sniffling.

Nope. I dashed right past the reception area without so much as a glance. "I did. You were absolutely right about them. They're gorgeous."

She held me at arm's length, her eyes shimmering like emeralds. "You mean it?"

"I don't think the flowers could be lovelier," I said,

trusting what Rox had told me earlier. "Thank you. Everything looks picture perfect."

"Sweetheart, I love you. You deserve the perfect day."

"I love you too, Mama." No sooner than the words left my lips, hot tears flooded my eyes.

No, no, no!

"Turnip, turnip, turnip. Come on, turnip, don't fail me now!" *Please!*

"It's not working," I yelped, lunging for the tissue box on the desk.

"Think of something else."

"Like what?" Rutabagas? Brussels sprouts? Parsnips?

She pinched the back of my arm. Hard. "Like that."

"Ow!" I dropped the tissue and glared at her.

"I know. Sorry, hon. Desperate times call for desperate measures." Her full lips curled into the kindest of smiles as she peered into my eyes. "It looks like it worked, though. No more tears. And no more—what did Duke call it?—'mushy stuff' until after the wedding and your pictures are taken." She plucked another tissue to tenderly blot my cheeks. "So, I will tell you how very proud I am to be your mama later," she said, looking adoringly at me. "Deal?"

"Deal," I choked out, turning to the mirror before the floodgates reopened. Amazingly, my hair still looked good, all credit going to the power of Donna's miracle hairspray, but I had ruined my makeup. "Will you be able to fix this mess in the next ten minutes?"

"No problem, sugar," my mom said, laying out her arsenal of beauty products in the bathroom as we heard a knock at the door. "That'll be your grandmother. You let her in and then get your hiney back here. We have a wedding to get you ready for!"

Chapter Thirty-Three

"Charmaine, I couldn't be prouder to walk you down the aisle if you were my own daughter," my great-uncle Duke said twenty minutes later as we approached the gazebo draped with flowing white chiffon and floral garlands.

While the wedding march faded to background noise in my ears, I hugged his arm a little tighter, my heart so full of love I thought it might burst. "Oh, Duke. You're gonna make me cry." And I absolutely refused to say turnip one more time today.

"Don't cry, honey." He patted my hand. "Today isn't a day for tears. Although you wouldn't know it by looking at the women in our family."

Sure enough, my mother, Gram, and Alice, standing in the front row with Barry, were all dabbing tissues at their eyes.

I smiled at the three women who helped raise me, grateful for everything they did so that I could be here today, marrying Steve.

Behind them in the second row was Lucille, Hector and his wife, and Courtney, none of whom were crying. Thank goodness. Instead, they were all smiles. Same with

Frankie, Ben, Shondra, and their spouses, as well as Karla and my other work friends filling a couple of rows. And holy cow! Even Patsy looked happy to see me. No happier than Heather standing next to Kyle Cardinale, though.

I did a double take as we passed, which made Heather laugh. Was Kyle her wedding date?

As if reading my mind she shrugged.

Whoa. I hadn't expected to see those two together, but given the way my wedding day had unfolded, maybe I shouldn't have been surprised. The stars seemed to have aligned in the last few hours.

"Someone looks happy to see you," Duke said when Stanley winked at me from the third row on Steve's side, where he was dwarfed by six-foot-six Georgie Bassett and several of Steve's pals from high school.

I winked back at Stanley. "He's wearing a suit. I don't think I've ever seen him in anything other than flannel."

"Yeah, he and I can clean up okay. But I wasn't referring to Stan."

I glanced back at half of the Port Merritt police force. "Wanda?" I guessed since the chief's secretary was the only one in that row with a big smile on her face.

"No, I meant *him*," Duke said, pointing to the good-looking guy in the charcoal three-piece suit waiting for us at the end of the aisle runner.

With his eyes locked on mine, Steve mouthed, *"Wow."*

If I hadn't been glowing with happiness before, the joy flaring inside me had to be radiating through my pores.

So grateful for the love of this man, I smiled to send my thanks to his wonderful mom, Debbie, in the front row with her husband, Gavin, and a couple of Steve's cousins.

Debbie blew me a kiss, and my eyes burned with happy tears as I turned my smile on Gram and my mom, both of whom were beaming at me. They were also mercifully dry-eyed.

Good! Because if I had seen them openly weeping, I was going to lose what little control of my tear ducts I had left.

"Well, kid," Duke said as we took our final step on the white runner. "This has been my honor."

I looked up at him. "The honor has been mine."

Taking my hand, Duke gently kissed it. "There's no one more worthy of our girl than you," he said, placing my hand in Steve's.

"Thank you," Steve whispered, his eyes glistening as his fingers tightened around mine. Then he smiled down at me. "Hello, beautiful."

Even though he had said those words to me before, I had never felt truly beautiful until that moment. "Hello," I croaked and had to clear the emotion from my throat. "Are you ready to do this?"

"Very ready."

As if that had been everyone's cue, Duke joined Alice in the front row, the music stopped, and I turned to hand my bouquet to Rox.

In one swift movement, she also dabbed away a teardrop that had spilled over my lashes. "Thank goodness for waterproof mascara. Now knock off the waterworks. You know how emotional I get when I'm preggers," Rox said, taking a swipe at her own leaky eyes.

"I love you, too," I said and then met Donna's gaze. "Both of you. And there's no one I'd rather be up here with."

"Except for this guy, maybe," Eddie whispered, cocking his head toward Steve.

I took Steve's other hand in mine and squeezed. "There's no maybe about that."

Judge Witten, standing on the first step of the gazebo motioned for everyone to take a seat, and ten minutes later, Steve and I shared our first kiss as man and wife.

And I'm pleased to let you know that I didn't cry once the rest of the evening. I cannot say the same for my mother.

Epilogue

"Does Sarah want some of Daddy's bacon?" Steve asked our ten-week-old daughter, making her smile at every touch of the crispy strip in his fingers to her little lips.

Since Duke's month-long trip to Italy with Alice had begun on this first Saturday of October, when I was back from my maternity leave, I ached to see my baby. But not while being teased to eat solid food!

"Hey!" Between flips of pancakes, I aimed my spatula at my husband. "Don't be giving my daughter any bacon!"

Dropping the bacon to his plate, Steve grinned at me from his usual seat at the counter. "But she loves it, just like her mama."

"She can love it later. Right now, she gets to love these milk machines," I said, pointing to my chest.

"And she thoroughly enjoys those." Steve touched the tip of her button nose with his finger. "Just like her daddy."

Stanley hooted from two seats away.

With heat flaring my cheeks, I waggled my spatula at him. "Pretend you didn't hear that, Stanley."

"That horse is already out of the barn, kiddo," he

quipped and then raised his coffee cup to me. "Glad you're back."

"Me, too, and thanks again for the present." I smiled at sweet Sarah Eleanor Sixkiller. "I think that pink little number she's wearing is the one that you gave her. It's a perfect fit."

Stanley nodded with approval at the baby wrapped in a matching pink receiving blanket. "Perfect indeed." He cut me an impish grin. "The outfit ain't bad either."

"I couldn't agree more." I heard the kitchen door bang shut behind me and hoped it was Lucille, because one of my waitresses had gone home sick.

"Good morning," I said with a sigh of relief as Lucille stowed her purse in a locker. "Thanks for coming in."

"Not a problem. But I can't stay past two. I got a hair appointment at Donna's." Lucille's lips curled with pleasure as she approached. "I want to look my best for my date tonight."

Her date? "But I thought you were babysitting for me tonight." Because Steve, Gram, and I were meeting my mother and Barry at the Grotto to celebrate the release of Marietta's new movie.

"I am," Lucille said, her eyes lighting up at the sight of Sarah in Steve's arms. "And there's my cute little date."

"Shucks," Stanley chuckled. "Didn't know we had a date later. My day is looking up!"

"Dream on, old man." Lucille pushed open the swinging door. "I'm havin' a girls' night with this little one," she said, smiling with delight when Sarah latched onto her finger.

"Whew," I said under my breath as I plated two orders of pancakes and eggs. "Order up!"

I didn't need more problems with the help I had arranged for both here and at home. With Hector out so that he could attend his granddaughter's tenth birthday party, I was already scrambling to keep up on my first day back. But when I heard the jingle of the bell over the front door and looked up to see Lucas Mercer coming in holding Erin Lofgren's hand, I was very glad to be the one filling in behind the grill.

Pulling off my greasy apron, I washed my hands, and then went out to greet my guests.

"I've got this," I told Courtney, my waitress who typically handled the counter business during her shift.

While she headed to the coffee station to grab a carafe of the best coffee in Port Merritt, and Lucille started a new pot, I waited for Lucas and Erin to stop staring at the bakery and breakfast sandwich menu mounted on the wall.

"I can make some recommendations if that would be helpful," I said. "Everything in the case in front of you was freshly baked this morning. The ham and Swiss croissants are delicious, if I do say so myself."

"Charmaine?" Lucas said with a chuckle. "What the heck?"

"Hi, Lucas. Hi, Erin." I gave them each a friendly smile. "And welcome to Duke's."

Erin looked confused. "Do you work here now?"

"I do. I left the prosecutor's office not long after I met you, and bought this place."

"Wow, that's quite a change," she said.

"Change can be good." Since these two appeared to be a couple, I hoped that was true for them as well.

"How are things going?" I asked Lucas. "The last time I saw you was almost a year ago at Sydney's sentencing."

"Better." He gave Erin a sweet smile. "A lot better."

"What brings you to town?" I asked, noticing she was blushing.

She linked his pinky finger with hers as if they were once again high school sweethearts. "He's taking me to some of his favorite places on the peninsula to try to persuade me to move here."

I had a feeling that she wouldn't need that much persuasion. "Well, I'm very glad that you stopped by. Are you ready to order?"

"The best latte I ever tasted was what Lucas promised me," Erin said. "So, I know we're gonna need two of those."

"You'll probably want a couple of apple fritters to go with them. Also the best you'll ever taste," Steve said, holding Sarah in the crook of his left arm as he extended his free hand to Lucas. "Good to see you again."

"Hey, Steve," Lucas said, shaking his hand. "Great to see you, and who's this?"

Steve looked lovingly at our little angel, who cooed as if to maximize her cute factor. "This is Sarah."

"Hello, Sarah," Erin whispered to her and then looked back at Lucas, whose eyes were glistening.

"Excuse me for a second," he said. "I'm just gonna wash my hands."

Once he disappeared into the restroom, Erin met my

gaze. "One of his friends just had a little girl and named her after Natalie, so he's been a little raw the last few days. But he's right. Things are getting better."

I was pretty sure that I was looking at the reason why.

We chatted for a couple more minutes while I filled their breakfast order. Then, after I watched Lucas and Erin leave, I turned to Steve. "That was a nice surprise."

"You mean them being together?" he asked as we headed back into the kitchen.

"Yes, all these years later, they're dating again. I mean, it was obvious when I interviewed her that Erin still had feelings for him, but I sure didn't see this coming."

"These things can take some time."

"That's certainly been my experience." Especially with Steve.

"And it's been my experience that the best things are worth waiting for."

"Are you referring to me or the baby?" I asked, unable to wipe the smile from my face.

"Both." Steve grinned. "Of course."

"Good answer."

THE END

Author's Note

While I have loved writing each and every Working Stiffs mystery, I knew that once I gave Char and Steve their happy ending, it would be the end of the road for the series. I hope you found *Better Wed Than Dead* to be a worthy conclusion to their story.

This won't be the end of my books set in Port Merritt, though. Nor will this be the last time you'll be able to spend some time with Char at Duke's Cafe. She and Steve will appear in my next book, a stand-alone novel that has been percolating in my brain for years. Like with Char's story, this will be a book about coming home and dealing with family, change, and the challenges of "adulting." There may even be a mystery to solve as the story unfolds—just not a murder mystery. If you follow me on Facebook or subscribe to my newsletter, I'll have more information about this book as it grows from the ideas in my head into words on pages. Until then, I thank you for allowing me to share my Working Stiffs Mystery fictional family and friends with you. It's been both a pleasure and an honor.

~ *Wendy*

About the Author

Wendy Delaney writes fun-filled cozy mysteries and is the award-winning author of the Working Stiffs Mystery series. A long-time member of Mystery Writers of America, she's a Food Network addict and pastry chef wannabe. When she's not plotting her next story, she can be found on her treadmill, working off the calories from her latest culinary adventure.

Wendy lives in the San Antonio area with the love of her life and is a proud grandma. For book news please visit her website at www.wendydelaney.com, email her at wendy@wendydelaney.com, and connect with her on Facebook at www.facebook.com/wendy.delaney.908.

Made in the USA
Monee, IL
05 December 2024